THE
LIBERATORS

Also by Philip Womack

The Other Book

THE LIBERATORS

Philip Womack

BLOOMSBURY

LONDON BERLIN NEW YORK

Bloomsbury Publishing, London, Berlin and New York

First published in Great Britain in February 2010 by Bloomsbury Publishing Plc
36 Soho Square, London, W1D 3QY

A CIP catalogue record of this book is available from the British Library

ISBN 978 0 7475 9552 6

FSC
Mixed Sources
Product group from well-managed
forests and other controlled sources
Cert no. SGS - COC - 2061
www.fsc.org
© 1996 Forest Stewardship Council

Typeset by Dorchester Typesetting Group Ltd
Printed in Great Britain by Clays Ltd, St Ives Plc

1 3 5 7 9 10 8 6 4 2

www.bloomsbury.com

For R.S. Christie

λέγουσι δ᾽ ὥς τις εἰσελήλυθε ξένος,
γόης ἐπῳδὸς Λυδίας ἀπὸ χθονός,
ξανθοῖσι βοστρύχοισιν εὐοσμῶν κόμην

An outsider has come, they say,
Howling out enchantments: a sorcerer, from Lydia.
His hair smells sweet, his golden curls like lightning.

From *The Bacchae*, Euripides, lines 233–235
(author's translation)

Chapter One

Blackwood darted through the crowds like lightning, his feet pounding on the pavement, splashing in puddles. The chill of December seared through his bones. Around him the press of people on their Friday shopping trips surged and flowed; a flock of pigeons scattered, startled. Blackwood pushed past an old lady, overturning her trolley. He saw a railing ahead of him, checked behind, and leaped over it in one bound, landing lightly on the other side. It was raining, and he was panting, and he could feel the taste of blood in his mouth, and drops of tangy sweat rolled down his cheeks. The stab wound in his shoulder throbbed. He had been running for half an hour, and he had lost all communication with Hunter, and one of the Liberators was just behind him.

Blackwood's heart thrummed. The crowds parted, and he saw the Liberator – laughing, his hands in his pockets, his long hair blowing in the wind, mouth open like a dog about to bite; an unholy aura of brightness surrounded him. Blackwood ran faster. Two Acolytes had chased him all the way from Hyde Park, and now here he was, approaching Paddington Station, its bulk looming. How had he let himself get into this mess? He'd been so stupid. But he still had the Koptor, and that was the important thing.

The Acolytes, he thought, he could deal with. He could escape them, outwit them, he was strong, young. But he didn't stand a chance against the Liberator – and then the Koptor would be lost, and then . . . He couldn't let that happen. He sent up a prayer, and sped across a road, diving over a car bonnet, stumbling a little, but picking himself up and carrying on. A gust howled over him, making his coat billow out; he threw it off, and it floated away, like a strange bird.

The object he clutched was glowing and humming. It was too precious to lose; it was the only thing that could stop the Liberators. Blackwood gritted his teeth and leaped over a dustbin, and the Acolytes quickened their pace.

He paused at the corner of the street, and looked over his shoulder, peering at every face. The two Acolytes were running towards him, their expressions set into hardness. He recognised them. He glanced ahead. It is not over yet, he thought, and he continued to run. He was breathing harder, ragged and gasping. Haring down the street, he slipped and slid on icy puddles. He ignored his freezing feet. His muscles were beginning to ache. He had to push himself. There was only Hunter left; he could not afford to abandon her.

Ahead of him were two women, marching towards him determinedly; behind him was the tall, laughing figure of the Liberator. Pushed on by fear and adrenalin, Blackwood dived into the railway station; saw Acolytes approaching from the other side; with a terrible shock he realised that the only avenue open to him was underground. They're driving me down there, he thought. They must know he'd got the Koptor. But maybe he could hide it, maybe he could pass it on to somebody else. . . . Please don't let me fail, he thought, then inhaled deeply, filling his lungs, and went down the escalator to the tube station.

He jostled through a group of commuters, making them turn and stare. There was a stream of people going through the barriers; he stood close behind one, slipped through, and stumbled forwards.

Blackwood tripped down the escalator and paused at the entrance to the northbound platform, ready to turn down it, to jump on a train, to escape.

But how could it be? There was an Acolyte – no, two Acolytes – coming towards him, dressed like normal office workers, but he could see it in their eyes, he knew it – he backed away, and sprang down the other tunnel, the white walls flashing by him, the posters screaming messages he didn't listen to.

He reached the platform. If only a train would come, he might have a chance to get away; but turning, he saw four more Acolytes approaching from the other end of the platform. He looked up and down, left and right. He looked at the Koptor in his hand.

Blackwood took in the other people on the platform in an instant: an old man, quavering, wobbling on his stick; a row of tiny children; some rowdy young men. And then Blackwood felt a disturbance in the air, and he knew that the Liberator was nearby. He couldn't give up the Koptor. He must dispose of it. Pass it on to someone innocent, someone who could continue the work.

Freedom, thought Ivo, tasting the word, stretching his arms out as if he were flying. My own adventure into the centre of the earth. Darkness behind me, darkness ahead.

Ivo was thirteen and a half, and he had just left his new school for the winter holidays. It was Friday afternoon, two weeks before Christmas. That day, after lunch, he'd taken a train with a lot of other students, and they'd all splintered off, saying their cheery good-byes, making plans to meet soon. He was now alone, riding the escalator down into the chasm of Paddington tube station. The hum of the machinery was edgy and scuzzy. He folded his arms in again, to let a rushing commuter past, and rested on his suitcase, which crouched on the step behind him, heavy with books and discarded school clothes.

He loved riding down escalators – and today he revelled in the sense that he was travelling somewhere otherworldly, perhaps even the kingdom of the dead, for who knew what lurked down there? He was coming to London, on his own, for the first time, and he was so excited he could barely restrain himself from shouting. Ivo held out his arms once more for a moment, as if embracing it all, feeling for a second that he was hovering, and then he came to the end of the escalator and into the maw of the underground station, his bag hitting the floor with a clunk. He bought an Oyster card, went down one more escalator, lugged his bag on to the platform and stood, just behind the yellow line, waiting for a train.

There were hardly any people on the platform to begin with. Ivo could hear the distant rumble of trains, like monsters in the deep, and for a moment it felt as if he might be one of the only people in this strange under-ground city, but more filtered through – tourists with cameras slung around their necks, a raucous rugby team on their way to a match, a row of tiny red-capped children in pairs being marshalled by some stressed adults.

Somebody bumped into him and then gripped him by the shoulders. Fear clutched at Ivo. It was a man, tall and thin, young, with crazed, shining eyes. His black hair was plastered to his forehead, his cheeks were reddened; a fat vein throbbed conspicuously in his forehead. The man was panting heavily. Ivo was so shocked he could not speak. Then the man leaned into him. Ivo could smell sweat and a powerful sense of dirt. He noticed that the man's clothes were torn, and he saw what looked like a knife wound in his shoulder, barely cleaned up. Ivo stood frozen, a sick taste rising in his throat. The strange apparition said, in a clear, but low whisper, something that Ivo did not under-stand, that sounded like 'Remember: Kop-tay thur-son', and then grabbed Ivo's hand and thrust some-thing into it.

'Keep it safe. Keep it hidden. They have found me. Remember: *Koptay thurson*. There is no more time. I am Blackwood. They are coming.' He leaned in closer still. 'No one has seen us. You must continue.'

The man released him and moved on quickly, the

incident over in moments and to any passer-by it would have looked as though the man had simply bumped into Ivo and muttered his apologies before hurrying on. The man stood a few paces down the platform from Ivo. Ivo began to say something but the man turned to him and he had such a crazed look about him that Ivo's words perished in his mouth.

Ivo opened his hand. Inside it was a small black object about the size of a mobile phone, which felt heavy and cold. He thought about throwing it away, but instead, bemused, and uncomfortable at the man's insistence, he pushed it into his pocket.

A brightness dazzled him, and Ivo became aware of a man who seemed to radiate power walking past him down the platform. He was wearing a red coat that was embroidered with yellow, green and blue flowers, a purple scarf looped around his neck. The man had long blond hair that fell to his shoulders, but his back was to Ivo, and for some reason Ivo was rather glad that this was so. He moved with a liquid, grumpy grace, stopping behind the man who had bumped into Ivo. The madman – did he say his name was Blackwood? – stiffened and straightened, but did not look behind him. Ivo felt an obscure sense of danger rising within him.

He noticed that four or five other people had

positioned themselves behind the man in the red jacket. This would not have troubled him, but they all seemed to share a purpose. Looking around, Ivo saw that the other people on the platform were oblivious to all this. There had been bombs on the underground, attacks at airports; people were nervous, unfriendly. A newspaper fluttered beside Ivo's feet; its headline warned of global economic meltdown.

A semicircle had formed around the madman, as if to make sure that he could not move off, but he made no attempt to escape. What is going on here? wondered Ivo. It looks like they're trapping him.

The train roared into the platform, and Ivo shook himself; he was overreacting. The rush of air whipped his hair and scarf, momentarily covering his eyes; he pushed his scarf down. A mechanical, patrician voice warned him to 'Allow passengers off the train first, please.' He shifted himself and his bag into the next carriage along from the man in the embroidered jacket, and the doors swooshed shut, the train juddering into action. Ivo noticed that nobody else, apart from the little group around Blackwood, had got into that carriage. All had been obeying some unheard signal that was telling them to stay away, as if they had seen a suitcase with no owner.

The moment they entered the tunnel, lights flickered:

the carriage went into darkness, and then the cold, clear artificial brightness flooded back on. Ivo's excitement at being in London on his own had tempered, now and he held on to a pole for support watching a young mother holding her baby carefully. She smiled at him. He smiled back, and brushed away some scraggles of brown hair that had fallen over his eyes. He saw himself reflected in the window, wrapped in a long, black overcoat, his school scarf, orange and green, warming him, and above he saw the carriage lights repeated endlessly, hanging like full moons.

There was a scuffling noise in the next-door carriage. Ivo strained to look but could not make out anything past the packed shoulders of the people around him. His anxiety suddenly vanished; he began to feel inexplicably elated, and he sensed a bubble of happiness burst in his stomach. He felt as if a shaft of sunlight had speared through him. He had to share this with everyone. He looked round at the other people in his carriage, and they were all smiling too. It was a joy that Ivo had never felt before – pure and unmixed. The young mother was giggling, the baby emitting peals of gurgles. The rugby team were guffawing, slapping each other on the back. Ivo too began to laugh, not caring that he did not know what he was laughing about. Laughter filled his ears, rolling like breakers on a shoreline. Ivo felt that he could do anything, become anything; he felt as strong as a lion, as free as an eagle.

The lights flickered again, then went out completely. Through his snorts Ivo could make out dim shapes, smell the musty, stale smell of the tube that had taken on a sharper edge – something like lush vegetation, something like fresh woods after rain, something like wine. All around him was laughter. It was beginning to sound frenzied. The lights flickered on and off, like a strobe, and Ivo saw the distorted faces of his fellow passengers, but this made him laugh even more.

A scream rose above the hysteria, but nobody stopped laughing. And that was when it began to change, and Ivo began to feel scared: it was madness that had infected the carriage, and Ivo felt himself borne helplessly on this crashing wave. He didn't want to help whoever was screaming. Instead he just doubled up, mirthlessly choking out laughter, at the whim of some greater force, a huge, physical presence, ruthless, merciless, endless. Ivo clutched his head. He could only think of himself.

When the noise and the laughter stopped, all that could be heard was someone weeping. The lights flickered back on and Ivo blinked in the sudden glare. People stirred, voicing their fear, their confusion. The baby started to cry, its mother holding it very close to her, her bag falling to the ground as she whispered softly to it.

Sense began to return to the passengers. The train was pulling into Edgware Road. People shouted through doors to find out what was going on.

'Shall we pull the alarm?'

'Was it a bomb?'

'There was no explosion.'

'Is anybody hurt? I'm a doctor,' said somebody, but nobody answered. Nobody was hurt physically. The train benignly opened its doors. Everybody in the carriage glanced uneasily at each other, wondering what they should do. There was no announcement from the driver. People filed out, uncertainly – confused, frightened. Then there began a wailing of horror in the carriage next to Ivo's, and a crowd formed.

'Oh my God . . .' shouted someone. 'Keep those children away.'

'He's dead! He's dead!'

'Who was in that carriage? Stop them!' yelled somebody.

The tiny red-capped infants were hurried off the platform. Ivo, ignoring a man who tried to block his path, elbowed his way out and pushed to where he could see into the next carriage. It took him a while to realise that the small, soft, glistening thing he was looking at, lying on the blue checked seat, was a severed human hand.

The arrival of officialdom was announced by three men in reflective jackets, who immediately started jabbering into their walkie-talkies. Ivo was pushed away by the crowds towards the exit. Sickness surged through him. He knew the dead man was Blackwood. He'd been dismembered. How could this have happened? thought Ivo. What force could possibly rip a human body apart?

Disoriented, Ivo let himself be pulled along by the crowds away from the platform; before he knew it he was on the other side of the barriers, back above ground. He noticed with a grateful sigh that he was still holding on to his bag. As if in a dream, he pulled out his mobile phone and dialled a number. Policemen stormed into the station; an ambulance drew up outside; nobody paid any attention to him.

He listened to his phone. As his Uncle Jago picked it up, he saw, moving in the opposite direction from everyone else, cool and calm, the man in the embroidered jacket, his blond hair falling unconcernedly around his shoulders. Someone should stop him, Ivo thought. But he couldn't say anything. And he could only hear his Uncle, saying his name, over and over again, and then he slid to the floor.

Chapter Two

Rumbling, a low shaking like nothing he'd ever felt before, enough to tear the world apart. A ruined castle on a hill; a pillared, grey building, glowing with green lights; a blade slicing through light, slicing through his wrist, slicing off his hand . . . Ivo woke abruptly, clutching his hands together; they were both still there. He was panting, his heart thundering, juddering faster than he believed it could. He was in a room he didn't recognise. He stared ahead, unable to move, the paralysis of sleep enveloping him. The curtains of the room were closed. He heard gentle voices, and forced himself to turn to them.

'He's awake!' said one. A woman rushed over: it was his Aunt Lydia, he realised with a surge of relief. She was like a willow tree, thin, wavy, trailing scarves and necklaces, her fine-boned, delicate face surrounded by a mass of dark, silky hair. Her eyes focused into something like concern. Jago Moncrieff and Lydia Cathcart were his uncle and aunt, and Ivo was to stay with them for the whole of the Christmas holidays.

'Dear boy – dear Ivo – how are you feeling?' Lydia asked. She stood by the side of his bed, her scarves trailing around her, her hands held together in front of her, almost like a nun praying.

'All right,' said Ivo, though it was a lie.

'You passed out, darling, and Jago got you from Edgware Road.'

'Poor chap.' It was his uncle's voice. 'A woman answered your phone and told me where you were. Clean out, you were. You were lucky, old horse.'

'The doctor said there was nothing wrong, so he gave you something to make you sleep. You've slept all night. It's morning now,' said Lydia.

'What . . . what happened?' asked Ivo.

Lydia looked across the room to Jago, who came across and sat down on Ivo's bed. While Ivo's father looked like a cheerful sort of robin, Jago looked like a hawk. Jago was the elder of the two brothers. Everything on his face was finely drawn; it always amazed Ivo that someone with such cruel features – those of a dissolute Roman or a Renaissance poisoner – should be so nice.

'Awful business, it was. Evening papers had a field day. They don't know who to pin it on – terrorists

14

haven't claimed it. Only one dead, they say. Seems a little odd, don't you think?' Jago stood up. A purring sounded, and Ivo felt a heavy, warm object land on his bed. He reached out a hand and felt soft fur.

'This is Juniper,' said Lydia. 'She likes your bed. I'd be careful of her though, she's pregnant.' As if listening, the cat hissed, and jumped heavily off again, slinking into a corner.

A buzzing noise came from Jago's pocket and he pulled out his Blackberry; this turned out not to be the source of the buzzing and he located a phone. 'Oh dammit. I have to go. Global economic meltdown, you know the drill, only Jago can save the day. Even,' he said sighing, 'on a Saturday.' He reached across and patted Ivo on the shoulder. 'We'll look after you. Shame it happened on the first day of the holidays though, eh?'

Ivo sighed. It wasn't as if he needed to be reminded. Jago marched out of the room, the door banging shut behind him.

'I'm fine, really,' said Ivo to his aunt.

'You might think that, dear Ivo, but you've had a nasty shock and the doctor says you're to stay in bed. All right? Now, I've got a client here, so do try to be quiet. I need to concentrate,' said Lydia. 'And then I'm going to be working on the guest list for my charity thing. It's at the National Gallery.' She went over to the window and pulled open the curtains, letting in the grey light of morning.

'OK,' said Ivo, and snuggled under the sheets.

'If you need anything, call down to the kitchen – the phone's here, the number's 21 . . . or is it 22? – it's written here, anyway. Christine will help you with anything you need. There's a pile of DVDs over here, and some books, and things.' Lydia was shimmering out as she said this, her thoughts already miles away, in colour, shade, angles and light. 'We'll all have a lovely supper this evening.'

Ivo nodded, and as she left he turned over and curled up. Juniper mewed in the corner, and skittered back to the bed. 'You're all right, really, aren't you?' said Ivo to the cat as she tried to get up on to his duvet; eventually she settled for a corner by the bedpost.

Ivo was already plotting to escape. No way was he going to stay in bed all day. Besides, he wanted to find out more about what had happened on the tube. And now what his Uncle Jago had said was bait to him. This was what he'd wanted, after all. London, with all its excitement, lay in front of him.

He also knew that if he didn't go out and do something, he would brood. Whenever his thoughts drifted, a speeded-up slideshow flashed through his brain –

the panicked, desperate look in Blackwood's eyes, the shouts of the passengers, the bloody hand, the embroidered jacket, and the terrible coolness of the man who had been wearing it, walking slowly away in the opposite direction, and then oblivion.

The sound of Aunt Lydia's footsteps faded away. Ivo immediately jumped out of bed. The room was big – bigger by far than the tiny cubicle he had at school, which was just about large enough for a bunk bed and a desk. For a moment he found himself missing it – that small space which he had somehow managed to make his own, in fifteen long weeks. His room at school – his 'bolter' as it was called in the school slang – was cosy, and looked out on to a quadrangle that was never still, always full of students rushing backwards and forwards.

He got up from the bed and went over to the window and looked out into the unappetising gloom of the morning. His room, he decided, was right at the top of the house. He could see the quiet square beneath him. There was a patch of green in the middle, surrounded by trees and railings. That, he thought, might be a good place to start exploring.

Someone had unpacked for him and put all his things neatly away, and removed anything that needed washing. He noticed with a pang that a postcard from his parents had been placed on the mantelpiece, along with some money and an *A–Z*. There was also a key, which he assumed was for the front door.

The room was dotted with lively pictures and shelves of old children's books, spotted and brown with age, and Ivo felt glad to be there, the creamy wallpaper calming him somewhat. He dressed quickly, pulling on a jumper and his jeans. A thought struck him and he rummaged in his pockets.

He found what he was looking for: the black object which Blackwood had given him. He considered it for a moment, holding it in the palm of his hand. It was made out of some sort of stone, he thought. Shrugging, he put it back in his pocket. There would be time to think about it later.

He put his head round the door and looked out on to the landing. He *was* at the top of the house – a large skylight opened to the heavens, the grey December sky louring overhead. There were four other doors, all firmly closed. He edged towards the banisters and looked down. There was no sign of life. Good, he thought. Then he heard a sudden movement, saw a flash of colour.

Just for a second, he was sure the man in the embroidered jacket was walking down the stairs. He felt an overwhelming horror and shook himself. Don't be ridiculous, he thought, it's a flashback, it's not real. I'll have loads more, probably. I'll just have to get used to it. He breathed deeply, and poked his head back over the banisters. Of course there was nothing there. There never had been.

He went down the staircase slowly. All along the walls were framed paintings – some, he assumed, were by Lydia. He recognised a couple of faces in portraits, cousins and so on. There were three noisily ticking clocks, two barometers (showing different readings), some maps of counties where the Moncrieffs held land (not as many as there used to be), family photographs, some posed, stiff in black and white, and others in relaxed, laughing colour, school certificates, a Venetian mask and an 'amusing' picture of some dogs dressed as humans relieving themselves on a street. Scarcely an inch of wall was bare. When it was, it showed cream and crimson stripes.

His shoes made very little noise on the stairs, which had a thick blue carpet running down the middle. Down a flight he passed what he guessed were the family bedrooms. He heard voices as he came down the next flight on to the first floor, and saw a long, low room full of light through an open door.

He caught sight of his aunt's back as she sat in a chair, an easel in front of her, talking softly to her subject. He didn't want to alert her to his presence, so he tiptoed past. He strained to catch sight of the painting – but all he could see was a mass of colour that had not yet resolved itself into a figure.

He sped silently down the last flight, out into the hall, the floor of which was tiled and cool. Doors led into the drawing room, a sitting room and a study, and one more flight, which he didn't set foot on, he guessed went down into the kitchen in the basement.

Ivo felt a tingling all over him. It was time to test the waters of his new kingdom. London was unknown territory, just as hostile to him as the bleakness of the Mongolian steppes was to his parents. His early years had been spent at his father's house in Devon. Trees rustled by his window, a stream that could be forded ran nearby. He had no brothers and sisters, and had grown used to being on his own in the forests and fields. But all the same, he had yearned for bustle and movement, for people, lights and action. He went up to the huge black door, opened it, and stepped out into the street. The city, vast, abrasive, alive, was waiting.

'London, you are mine,' he said under his breath, and strode out into the street.

Grey clouds were weighing down, filling the sky with their gloomy presence, threatening at any moment to explode in rain that had the cold sharpness of knives. Ivo pulled his coat around him more tightly. It wasn't thick enough for this weather. He muffled his mouth in his scarf, feeling it warm up with his breath, but it soon became uncomfortable and he pulled it down, letting the wind in. He could feel it chapping his lips. Trees loomed, houses squatted, cars shot by.

He had gone to the garden in the middle of the square, but the gates had been locked and he didn't have a key, and when he'd tried to climb over the fence an angry keeper had shouted at him. He'd forgotten to bring the *A–Z* with him, but he didn't want to risk going back to pick it up. He didn't know in which direction he should walk to get to anywhere interesting. Even if he did, he reflected, he didn't know where he should go.

Sighing, he stumbled down one of the roads that led off Charmsford Square and then, wandering through a street full of chic shops and hairdressers, he came across a newsagent's. A board in front of it screamed in fake handwriting:

TUBE TERROR

He went in and bought an *Evening Standard*, and then, driven by the cold, slipped into a small greasy spoon

next door to the newsagent's. It was crammed full of formica tables, each with a bottle of ketchup and mustard nestling in the middle, a plastic menu card stuck in between the salt and pepper cellars. There was a muggy, homely smell in the air. The customers were few, and slow, muttering quietly amongst themselves.

As he waited for the waitress to bring his tea, he settled down to read the feature:

It wasn't a bomb. But at five fifteen on an ordinary Friday afternoon, the passengers of a southbound Bakerloo line train might have been forgiven for thinking so. Just before the train pulled into Edgware Road station, the lights went out. 'I thought I was going to die,' said Joan Freeman, 42, of Dulwich. 'There was a terrible screaming. I thought, "This is it."' Reports are confused, but it is known that there was one fatality. Charles Blackwood, 28, was killed on that carriage by what eyewitnesses are calling 'a terrible force'. His body was dismembered . . .

Ivo stopped reading. The soft, glistening thing he'd seen had been Blackwood's hand. Trying to ignore the sickness in his stomach, he returned to the paper. The waitress put a cup of tea on the cold table and he thanked her, and began to slurp at its warmth.

The article was accompanied by a photo of Blackwood. The tea swirled uncomfortably in Ivo's guts. The man who'd given him a black stone. His face had seemed so ordinary, and yet possessed by madness. Was everyone like that? he wondered. Did everybody carry madness inside them, like a germ waiting to multiply? He carried on reading the article.

Passengers report being taken over by an uncontrolled hysteria, leading to suspicions that some sort of laughing gas was released, though so far this has not been confirmed. Several people are being treated for shock. Police are investigating all leads, and appeal for any information.

Ivo scanned around for a mention of the man in the embroidered jacket. There was a piece entitled '*We all stand firm*' with a picture of the Mayor of London beneath; another read '*MI6 Rule out Al Qaeda*'; on the opposite page the headline screamed 'Shares in massive dive'. There was no mention of the man and he wondered if anyone would have told the police about him. Somebody else must have seen him, in that jacket. Was it worth bothering the police about, when they had so much else to consider? No doubt everybody else on that tube had their story to tell and were flocking to the police stations.

He flicked through the rest of the newspaper, moodily speeding past articles he had no interest in ('*Ten ways to stay slim this Christmas!*'; '*How will the global credit crunch affect YOU*'). There was a big feature piece in the Londoners' Diary about two brothers who were 'taking London by storm'. They looked interesting and he began to read. Julius and Strawbones Luther-Ross had thrown a party the night before, for some charity or other, which had taken place in a disused warehouse on the Thames. Those guests who had found the warehouse (several had not, as it was so obscure, and had wandered the banks of the river for hours) had discovered a sort of private play going on, and had been drawn into secret rooms, given champagne, and had generally been alternately frightened and amused.

Engrossed, Ivo hardly noticed the door to the café being pushed open wildly, and two people come rushing in. One of them dashed past Ivo's table and knocked over his mug of tea, spilling it all over his paper.

'Hey!' he exclaimed. But when he looked round, he couldn't see anything. He turned to the door and saw a man enter, a blue T-shirt flapping on his skinny body, and jeans looking somehow out of place. He was angular and pasty, his mouth curving in a sneering smile, his brown hair ruffled and unkempt. A pair of glasses hovered anxiously on the bridge of his nose. Ivo watched him storm right into the café, look around, then accost the waitress. She shrugged. The man gesticulated, and then cast round the room again.

'You,' he said, pointing at Ivo. 'Did you see a boy and a girl run in here?'

Ivo shrugged, and said, 'No.' Something stirred in his memory.

The man looked around, cursed loudly, then strode out and banged the door shut. One of the waitresses was mopping up the spilled tea and offering Ivo another cup.

'Don't worry,' said a voice. 'We'll get it.'

Ivo looked up to see a boy and a girl, faces flushed with laughter and running.

'Sorry about that,' said the girl, sitting down at Ivo's table. Her long, thin face was friendly, her eyes a dark blue, her hair very blonde. She was wearing a military-style jacket which was slightly too big for her.

'That is the last time I'm helping you two out,' said the waitress, smiling at them.

'Thanks, Jeannie. Three teas, please,' said the boy. He had almost the same face as his sister, a little

25

rounder perhaps, and his eyes were the same shade. The only difference was that his hair was black, and short, and shiny. He was skinny, and nervy, like a new-born foal, thought Ivo.

When the waitress had brought them teas and tutted at the boy, they introduced themselves. The girl was called Miranda, the boy Felix. Their surname was Rocksavage, a name which Ivo instantly liked. Felix was the elder by eighteen months – he was nearly sixteen – though Miranda said he often behaved as if he were younger. They were home for the Christmas holidays too. Most of their friends, they said, were skiing, or in the country, or on beaches somewhere, and it was very bad luck on them being in London.

'There's nothing to do,' said Miranda, flopping her head down on to the table and sighing theatrically, but when she looked up again Ivo saw that her eyes were laughing, and he couldn't help laughing too.

'Really? There's nothing to do in London?' he said. This came as something of a shock to Ivo, who'd always imagined that you could never be bored in London. 'At least you're not in Devon,' he said, remembering the emptiness of the fields, his nearest friend an hour and a half away by car.

'God I wish we were in Devon,' said Miranda. Felix raised an eyebrow, and pulled his bright red jumper sleeves down over his hands.

Mopping up the newspaper as best as he could, Ivo asked them who they had been running away from.

'That *man* is our tutor,' said Felix. 'He's called Perkins. I don't think he has a first name. We're meant to be doing five hours a day with him. Even,' he added mournfully, 'at weekends.'

'That *sucks*!' said Ivo. 'Why are you doing that?'

'Our parentals,' said Miranda, 'are, how can I put this, a little obsessive? About our marks, and so on. They want us to succeed.' She said the last phrase with a despairing look, and jangled the bracelets on her arm.

'That's actually not true,' interrupted Felix. 'Well, it sort of is. Basically, they want to keep us out of trouble. We didn't behave very well, and so our rentals made a deal with us. We work, every day, with a tutor, for the whole Christmas break, and then we get to go on a cool holiday at Easter. If we don't behave, then it's no holiday, and even MORE tutoring.'

'That's not much fun, is it?' said Ivo. 'And on Saturdays too?'

'Yup. And on Sundays. But it's OK,' said Felix to Ivo's incredulous stare, 'we've given Perkins the slip for the last three days, and he's too scared of our parents to tell them – he doesn't want to lose his job. God

27

knows they pay him enough. And we get some afternoons off. Even Perkins has to live, apparently.'

Ivo laid out the newspaper, which was still just about readable.

'You heard about this bomb thing?' said Felix.

'It wasn't a bomb,' said Ivo, then without really thinking, 'I was there.'

'No way!' said Felix.

'Yeah,' said Ivo, feeling at the same time rather proud and rather ashamed of himself for feeling proud. In order to deflect attention from himself, he spread out the paper. 'Look,' he said. 'It's all here in the report.' It was illustrated with pictures of the tube platform, and of disorientated passengers emerging blinking into the afternoon gloom of the streets above, their overcoats swathed around them like shrouds.

'That's strange,' said Felix, looking closely at the newspaper.

'What, you?' said his sister.

'Shut up. Look at that picture.'

'Yeah, she *is* fit, Felix, but we don't all want to look at her,' Miranda poked her brother in the ribs.

'Shut *up*. Look.' Miranda and Ivo gazed at the tea-stained pictures, wondering what on earth it could be that Felix had spotted.

It was Ivo who noticed. He looked at Felix for

confirmation, and felt his heart beating faster when Felix nodded. Standing just behind a pretty girl on whom the camera was focused was a face that Ivo recognised. It was the face of one of the men who had gone into Blackwood's carriage. And the face of the man who had chased Felix and Miranda into the café. It was their tutor.

Chapter Three

The bespectacled face stared out at them from the newsprint. Miranda sat up straighter, her eyes flashing uneasily; Felix leaned forwards, his face set into a quizzical expression, whilst Ivo toyed with a packet of sugar. Around them the room was hushed, the waitress rushing back and forth, the cash register ringing out every now and then. Occasionally the door would bang open and a gust of sharp cold air would enter; people would stand for a moment, blinking, and then settle into a quiet corner. A dog snuffled glumly under a table.

'Now that is weird,' said Ivo. 'He got on to the carriage where Blackwood died, I'm sure. And you know what was even weirder? They were trapping Blackwood. He was running away from them, I know it.'

'What do you think he was doing there?' asked Miranda. 'Perkins, I mean. Do you think he's got something to do with the bomb? Oh my God I can't believe it. If he has, our parents will go *crazy* . . . oh my God, Felix, how can you just *sit* there when something like this happens?' She kicked her brother, who threatened to punch her back in mock anger, curling his hand up into a fist, and distorting his face into an excellent imitation of a sneer.

'It *wasn't* a bomb,' said Ivo. His voice made the two stop.

'Well, I don't know what to call it. What would you call it?' There was a challenge in Felix's voice.

Ivo shrugged. He was feeling uncomfortably hot. Suddenly this friendly café seemed to be closing in on him, the builders at the table next to him appeared larger, more threatening, the waitress to be glaring at him, and slicing through his thoughts was the image of the hand, soft, glistening, bloody, three times as large in his imagination as it had been in real life.

'I'd call it murder,' said Ivo.

'Murder? Who was murdered?' said Miranda, leaning forward, her eyes lighting up with interest. 'We love a good murder story. We've got all the Agatha Christies, and Felix has started on Dorothy Sayers, but I don't like those so much, do you?

'Not really,' said Felix. 'Although I quite like those Father Brown ones, have you read those?'

Miranda began speaking in a reporter's voice. 'Intrepid ace Ivo Moncrieff stumbles upon a conspiracy and saves the day!'

Felix joined in, laughing, but Ivo cut through it.

'I don't . . . This is serious. This is real, and it's . . .' He stopped, not wanting to mention the black stone, and the strange words which Blackwood had said before he had died. '*Koptay thurson*. Remember: *Koptay thurson*.' He had known he would die, Ivo had seen that in his eyes. This was his last, desperate act, giving the object to a boy he didn't know. And why had he done that? It would be mad, an empty gesture, unless . . . unless he had not wanted those following him to get it. Which must mean that it was important, and, now Ivo had been entrusted with it, that he too was in danger. Those people, and the tutor, Perkins, could they really have torn Blackwood apart?

'I need . . . *I* need to find out what happened,' he said. He felt in a choking way that a net was being drawn around him, that the dim, vague future was forming into a clearly defined and dangerous path. His quiet life had so far been undisturbed by anything more exciting than being told off by his housemaster for having an untucked shirt. Now he was embarking into the unknown, and it was scary, and it was exhilarating.

Miranda pushed her hair back, tying a blue scrunchie round it. 'I wonder if this has got something to do with what Perkins was up to the other day? I hope not.' She lifted her tea in her long white hands.

'You know what?' said Felix. He aimed a jet of air at his purple-black fringe. 'I think you should come with us.'

'Why's that?' said Ivo, folding up the newspaper and stuffing it into his rucksack.

'We found something *strange* . . . you should see it. It might help you find out about what happened. Who knows?'

'Yeah, and if it doesn't, it's pretty cool anyway.'

'What is it?' said Ivo.

'That, you'll have to wait and see. Coming?' said Felix, in a deep voice.

Ivo nodded, pleased that he had made two friends so quickly. They left the tiny café, paying for the teas, joking with the waitress as they did so, and then Miranda grabbed Ivo's arm, leading him out into the street. Horns beeped aggressively, sirens wailed in the distance, a pall of fear hung over London as its citizens mobbed around, uncertain of the dangers that hid in their midst. Ivo felt it creeping into the cracks of buildings, emanating from the ground itself.

It was raining, and they began to run, slowly at first,

then leaping over puddles, whooping round corners, and Ivo began to feel free and happy. They dashed through knots of startled pedestrians, drab workers on their way back to offices; laughing and shouting, they then turned a corner.

'Hey,' said Ivo. 'This is where I'm staying. My aunt and uncle live here.' Charmsford Square, it was, though it looked far from charming, the houses looming grey and grim. 'Lydia and Jago Moncrieff.'

'Awesome!' said Felix. 'We're on the corner.'

They headed over there and jumped, jostling, up the stairs to the door, Ivo suddenly anxious that Lydia might spot him out of the window.

'Quick,' he said, as Felix fumbled with his keys, and soon they were all piling into the hall. 'What about Perkins?' said Ivo.

'Perky? It's OK, he'll have taken himself off to the Science Museum or something so he's got something to show our rentals. He'll buy a souvenir and pretend he took us with him. He did that the other day.'

'He'll run out of places to go soon, and *then* he'll be in trouble.' Felix and Miranda laughed. They had a very similar way of laughing, and Ivo felt an envious pang as he watched the siblings share their joke. As they marched on ahead he trailed behind them, feeling shy and awkward.

Ivo looked around in amazement. Their house, identical on the outside to his aunt and uncle's, was inside nothing like the comfortable, homely clutter of 43 Charmsford Square. It was all steel, black and white squares, abstract sculptures and acres of empty space. The whole right wall of the hall was an aquarium, filled with tropical fish, glowing with blue light; and the stairs that led up to the first floor were made of glass too. Ivo watched an octopus making its way up, and let out a small gasp.

'You like?' said Miranda, her face tinged from the blue glow.

Ivo nodded, dumbly. 'I . . . I think so,' he said, although he wasn't exactly sure whether *like* was the right word to describe his feelings.

'Ma's an interior designer. This is like, the *eighteenth* time she's changed the inside. You can never put anything down in this house because you never know when everything will change,' said Felix. 'It is *so* annoying. I once left my iPod on a green chair in a green room, and when I came back downstairs about three hours later the whole thing had gone. There was like a red chair and some builders and Ma said she'd no idea where my iPod had gone. Dad hates it even more.'

'Yeah, he's always leaving papers on the table and

finding them gone. And he's a politician,' continued Miranda. 'Lots of secret files and stuff.'

'Yeah, *secret*,' said Felix sarcastically.

'So where are we going?' said Ivo.

'I just need to get a couple of torches, and then we'll show you.' Felix disappeared off down the corridor; Ivo stood fascinated by the aquarium, watching the fish. Miranda sat, somewhat disdainfully, in a chair, tapping her foot on the ground.

'Where are your parents?' asked Ivo.

'Ma's at her office, in Mayfair,' answered Miranda, 'and our father works in Whitehall somewhere. Pretty dull, actually. They know your aunt and uncle – they've been to Christmas parties over there. I know I heard Daddy asking if we should get Lydia to paint Ma.'

At this point Felix returned, grinning. 'You two getting on OK?' he said. Miranda made a face, and Ivo blushed slightly.

'Come on,' said Miranda impatiently, and opened the front door, ushering Felix out, who made a mock bow as he left. Miranda turned to Ivo and grimaced, shooing him out in front of her. Back out in the cold, Felix pattered down the steps, jumping down the last couple, and gestured to them to follow.

'So . . . what's up?' said Ivo, slightly nervously.

'Well, last week,' said Miranda, 'me and Flixter gave old Perky the slip. It was Tuesday, and our parents were really busy, and there was no one else in the house, and so we thought we'd just leave. So we did. We thought we'd wait for him to leave too, and then we'd go back in the house. We were hiding in the square garden, and we saw him go out, and then, I don't know why, we thought it might be funny to follow him, because . . .

'Because,' chimed in Felix, 'we couldn't really believe that Perkins had any sort of existence outside our house.'

'I mean, you know, you've *seen* him,' said Miranda. They were walking along the south side of Charmsford Square, the side on which the Rocksavages had their house; the Moncrieffs were on the northern side. They turned right, down towards the Marylebone Road, and crossed it at the lights, jumping up and down from the cold.

'And we followed him, laughing quite a lot, obviously,' said Felix, 'and really not being very good spies at all.' They entered a small side road, on which there was nothing but an abandoned office block and a couple of half-derelict houses.

'We were just about to give up and go home,' continued Miranda, 'when we saw him stop here.' She pointed to the office block. It looked very dejected. There wasn't a single window that didn't have a crack in it, and it was plastered with signs that read '*DANGER*' and '*CONDEMNED BUILDING*'.

'So he went in *here*?' asked Ivo.

'We didn't actually see him go in,' replied Miranda.

'But he must have,' said Felix.

He led them round the side of the building. Ivo shivered, both from the icy air and from excitement. He exchanged a glance with Miranda, and felt that she shared his trepidation. Felix raised an arm, pointing at a pair of doors that looked like they led into a cellar. 'He came round here and then disappeared. He must have gone in here.'

'So whaddya think?' said Miranda. 'Shall we have a look?'

'We didn't go in before,' said Felix. 'Miranda was scared.'

'*Miranda* was scared? You were the one who suddenly started squealing.'

The siblings stood facing each other for a moment in silence, and then turned to Ivo, who nodded quickly. Felix bent his head once, as if confirming his thoughts about Ivo, and said, 'Good man. Help me open these.' He aimed a kick at the doors, and Ivo did so too. Thump after thump, they kicked at them, until eventually the lock caved in.

Miranda jumped from foot to foot, rubbing her hands. 'God, I'd go in there now anyway,' she said. 'It's so cold out here.'

Ivo peered into the opening. He could just about make out a flight of steps leading down into the darkness. He stopped at the edge.

'You all right?' said Felix.

Miranda was already on the third step down.

'Can't catch me!' she called, and, suppressing his fears, Ivo followed her, Felix coming close behind.

Blackness. Ivo could hear his heart thumping.

The passageway was musty. It was tall enough to stand up in, and wide enough for Ivo not to be able to touch both walls at once. He could hear the earth around him, full of subtle noises. He imagined creatures slinking in their tunnels, the tube trains sliding in and out of platforms like hideous white snakes, fat with their human cargoes. Ahead he could hear Miranda feeling her way along the walls, occasionally giggling and shrieking a little. Behind him was Felix, relaxed, whistling under his breath.

Something jumped at him – a face, ghastly, half-illuminated. Ivo faltered for a minute; it was Miranda. She pointed the torch at her own face, showing only her cheekbones and her forehead.

'What is this?' said Ivo, in hushed tones.

'Who knows? Follow me.'

Felix appeared. 'Here, take this.' He pressed something cold and hard into Ivo's hand. 'Maglite. Come on.'

They crept on. Damp filtered through Ivo. After about five minutes or so, during which Ivo began to feel that he was becoming hypnotised by the darting beams of light from the torches of Felix and Miranda ahead of him, his own showing up patches of damp and mould and brick, the wall that he had been running his finger along came to an abrupt end.

'Look,' said Felix. 'There's a door here.' A faint light was coming from the other side. Felix took the handle. 'Ready?' They looked at each other.

'OK,' said Miranda. 'Three . . . two . . . one.'

Felix pushed at something, and switched his torch off, pulling Ivo with him.

Light flooded Ivo's eyes, making him blink in the shock. He took in a large, cold, institutional-looking room, with stacks of containers placed around the edges – dozens of them, all piled up higgledy-piggledy, with papers and tools and bits of old electrical equipment pouring out of them. The space was about the size of a classroom, and there were doors at both ends of it. A few fire extinguishers provided a splash of violent colour against the uniform whiteness of the walls. The lighting was fluorescent and bright, casting long shadows over the mass of objects. There were desks, and office chairs, and even what must have been an old computer – a large, cabinet-like thing with spools of tapes and many incomprehensible switches. Ivo half expected it to turn itself on and start buzzing, like some haunted machine, but thankfully it remained still.

'Pretty cool, huh?' said Felix, running into the middle and flopping on to a chair, releasing puffs of dust. 'God knows what Perky was doing down here. This place has been abandoned for *years*,' he said, holding up a desk diary that said 1965.

'Maybe there's a whole network,' said Miranda.

'I think it's, like, something to do with the Cold War,' said Felix. 'You know, bunkers and stuff, and biological warfare and nuclear weapons.'

'Weapons of mass destruction,' said Miranda.

'You're a weapon of mass destruction,' said Felix. Ivo laughed.

'That's right, Ivo, laugh at Felix. He is *so* funny I can hardly contain myself.'

Miranda grimaced and sat down. Felix leaped up and grabbed the back of her chair, spinning her around faster and faster, Miranda shrieking with delight. 'Spin me too!' said Felix, jumping on another, and Ivo did, and soon they were all laughing.

'What was that?' said Felix suddenly, stopping himself with his feet. Ivo's snorts died down. Miranda came to a creaky halt. They fell silent. A rhythmic, clanking noise was coming from nearby: noise like people walking. The three looked at each other for a second. Unease had slithered into the marrow of their bones. Ivo could feel warning signals flashing through his body, as if he were a small mammal that could sense the presence of a hawk above him. He obeyed those signals instinctively.

'Come on, hide,' said Ivo, surprised at himself, dragging Miranda and Felix behind a stack of large boxes that stood next to the entrance they'd come in by. Ivo pulled them down just as the doors on the other side of the room were flung open, and they heard the marching of feet and the murmur of voices. Through a crack between the boxes, Ivo could see the shapes of some figures. He motioned to Felix and Miranda to keep quiet. Miranda shrunk down next to her brother, who put his arm around her.

They watched as the figures came into the centre of the room, and heard somebody throw themselves into a chair. 'So,' said a voice, 'we eliminated Blackwood.' An ecstatic cry filled the air, coming from many people's throats, sounding like a pack of hounds. 'One more gone! But . . .' and the voice changed a little, became a little entreating, 'he did not have the Koptor.' The word shot through Ivo's brain like a bolt.

'It has been lost. Now,' he said, over mutterings, 'there is nobody to blame for this. It was to be expected. So we will set our best agents on it, and perhaps we ourselves will take an interest if there are no developments. We must find it! Perkins, I will entrust this to you.' There was silence after he spoke. Then, hesitantly, someone said, 'Will you show us?'

'Ah. You want to know what it feels like? To be free?'

Ivo could feel expectancy in the air.

'Yes,' came Perkins' voice and others added their assent.

'Well . . . it would not be good to spoil it now, would it? Maybe, just a little . . .' The voice began to sing, sonorously, two syllables – a long 'eee', and then 'oh'. Eeeyoh, eeeyoh. It was a wonderful sound. It made Ivo's skin prick with pleasure. The other people in the room joined in. A strange light spilled out to where the three were hiding, and they slid further back. They could no longer see anyone. Ivo let the sounds wash over him, and into him, let the voice become a part of him. He could feel it stretching into every inch of his body. He was alive with it. Happiness coursed through him. He could see that Miranda and Felix were experiencing the same thing, and suddenly knew this was wrong, just like it had been on the tube. Don't give in, he commanded himself. Felix released Miranda and sprang forward and, alarmed, Ivo grabbed him and held him back.

'I want to see!' he hissed at Ivo. 'Get off me.' Ivo shook his head and pinned Felix's arms to his sides. Miranda, who had shut her eyes, opened them. Taking in the situation, she too put her arms around Felix and held him back. Felix struggled a little. He kicked out, and a box almost toppled over, but the people in the room were too wrapped up in their chant and did not notice.

Time expanded. Ivo became aware of the ache in his calves from crouching. He put his hand to the floor to support himself. At last the chanting came to an end and the ecstatic feeling ebbed from the room, like the last rays of the sun behind a hill.

'There. You see.'

A murmur of wonder passed through the group.

'Now, let us go.'

Ivo waited until the last footstep had gone, and then released Felix. The lights went out.

'What the hell did you do that for?' snarled Felix.

'Stay quiet,' Ivo whispered. 'Hold on to each other's jackets. Keep together. Follow me.' Ivo felt his way to the wall and edged round it, knowing that the door was near. He soon found it and reached up for the handle, opening it with barely a sound. He crawled into the tunnel, feeling Miranda behind him. Once through he stood up and helped Miranda to her feet, Felix hot on their heels.

In total silence they stumbled back through the tunnel, torches blurring and jittering in front of them. The journey seemed to take for ever. Miranda fell, Felix caught his arm on a nail in the wall, Ivo tripped and banged his head.

Only when they emerged out into the freezing street and had closed the heavy doors did Ivo feel he could speak. He rubbed his hands together, ignoring the cold in his bones. It had begun to drizzle slightly. Felix was still glaring at him.

'I was enjoying that! Why did you stop me?'

'It . . . it was dangerous!'

Felix growled in anger and turned to go, thrusting his hands deeply into the pockets of his jacket, striding on ahead, his eyes fixed upon the ground. Ivo noticed he was shaking. Miranda, glancing apologetically at Ivo, said, 'Come on, we have to follow him. I've seen him like this before. He'll calm down soon.' They kept a few paces behind Felix, who stalked on angrily. They crossed the Marylebone Road and made their way back into Charmsford Square. Felix, fiddling with the latch, flung open the door and stomped inside, scaring the fish as he entered; Miranda and Ivo went after him, into the kitchen.

'Jeezus,' said Felix as they came into the clean, bright, stainless-steel kitchen, with its table shaped like an hourglass and its two enormous fridges. The three of them were very dirty, their hands filthy with black dust. Ivo's jeans had a rip in them, and Felix was bleeding, whilst Miranda had lost one of her bracelets. They washed in the sink. Miranda automatically put on the radio and poured glasses of orange juice, her briskness hiding her anxiety. Tinny, cheerful pop music filled the room. Felix rootled around in a cupboard for plasters, and eventually found some, muttering under his breath, 'You can never find anything in this damn house.'

'What the hell were they doing?' said Miranda finally. Her eyes were wide and afraid, liquid like a hunted animal's.

'I don't know what it is but it's happened to me before,' Ivo said hesitantly. 'On the tube. It's the same, the hysteria, the . . . I don't know, the elation. That's why I . . . that's why I stopped you.' He caught Felix's

46

eye and saw a softening in him.

Miranda suddenly sat down, trembling, spilling orange juice. Felix comforted his sister silently, the two of them sharing each other's confusion.

'We've got to find out what's going on. This Blackwood guy. Who was he? You still got the paper?' asked Felix, a little brusquely. 'That feeling . . . it was amazing. We have to find out more about it. Perkins . . . to think that he was hiding that all the time! I wouldn't have thought it of him, the little runt.'

Ivo nodded, though he was a little alarmed at Felix's enthusiasm for the feelings that had overcome them in the underground room. He pulled the newspaper out of his rucksack, scanning the articles. 'It says Blackwood's name, and that he lived in Kensington.'

'We have to go there,' said Felix.

Ivo nodded. He had to make sense of what had happened on the tube, and of what Blackwood had said: '*Koptay thurson.*' The man who led the chant had mentioned something called a 'Koptor' – did that have something to do with it? And they were setting their agents after it . . . Ivo wondered whether to mention the strange object Blackwood had given him, but it didn't seem like the right time. He somehow didn't want Felix and Miranda to think that he was any more implicated in this than they were. It was enough, for now, to have them on his side. How strange, he thought, that one moment you can be sitting in a café, quietly drinking tea, and the next you have been plunged into something beyond undersanding and terrible.

They made plans to meet, and Felix and Miranda promised to keep an eye on Perkins. Ivo left the house slowly, his thoughts twisting and jumbling.

Chapter Four

It wasn't raining any more, and in the pure winter sunlight the houses looked almost unreal, as if they were in a television adaptation. Ivo half expected a horse and carriage to come trundling round the corner. Some houses had already put Christmas wreaths on their doors, and he could see into drawing rooms with cards filling up mantelpieces, and presents jostling for position under trees spilling their needles on to carpets. Here and there the sound of carols rippled from windows.

As he walked across the square to Number 43, Ivo wondered how deeply Perkins was involved with the murder. It could be a coincidence that he had been there at the station. But not that he had been in the underground room. Perhaps Perkins was after the thing Blackwood had given him – if Perkins was in league with Blackwood's killers, then Ivo would have to be very careful. He felt sure he could trust Felix and

Miranda – he was positive that they would tell him immediately if they found anything out. He had liked them both immediately – Miranda with her hair blonde like the sun, and Felix with his eyes like burnt toast.

It was now just after lunch. He'd been away from the house for almost three hours. He quietly inserted his latchkey, pushed open the shiny door to Number 43, and went in; Lydia didn't hear Ivo coming up the stairs, engrossed as she was in painting her new client, so Ivo managed to sneak in without mishap. Juniper had settled on his duvet, and as he shooed her off, she hissed at him, baring her claws. 'Leave it, Juniper,' he said, and he slipped into his warm bed, and for the next three hours or so he dozed, haunted by what he'd seen. He knew that it was all connected and that he was now inextricably linked to this odd series of events, and he fell asleep, fighting against the nightmares which scratched at his mind like a cat at a piece of furniture.

When Jago came up at about seven and sat concernedly at the end of his bed, Ivo was gently snoring.

'Ivo . . . Ivo, old boy, wake up,' Jago was saying. 'Supper's at eight and we've got a guest.'

Ivo woke, startled, and glanced about him. 'It's all right, old horse, it's all right,' said Jago. 'Are you up for some supper? Don't feel you have to. But it might do

50

you good, and Lydia would like you to meet her guest. You know what Lydia's like. Well, you don't. But you will soon.'

'Who is it?' said Ivo blearily, trying to wipe away the imprint of Blackwood's severed hand, which had burst on to the cinema screen of his memory.

'Some chap called Julius Luther-Ross. Don't know anything about him. Appeared from nowhere, suddenly he's everywhere. Don't know anyone who went to school with him – or university. You'd think he was a Kennedy from the way Lydia bangs on about him.'

Jago's Blackberry whirred and beeped; he picked it up and spoke commandingly into it. When he hung up, he smiled at Ivo. 'Another crisis averted.'

Ivo scrabbled for his rucksack and found the page in the Londoner's Diary. 'Is this him?'

Jago took the paper from him, his hawk-like features screwing up in a thoughtful expression. 'Julius Luther-Ross. Yes, that's it. Odd name. Not one I know. Not Scottish, that's for sure. Not related to any Rosses I've ever heard of. Bags of money though. Don't know where it came from. Not the city. Lydia's painting his brother. Of course, Julius is helping her with this enormous party that she's throwing at the National Gallery.' He said the last sentence with weary irony; Jago always pretended not to like whatever it was that

Lydia got up to, but he inevitably ended up enjoying things much more than she did. 'You don't have to come down if you don't want to,' said Jago, genuine sympathy in his voice; his Blackberry vibrated again and he swore. 'Damn these people all to hell. Hello?' he spoke once more into it, issuing instructions with the swiftness and concision of an army officer.

'It's all going down the chute,' he said after he'd hung up. Ivo noticed he looked tired. 'Luckily we're all right, but after tomorrow . . . there's trouble in the air, Ivo. But don't worry about it. Still . . . it's going to be chaotic.' His phone rang, at the same time as his Blackberry, and he swore even louder. 'Right,' he said, 'I've got to go and deal with this. Do you think you'll be coming down?'

Ivo decided that he was definitely going to go down for dinner. He wanted to meet this Julius Luther-Ross, to see what it was that the rest of London saw in him.

'Do I need to be smart?' asked Ivo.

'Not really. Just . . . er, wash up a bit,' said Jago, ruffling him on the head, and then he left the room with an odd smile on his face, fielding both calls at once.

Ivo immersed himself in a shower in the bathroom that opened into his bedroom, the hot water enveloping him like a sheet, put on some clean clothes from the pile which had been thoughtfully placed on the green and gold ottoman that guarded the foot of his bed, did what he could with his hair (which meant flattening it with water) and about twenty minutes later he had stumbled down the stairs and slumped into the drawing room.

He was now sitting, very awkwardly, on the edge of a chair, a small glass of wine held between his hands. Lydia had given it to him as he entered. He rolled it between his palms, warming it. He liked the colour of red wine, so deep and dark and inviting. He had not been in the drawing room before, and he took the opportunity to look around it.

It was not over-formal, but cosy, with comfortable, straight-backed chairs with rather tatty upholstery huddled around the edges; a large table was bursting with art books and magazines; a baby grand piano stood in one corner, on whose top reclined several family photographs, including, Ivo noticed, one of his own mother and father holding him as a toddler. He had a silly smile on his face.

The wallpaper was blue and white and above the mantelpiece was a painting of which Jago was extraordinarily proud. It was always mentioned when people talked about Jago and Lydia Moncrieff. ('You must see that painting they've got in their drawing room, it's by some Italian chap.')

It had been bought by one of Jago's (and Ivo's) enterprising ancestors on his Grand Tour of Europe. It was not an 'old master', but had been done by somebody's pupil. It showed a young man leaping in the middle of a collection of nymphs, lions, satyrs and tigers; near them was a woman who stood at the edge of the painting, looking away, unaware of their presence. The colours were bright, the figures almost like in a photograph, every fold of their clothing and every leaf on their brows standing out sharp and clear.

To Ivo, the woman's face seemed extraordinarily sensitive, and it was almost as if he could feel what she did. She thought that she had been abandoned on the lonely sand; she thought her fate was to die alone. Ivo looked at the band of people coming up behind her, and wondered if it would be a better or worse fate to go with them.

'Bacchus and Ariadne,' said Lydia quietly, noticing Ivo staring at the painting. She was sitting in the recesses of a plump armchair. 'She was abandoned by Theseus, the man who she'd loved enough to betray her own family. She is about to be rescued by Bacchus. Rescued? Or imprisoned. Some say he turned her into a constellation – imagine! Wheeling through the blank depths of space for eternity, your consciousness transformed into something entirely other.' Her voice, lilting and strong, bore into Ivo. 'Look at it more closely,' said Lydia. 'Notice anything strange about it?'

Ivo got up and moved closer to the picture, holding his drink carefully so that it wouldn't spill. He inched towards the fireplace and peered at it. There *was* something strange about it – none of the other figures were touching the leaping young man, and if you looked at it from a certain angle, there was a negative version of him, just beside him, as if a figure had been painted out. Ivo noticed this double, and looked inquiringly at Lydia; but at that moment Jago came in, followed by someone else, and Lydia perked up enormously. Her whole body was animated, and she raised herself from her armchair, standing tall and straight, her arm outstretched and open in a welcoming gesture. Her face turned in an instant from lugubrious to sparkling, and her lips parted to form the words 'Darling Julius . . .'

Ivo observed the man carefully. He was wearing a dark blue suit, with low-key pinstripes, and it looked as if every move he made was posed by a photographer. He was very still. His blond hair was not slicked back, but rather messy, although it did give the impression that it had been carefully arranged to look that way. His suit had obviously been made for him; his tie was knotted perfectly. It was blue silk and had little green vine leaves on it. His face was long and looked as if it would never run to fat. His skin was pale, unblemished, startling, like a dove's feathers, which made his eyes prominent – they were, thought Ivo, the colour of the wine in his glass; but then he saw that it must be a shadow falling across Julius's face, and when he turned his eyes again to Ivo, they were a normal shade of blue.

For a second he did not seem to have noticed Ivo at all, and then he moved forward, fluidly, gracefully. He extended a hand, and Ivo leaped up.

'This is my nephew, Ivo Moncrieff,' said Lydia vaguely, as if she had temporarily forgotten who he was, and Ivo found himself blushing slightly. But as Julius looked at him, Ivo's blush burned even deeper, for being under that gaze was like being on a stage and having the glare of footlights on you. Ivo's mind suddenly blanked.

'Ivo – an excellent name,' said Julius, his tones soft and understated.

'Why is that?' asked Ivo, in great confusion, blurting out the words before he'd thought about them.

'Because ivy is the greatest plant – it lives by clinging to others, but in fact it has the most power. Slowly, it can bring down whole buildings. Is that not so, Lydia?'

'Yes, Julius darling, it *is* rather like that, isn't it? Now let's all sit down and have a drink. Christine has made the most extraordinary cocktail with the most extraordinary name – you can't *think* what she's called it,' she continued chattering to Julius, pouring drinks from a jug.

Ivo was relieved that Julius had taken his skewering eyes off him, and sat down again unobtrusively.

He was rather left out of the conversation after that, and as they finished drinks and moved into dinner, he began to wish he hadn't said he would come down. He could have been upstairs checking the news. He wanted to see if anything more about Blackwood's death had been reported, and to find out about what Blackwood had said to him. *Koptay thurson*. Odd sounds, not from any language that he knew of, he thought; it didn't sound like French or Latin. Maybe it was Scandinavian or something . . .

Dinner went on – there were five courses, one after the other, with wine filling Lydia's and Julius's glasses, glowing rich and dark. Jago, having to work early the next morning, despite it being a Sunday, abstained, but cheerfully made up for it by attacking each course with relish and having at least twice as much as anybody else. It was, thought Ivo, amazing that he could eat so much and yet be so thin.

By the end of the meal boredom was throbbing in his head like an ache. So he was extremely pleased when Lydia glanced over to him and said, 'Now, darling, why don't you go on up to your room, Julius and I are going to talk shop.' Not, thought Ivo, that you've been talking anything else all night, but he didn't say anything, and got up hastily from his chair. He kissed Lydia goodnight, and Jago squeezed his shoulder; as he passed Julius, unsure, he offered him his hand. Julius turned slowly to look at him, and smiled, not taking the proffered hand; something clicked in Ivo, and he turned and fled up the stairs.

Halfway up he became aware of a flicker of movement ahead of him. What was it? He stalled in his tracks, one foot on the stair ahead, one foot perilously below; he clutched the banister. Could it be? He thought he saw a flash of red, yellow, blue and green bursting round the corner, the jacket he'd seen on the man at the tube station; suddenly it felt as if a ghost had walked out of his brain and he was trapped in a nightmare. He felt clammy and frightened.

'Don't be stupid,' he said to himself. 'Go and have a look. There won't be anything there.' He filled his lungs with air, and cautiously climbed the remaining steps on to the landing. The flash of colour had gone off around the corner. I have to see, he thought. Slowly, each step making very loud creaking noises, he trod down the passageway; there was only one door, and it was ajar.

It was the door to Lydia's studio. There was a light

on in it, and a low hum of classical music – Lydia often liked to listen to the radio as she was working. She must have forgotten to turn it off.

He pushed open the door further, and then jerked back – was that a laugh? No, it was on the radio, a squawk of clarinet, a bristle of violin. He inched further into the room. There was the easel, not three feet away from him, and there was Lydia's stool, her brushes neatly put away, a cloth over the picture; and there was the armchair in which her subject sat.

For a moment Ivo stood paralysed, shots of fear flowing up his veins; there on the armchair, wrapped in the embroidered jacket, was a person – but his eyes were green, with no pupil or iris, just wholly, entirely green. His skin was mottled and liver-spotted and wrinkled and his hair was like a black horse's mane, falling and falling down his back, and the grin revealed teeth pointed like rusty nails.

Ivo, wits blown away, feeling like a rabbit being shot at, turned on his heel and banged the door, and dashed up the stairs, leaping the steps three at a go. It's not real, there's nothing there, he thought. When he got to his room, he pulled the door to and turned the key in the lock; he sank, breath heaving out of him, into a corner. He had to stop seeing things. He had to take his mind off it, find the root of the problem.

There was a computer lurking in the corner of his bedroom. He went over to it and turned it on. After a couple of moments of thought, he pulled up a news website. The main story was still the tube horror of the day before; the credit crunch, Afghanistan, the embattled Prime Minister, floods and a supermodel's baby were relegated to the sidelines. There was nothing new about Blackwood, as far as he could see. He typed the name into a search engine, but when a million results came up he realised the futility of that action. He picked up a few of the stories, but they all said much the same as the one he'd read in the paper.

He pushed his chair back and flung himself on his bed. He sent a text to Felix, asking how they'd got on with Perkins. A few minutes later his phone beeped. 'No developments,' it said.

Koptay . . . Maybe it was from Greek. Wasn't 'helicopter' from Greek? Was it *helios*, the sun, and *kopto*? What could *kopto* mean? He tried to remember, but couldn't.

Exhausted, Ivo extinguished the computer and, throwing off his clothes, sank into bed. Outside the roar of London, awake and frightened, ebbed and flowed; cars screeched round the square, foxes coughed, and rain spurted down; and after a long period of fluffing his pillow and rolling fruitlessly from one side of the bed to another, Ivo eventually fell asleep. Just after he did, he was briefly woken by the sound of the front door shutting, and Julius Luther-Ross left the house, climbing into a waiting car, and somebody else left the Moncrieffs' house and got into the car with Julius.

A scraping noise, insistent and low, awoke Ivo. He hovered for a second, imprisoned on the wrong side of sleep, seeing fantastical shadows around him. The noise was coming from the pile of clothes on his chair. He considered briefly whether Juniper might be trapped underneath; then he thought maybe it was his phone, on silent, vibrating quietly. Thinking it might be his parents, calling as they often did at odd times of the day, he heaved himself out of bed and lumbered heavily over to the chair.

He saw what he thought was his phone glowing inside one of his pockets. Sleepily, he put his hand into the pocket and pulled it out. But his fingers didn't find the buttons. Shaking himself a little more awake, he held the object in front of him.

It was, he saw, the black stone which Blackwood had thrust into his hands. Frightened, he dropped it as if it were hot; and then, curious, he knelt, and gingerly reached out to touch it. He grasped hold of it, feeling it cold in his hands. It gave him no shock, so he lifted it up, and held it out in front of him. Where was the light coming from? he wondered.

He moved over to where the desk was, and cleared a space, placing the object carefully on the table top. He could make out three letters on its side, glowing faintly.

FIN

The light that the object emitted was extremely calming; it made him feel as if everything were safe and ordered. He picked it up and examined it. It was totally blank, apart from the three letters. He pushed and prodded it a bit; it made a low mechanical noise, and a long, thin blade extended from its end. Though he was taken aback, it seemed entirely right that a blade should come out of it in this way. Experimentally, he swung the blade around, as if it were a sparkler, and its glowing tip left a trail in the air. He wrote his name in light, and watched it vanish; and then he wrote the three letters on the side of the object.

In a crisp, clear way he realised that this was a message. Blackwood. FIN. He wondered what it could mean. He sat, suspended, for a moment, feeling so peaceful and at ease that he almost didn't want to move back to bed; but then the object stopped glowing, and the blade retracted; and Ivo was left, standing in his boxer shorts in the middle of his bedroom. He sat thoughtfully on the end of his bed, before climbing back under the duvet; he held the object to his chest, and then stayed, lying on his back, staring at the ceiling as outside cars growled and the rain battered his window.

Chapter Five

Jago threw down his newspaper on to the break-fast table. 'I told you so,' he said abruptly to Ivo, who was drowsily eating a piece of toast. Jago put his hands behind his head and stretched. Ivo looked at the newspaper, which told him it was a Monday morning. The basement kitchen was warm, and Ivo was huddled in his dressing gown. He'd spent all of Sunday in a kind of trance, pootling around his room, watching films, and resting, and he still didn't feel quite right. He hadn't spoken to Felix or Miranda, or received any communication from them, and he desperately wanted to see them.

'*Apocalypse now!*' said the headline.

'A little over-dramatic,' said Jago, 'but quite close to the mark. The economy is in serious trouble. There'll be worse headlines soon, you can bet.' He sounded, to Ivo, almost pleased, as if he were relishing the situation. 'Well,' he said, 'you know sometimes I wonder what the point of it all is.' He stood up, immaculate in his suit, his hair slicked back, only the bags under his eyes hinting at any stress he might be under. He patted Ivo on the shoulder. 'See you soon, old thing, OK?' he said, and left the room.

Ivo nodded and took the newspaper. He scanned it for new information about Blackwood's death, but the credit crunch had forced the murder into the obscurity of the middle pages now, and there was only one small notice about it, which said that as yet nobody had been arrested or charged. Interestingly, it also said that the people who'd been in the carriage itself had all experienced some kind of amnesia. Ivo cast aside the newspaper, and continued to eat his toast.

Lydia came wafting into the kitchen at this point, followed by Christine. Christine had worked for Lydia and Jago for ten years, and was very thin and wore very long dresses of varying shades from purple to green. She lived in the basement flat, into which nobody was allowed, and from this sanctuary directed the households of the Moncrieffs in London and in the country. She cooked beautifully and always wore a black apron over her dresses (which never looked like the sort of dress that had been made to cook in). 'Yes, dear Christine, I think stew for lunch will be marvellous, that's a wonderful idea, of course we will have Strawbones with us then.'

'Well, you've got him now,' came a voice, and a man walked into the room. He was about six foot one, Ivo noticed, and he had the longest, blondest hair that he had ever seen on a man. It was glossy and shook and shimmered as he moved. He was very slim, and moved in a boneless way, his limbs seeming almost to be made of putty. His smile was radiant, lighting up his clear blue eyes, his red lips curving back to reveal rows of white teeth, with two elongated canines. He was wearing a dark blue shirt, faded jeans and a thick black overcoat.

'Darling,' said Lydia, kissing him absently on both cheeks, 'I am glad you've come early. I feel we're getting to a very important stage with the painting. Now, where are we, yes, this is my nephew Ivo, who's staying with us for the holidays.' Strawbones moved first to Christine, taking her hand and kissing it in a remarkably old-fashioned manner, and then he turned to Ivo and, straightening, held out his hand. Ivo stood up, holding his toast, and muttered through a mouthful, 'Hello.' He dropped crumbs on to his dressing gown and brushed them off, embarrassed.

Strawbones fixed him with his blue eyes and smiled. 'How lovely to meet you,' he said. 'I've heard a lot about you.'

'Have you?' said Ivo, surprised. He couldn't imagine Lydia talking about him to anyone.

'Of course! Your uncle and aunt have told me all about you, and about your family. They're away, aren't they, in Mongolia?' Ivo nodded and rubbed his eyes. He remained standing, and Strawbones, with fluid grace, motioned to him to sit down, and then, when Ivo had settled himself, sat in a chair opposite him. Christine and Lydia murmured together. Ivo poured Strawbones some tea from the large yellow teapot, and Strawbones inclined his head in thanks, making a gesture of mock servility, which made Ivo laugh. He couldn't tell how old he was – he could be sixteen, he could be twenty-five.

Lydia came over. 'Now, Strawbones, darling, I have to go up and phone your brother about the menus. Will you give me a few minutes and then come up to the studio?'

'Of course, Lydia, of course,' said Strawbones, smiling. 'I'll keep Ivo company, if he doesn't mind?'

'No, not at all,' said Ivo. Strawbones settled into his chair, and picked up his mug, sipping quietly at it. 'So how are you finding London?'

'Oh – good, I suppose,' said Ivo, unable to keep his disappointment out of his voice.

'Not been having much fun, then?' Strawbones

looked at him sympathetically.

'Well – I haven't been here very long, and I guess . . .' He stopped, unsure what to say.

'Jago tells me you had a pretty nasty time on the tube?' His voice was low, empathetic, inviting confidence. Ivo nodded.

'Yeah,' he replied. 'It was *nasty*. I saw . . .' He looked at Strawbones, and then looked away. 'I saw . . . that man's hand. They'd torn it off. I mean, who would *do* something like that?' He looked up into Strawbones's eyes; he was looking at him evenly, with an expression of quiet sadness.

'Look, Ivo,' said Strawbones, 'you've had a tough time. But hey – what do you say that I take you out? Lydia said you might need someone to show you round a bit. We can go and see a film, get some food or something. Might take your mind off things.'

Ivo looked up at him. 'Yeah,' he said. 'That would be great.'

Strawbones looked up at the kitchen clock. 'I think it's time for me to go up there,' he said, pointing to the stairs. 'See you later, OK?' Ivo nodded.

Standing up, Strawbones stretched, and emitted a groan which was half-yawn, half-cry; and Ivo was sure he saw, poking out of Strawbones's coat pocket, the head of a snake. It peeked out just a little, hissed, and flickered its forked tongue; Ivo was about to say something, but Strawbones turned and left. What's happening to me? thought Ivo. Now I'm imagining snakes. He shook his head violently, and drained the last of his drink, plonking the mug down with a bang that caused Christine to turn and look at him.

'How goes it, my little one?' she asked, and Ivo shrugged. Christine's English was almost faultless, and it was only occasionally that she made a mistake; she did however sometimes sound like a schoolbook. He got up from the table, pulled his dressing gown around him, thanked Christine for breakfast, and pottered slowly upstairs. He'd arranged to meet Felix and Miranda at eleven o'clock. He reached his room and got dressed, trying to shut out the image of the snake in Strawbones's pocket, then checked his emails to see if there was anything from his parents (there was – a shortish note telling him about their latest camp); there were a couple of messages from his schoolfriends, which he replied to, and then he called up a search engine, and tapped in the word 'Koptor'. No useful leads appeared. He tried 'FIN', and various combinations of both, together with Blackwood's name, but each time, frustratingly, he came up with nothing. He spent the next couple of hours listlessly playing a computer game, and then at ten to eleven he bounded down the stairs to go to Miranda and Felix's house.

He crossed the square, and rang on the doorbell, which was answered, Ivo found with a shock, by Perkins, grim-faced and wearing a black woolly jumper, who glared at him. Ivo was unable to say anything.

'Ivo Moncrieff?'

Ivo nodded, once, avoiding contact with his eyes. 'They're expecting you. Go on. They've got half an hour's break. You can talk to them for that long, then you're out.'

Perkins motioned Ivo through the hall, with its vast blue aquarium, and Ivo ran up the stairs to the first floor, where there was a small sitting room, in which Miranda and Felix now reclined, bickering quietly.

'Hey,' Miranda said when Ivo came in, and got up and gave him a hug. Felix acknowledged him with a swift nod. 'We've talked about it,' said Miranda softly, 'and Felix agrees with me now. He says that you were right to stop us. Isn't that right, Felix?' she said, turning to her brother, and Felix, looking away from Ivo, said, 'Yes, that's right.'

Ivo told them, as briefly and succinctly as he could, about what had happened to him on Saturday night in his bedroom.

'Fin? Like a fish?' Miranda slurped her tea, jingling an armful of bracelets.

'Or like "the end" in French?' Felix crossed one long, lazy, bony leg over the other. 'Or is it just a name? Some people are called Fin, aren't they? Or could it be, like, someone from Finland?'

'You're SO helpful,' said Miranda. 'That's F-I-N-N, anyway, bonehead.'

'I don't know. It could be any of them. Or all of them.' Ivo was leaning his head on his hand, his arms in front of him, moodily staring. He had placed the object on the table, and it lay there, the others too wary to touch it. Ivo picked it up, fingered it, and slid it back into his pocket, feeling its weight.

'It's a message. I don't know why, but Blackwood chose me to get this message. I think he must have been assassinated, and he wanted me to look after this. The people who killed him must have wanted this. So we have to guard it.' Ivo said this slowly. He had been thinking a lot, the thoughts sloshing around his mind like eddies in a river. 'But I don't know what the next step is. How do we find out anything about Blackwood? He was so strange, I almost think he didn't exist . . .'

Miranda and Felix looked at each other, Miranda with her eyebrows half-raised, Felix with a sort of smirk on his mouth. 'Well, Felix has actually done something useful with his life for once,' said

Miranda, elbowing her brother.

Felix ignored her and calmly patted his pockets, eventually fishing out a piece of paper. He passed it over to Ivo without a word. It was an address.

> *Charles Blackwood*
> *17 Cavendish Mews*
> *SW3*

'Blackwood's address? Where did you get this?'

Felix looked into the corner of the room. 'Well . . .' he said carefully, 'let's just say that it's on a need to know basis.'

Miranda made a face. 'He hacked into Daddy's computer. He's got access to loads of records in the government and stuff. Flixter, of course, knows how to get into them – much better than poor old Daddy.'

'It's in between the King's Road and the Fulham Road. I looked it up in the *A–Z*.'

'Felix! What a legend! Thanks! How can I pay you back?' Ivo exclaimed, almost jumping up out of his seat.

'Ah, don't worry about it,' said Felix. 'So what do you say? Shall we go and take a look? Might find something interesting there.' He wiggled his hands in a spooky way and Miranda threw a cushion at him.

'Yeah, definitely!' said Ivo. They spent the rest of the break chatting until the door banged open, without any ceremony, and Perkins marched in.

'Right, you two,' he said, picking up Felix by the scruff of his jacket, 'let's go. Time for some Maths. Hurray! You,' he said, turning to Ivo, 'clear off.' He pulled Felix, protesting, out of the room, and Miranda, apologising to Ivo, followed.

'I'll text you later,' she said, and left Ivo on his own.

Coming downstairs, he paused to look at the fish swimming in their blue prison, so brightly coloured, little flashes of fire in the coldness.

'They're beautiful, aren't they?' said a voice, and Ivo turned to see a rather haughty-looking woman, dressed in a cream suit.

'Oh ... yes, lovely,' said Ivo. 'Er ... I'm Ivo Moncrieff.'

'Jago's nephew? Yes, I know, you're staying with them this Christmas, aren't you? I suppose you've met my wild children?'

Ivo was a little flustered. 'Well ... yes, I suppose so ...'

She laughed quietly and said, 'I'm Olivia. Now you couldn't do me a favour, could you, and tell Lydia we're coming to her party, and that I'm dying to meet this Julius? Thank you,' she said, moving to the door and opening it, 'I'm sure I'll see more of you,' and Ivo, not quite knowing what had happened, found himself on the doorstep, the door closing firmly behind him.

Chapter Six

While the Rocksavages were doing their lessons in the afternoon, Ivo was sitting in the drawing room of the Moncrieffs' house, picking out a tune on the piano, when the door opened to reveal Strawbones, who swung back and forth on the door, smiling at Ivo. Ivo closed the lid quickly and stood up, uttering a garbled, 'Hello.' He was wondering what he could say to him. The piano stool scraped on the wooden floor.

'Want to go out?' said Strawbones. He pushed his curtain of hair back behind his ears. 'I've finished with Lydia for the moment.' He smiled again, curving up the side of his face in a fashion that made whoever he was with want to smile too.

'Where shall we go?' Ivo said.

'As the whim takes us,' said Strawbones, and went out quickly, leaving Ivo to follow in his wake. Strawbones was out of the front door in a flash, picking up his long black overcoat as they went. Ivo barely had time to get his coat and then ran after Strawbones, who was loping quickly ahead. They walked companionably for a while, and then got on to the tube: five stops south on the Bakerloo line and they were in Charing Cross Station.

Once they were outside in the freezing air, Ivo couldn't help but gasp in admiration as they approached Trafalgar Square. Ivo saw two of the great lions, gazing out magisterially over the traffic, and then as they neared he saw the base of the great column with Admiral Nelson standing at its top. The square had been infected with a sense of festivity: it was draped with lights, twinkling faintly in the dim daylight. Tourists, wrapped up in scarves and hats, mounted the lions and posed for photographs by the fountains. Ivo wanted to stop and gaze up at the statues, but Strawbones grabbed his sleeve and pulled him onwards towards the National Gallery.

The enormous building, taking up almost the whole of the north side of Trafalgar Square, looked as if it had been built as a palace: it had a huge central dome, two wings that spread on either side, and a vast entrance hall, with steps leading up to it. Many people swarmed up and down them, clutching umbrellas, scarves across their faces against the cold. Large, martial-like flags hung down from the roof, advertising the current exhibitions.

Strawbones didn't say anything, but pulled Ivo straight into the gallery, and up the stairs into the central hall. The first thing that Ivo felt was an enormous sense of space and peace. Huge, hushed galleries stretched out on either side. He wanted to linger, but Strawbones acted as if he knew exactly where he was going and dragged him on by the sleeve. The marvellous paintings on all sides went by in a blur. After a short while, they came to a small room with wooden floors and dark red walls. Two leather sofas were positioned in the middle, so that weary visitors could rest. Strawbones led Ivo over to one, and plonked himself down in it. It was comfy, and Ivo leaned back.

'Now,' Stawbones said, 'look at that painting.'

Ivo did so obediently. It was very familiar. It looked almost exactly like the painting in Jago and Lydia's drawing room, except that theirs was less colourful and had less action in it. This was a riot of tone and movement: there was a man leaping out of a chariot, and it felt as if he was leaping out of the painting and into the gallery.

'It's a Titian,' said Strawbones. 'Bacchus and Ariadne – like the one in Jago's room, but that isn't a real Titian, of course. And that one is . . . different. Do you know why?'

Ivo studied the picture in front of him, taking in the smiling, cheeky faun at the bottom, the two sedate leopards, the followers entwined in ivy. 'Well . . . in Jago's painting, there are two people in the chariot – but one of them has been painted out.'

'Right first time! You are sharp. Sharp as a spear,' said Strawbones, grinning his benevolent grin, his face lit up by it. Some tourists clustered around the sofa, hoping to sit down, and Strawbones pulled Ivo off. 'Here, please, sit down,' he said, as if it were his house, and he led Ivo slightly away, walking out of the room.

'There are two forces in the world, Ivo,' said Strawbones quietly, so that Ivo almost had to strain to hear. 'Two major forces, that is. One is shown in that painting you've just seen.'

'What do you mean – Bacchus?'

'Yes – or, as the Greeks called him, Dionysus. The god of wine. The Dionysian power. The power of freedom. And then, opposing that, is the Apollonian. Apollo, god of music, order, symmetry.'

'So why are there two people in Jago's painting?'

Strawbones grinned again, quite wolfishly this time, Ivo thought, and said, 'because sometimes two people can be Dionysus.' And then a crowd of people bustled past Ivo, and he lost sight of Strawbones, and when the tourists had passed, waving leaflets and maps, Strawbones had gone.

When Felix and Miranda had finished their lessons at five thirty, the two siblings came lolloping down the stairs and settled in the basement kitchen. Their mother was there, quietly writing in a large bound notebook; the radio was on.

'Hello, darlings,' said Olivia. 'How were your lessons?'

'Filthy,' said Miranda.

'Horrific,' said Felix. They glanced at each other. Their mother was bent over her work. Miranda was wondering about Perkins. She hadn't discussed it with Felix, but felt that she was bound to tell her mother what they'd seen. He could, after all, be dangerous.

Miranda said, 'In fact . . . Ma, I think there's something you should know about Perkins.'

'Oh really?' answered Olivia, with an amused glance. 'Has he been whipping you? Or performing other barbaric and cruel acts?' She laughed. 'You know our pact. You have lessons every day, and behave well, and you will get an amazingly cool holiday at Easter.'

'Oh Ma, don't joke,' said Miranda, anxiety creeping into her voice. 'You know the stuff that happened on the tube?'

'Yes,' said Olivia, 'horrible, isn't it?'

'He was *there*.' Miranda went up to her mother, and grabbed her by the arm, forcing her to look right at her.

'Oh I know, darling, he came straight and told me. He says he doesn't know what happened. The police took him aside – he's got total amnesia. Poor thing. I asked him if he wanted time off, and he said he didn't – so there you go. Pretty brave of him, don't you think?'

'Ma!' said Miranda, bursting with urgency. 'We hate him!'

'That's nice,' said Olivia, with an amused glance. They knew when they were beaten; Miranda retreated back to the sofa. 'I met your nice friend Ivo today,' continued Olivia.

'He is nice, isn't he,' said Miranda, and then said, 'Ow!' as Felix kicked her.

'Miranda fancies him,' said Felix.

'I do NOT!'

Their mother got up, slightly awkwardly, and pushed her hair back. 'I'm off up to the study,' she said. 'Lydia wants you to meet these Luther-Ross people. I'll tell you when, OK?'

'OK, Ma,' they both murmured, and she went out. Felix then turned to Miranda. 'Why did you say that to Ivo?' he asked. 'I mean about me agreeing with you? I don't.'

'You mean, when Ivo stopped you from going into that frenzy? Are you mad?'

'No!' said Felix, his eyes glistening. 'I felt it . . . I know what it is – I think I do, anyway – and I want to know more about it!'

'But Ivo says it can kill people!' said Miranda, shrinking from her brother.

'Yes, yes,' said Felix. 'But if harnessed properly . . . just think!'

'Well, I think you're crazy,' said Miranda, and pushed him. 'I'm going to watch TV. You can come if you like, but I think you need to calm down.' And she left him, long arms crossed over each other, eyes alive with fire.

Felix waited for a little while, and then, checking that no one was around in the hall, slipped upstairs. His father had a small study right at the top of the house – an attic, basically, with little more than a small table, an old computer and a few books in it. Felix slid into it. It was dark outside, street lamps casting their dim glow upon the ground. He didn't turn the light on. He switched on the computer, which took a few minutes to warm up, and sat down at the desk, one spindly leg dangling. He rubbed his hands in the cold. They never turned the heating on up here. Eventually, the screen lit up, and Felix tapped in the password that he'd found in his father's papers. His face took on an unhealthy green light. The system blinked, and up came the government data centre. Felix smiled, showing his long teeth, and continued his searches. He kept his ears strained for the slightest of noises. After a while he went to the door and looked out; then came back, and soon there was something wheezing out of the ancient dot-matrix printer. He'd found the plans for the tunnels, and, as yet, he wasn't sure what he was going to do with them. He folded them up and put them in his pocket, turned off the computer and went back innocently to the sitting room to join his sister.

Dancing flames threw shadows on to the walls. A large mastiff lay in front of the fire, its tongue hanging out; it raised its eyebrows slightly as a door opened and two men walked into the room. Outside it was night, the freezing sky picked out with stars, the orange glow of lamp posts tainting the pavements with a sickly hue. Inside the room it was sweltering, but the two brothers did not seem to notice. Their faces were very similar, looking almost as if they had been carved out of wax, devoid of any colour.

They sat down in heavy armchairs, on either side of the fireplace. The mastiff placed its head back on its paws, whining slightly; one of the men aimed a kick at it.

'Don't kick my dog, Strawbones.'

'I will kick it, if it whines.' He ran a hand through his thick blond hair.

Julius sighed. 'You are starting to annoy me,' he said. The flames flickered light over his face; smoke billowed, but neither man coughed. The dog whimpered and padded to the door; they ignored it. Strawbones leaned forwards, and lit a candle that stood on the table in between them; then he held the candle up to Julius's face. Julius tapped long fingers on the side of his face; his nails were long, and pointed, and very, very clean. 'Do you have to be so *blatant*?'

Strawbones began to laugh, at first quietly, and then louder; and then suddenly, in the middle of a spurt, he stopped. 'I did the job, dinn't I?' he said, imitating a Cockney. 'Don't blame me, guv'nor.' Then he returned to his normal voice. 'You just haven't got the *guts* for it, have you, old brother of mine?'

Julius stood up quickly and grabbed Strawbones by the throat, raising him up from his chair; he choked and grabbed at Julius's arms, flailing in vain. 'Stay out of trouble,' Julius rasped. 'You,' he said, gripping around his brother's neck harder, 'cannot afford to spoil everything. I will do more than this, next time.' He released Strawbones, who dropped back on to his chair, feeling around his throat.

'That really *hurt*,' he said in a whiny voice, and looked up at Julius.

'Do you swear?' asked Julius.

Strawbones looked right at him. 'I swear,' he said; Julius smiled. 'Of course I swear,' Strawbones whispered, and sat back in his chair, shaking with silent laughter. Julius returned to his seat. The fire burned out, and for a moment it seemed as if only their eyes could be seen, four little orbs glowing strangely.

From his window Ivo watched the Moncrieffs' pregnant cat Juniper heave itself along the road, and he felt it to be an omen. He had begun to believe that every movement of every branch, every flutter of a bird's wing, was a sign. She's hiding, he thought, or in flight from something. He watched a flock of sparrows bloom out from a tree, like a mushroom cloud, and speed off in the same direction, away from 43 Charmsford Square. Everything is running away, he thought. It was the next morning, Tuesday, and he had slept for only three hours the previous night.

The crumpled postcard from Mongolia caught his eye from where it was nestling on the shelf in between some other of his keepsakes. He went to it, the light from the window barely illuminating it, turned it over and read:

Darlingest Ivo,
We are thinking of you so much. We talk about
you every day. It won't be long now before we're
home. We'll be back for New Year's Eve.
Your ever loving parents.

He put it back on the mantelpiece and sat down at the computer, logging on to his email. After a couple of seconds he brought up on screen a small, grainy video. His mother's face, shining and pink-cheeked, appeared taking up almost all of it. 'Whoops . . .' she said, and then stood back. 'Er . . . Hello, Ivo!'

Ivo moved his mouth in response. The face disappeared, and then the camera was picked up and tracked over a huge, open space. It was arid, but there were sparks of life here and there – ground squirrels, clumps of grass clinging on, a motorbike shooting across the Mongolian plain like an arrow. In the distance was the faint glimmer of water. There was a moving figure, small, getting bigger, coming straight towards the camera. It resolved itself into a horse, and on it was his father. His mother laughed. 'Here comes Daddy,' she said. The horse slowed to a trot, and then a walk, and drew up in shot. Ivo's father patted the horse's neck, and then leaped down. His hair was blown back, and he looked exhilarated, his round face made ruddy by the wind. He came to join Ivo's mother. 'Hello, darling, I'm making a video for Ivo!' His father beamed, and turned to the camera.

'Ivo! We wish you could be here with us. Look – it's magnificent!' He took the camera from Ivo's mother, and tracked it over the landscape. 'They used to venerate the wolf. All this was grassland.' There was an edge of sadness in his voice. 'Everything depended on everything else. The grassland needed the wolves, and the herdsmen learned from them. It was a balance – complex, fascinating, every factor as necessary as a cog in a clock. It worked. The herdsmen worshipped Tengger, and when they died, they gave their bodies to the wolves so that their souls could fly up to Tengger. And then the farmers came, and slaughtered all the wolves. But the wolves are clever, Ivo – they moved on, they found a way to be free.' He stopped speaking and held the camera facing himself, and leaned in to Ivo's mother and said, 'We love you very much, darling.'

Ivo stopped the video. He was lost in thought, when the door opened quickly and Strawbones came running in and flung himself on the bed.

Ivo could see a tangle of blond hair, a yellow embroidered shirt and a pair of jeans, and the flash of a brightly coloured waistcoat, and he could hear sobbing, then Strawbones turned over, and Ivo realised it was laughter. The young man's face was completely crumpled up, and dry, racking sounds were issuing from his mouth, which was opened like a gash, revealing canines that looked like they would have no trouble tearing apart a raw steak. The red lips eventually closed, and Strawbones's eyes, which had been screwed shut, opened; on seeing Ivo, they closed again and the laughter began once more.

Ivo was unsure what to do, and embarrassed, and eventually decided that he should make his presence known; so he coughed, quite loudly, and Strawbones immediately sat bolt upright, although he seemed unable to do this for very long, for he quickly lapsed and relaxed, putting all his weight on one elbow. He was curiously long, thought Ivo, and limp, as if he didn't have any bones at all; his face, on the other hand, was defined as clearly as if a sculptor had chipped it out of marble.

'Er . . . hi,' said Ivo. He couldn't think of much else to say. 'Did you . . . want to go and do something?'

'Er . . . hi to you too,' said Strawbones, imitating Ivo's confusion, and giggled, though didn't quite fall back into his hysteria. He had a long red scarf around his neck, looped several times, in which he buried his head, the blond hair falling over it.

Strawbones, when he had finished, and taken a deep

breath, looked up, his eyes bright and his mouth grinning. He held out his hand in greeting, and Ivo moved forward rather awkwardly to shake it. Strawbones clasped it, and patted him on the shoulder.

'Ivo, my friend,' he said, 'I didn't know anyone was in this room. I didn't mean to barge in like that. Sorry. It's just . . . it's just some people will do *anything*.' He put his hands over his mouth and emitted a curious squealing noise, like a pig. Ivo realised that he was still laughing. He contained himself, and stopped, and looked up at Ivo once more.

'That's . . . that's all right,' said Ivo. 'Is . . . is Lydia painting you today?'

'Yes,' said Strawbones, and threatened to burst into laughter again, but managed to stop himself. He snapped upright and began rearranging some objects on Ivo's bedside table, placing books on top of each other and then knocking them all aside. Then he got to his feet, and began to sway; Ivo started to laugh, and Strawbones began to play up to it. First he jigged like a chimney sweep, waving an imaginary brush from side to side; he pretended to kill a standing lamp; he conducted a duel with an imaginary opponent, thoroughly enjoying the thrusts of his sword, and eventually, tired of his exertions, but obviously pleased with the reaction they had caused in Ivo, he collapsed upon the bed again, directing a beam of such joy at Ivo that he immediately lost all his inhibitions.

'Is Strawbones your real name?' said Ivo conversationally.

'No,' said Strawbones, suddenly serious.

'So why do they call you that?'

Strawbones shrugged. 'I don't know. I've had it for a long time. I suppose it's because I broke my arm about a million times when I was young. And my legs. I kept falling off horses and stuff. So they said my bones were made of straw, and my brother started calling me Strawbones, to annoy me, and it stuck, and then I ended up kind of liking it.'

'What is your real name?' asked Ivo.

'You wouldn't want to know,' said Strawbones, and all the light had gone out of his eyes. He threw himself back on the bed and stared at the ceiling.

Ivo, feeling rather shy, said, 'Why were you laughing so much?'

Strawbones stretched and yawned, like a cat, and said, 'Oh, at something very funny, that's all.' The young man sat up, and faced Ivo, a grin on his face. Ivo found that he desperately wanted to know what had made Strawbones laugh, and that he wanted to make him laugh too. Strawbones turned away from him, and was hidden from Ivo by a fall of hair; when

Strawbones turned back his expression was set.

Strawbones opened his lips slightly, and Ivo started back as a small, forked tongue appeared; Strawbones opened his mouth wider and a garter snake darted out, hissing, and slithered down softly on to a hand that was carefully put out for it. Ivo watched as the snake wove its way between Strawbones's fingers, emitting little, cross explosions. Watching Ivo carefully, Strawbones grinned, and suddenly the snake was gone. Ivo remembered the snake that had been in his pocket in the kitchen, which he thought he had imagined. Ivo froze. He didn't know what to think or say. Strawbones made no reference to the reptile. Ivo was about to open his mouth to speak, when Strawbones moved to the door.

'And now, shall we go down to the kitchen?' asked Strawbones quietly. 'I've worked up rather an appetite.' Ivo nodded, confused. Strawbones was so strange, so changeable. Ivo liked him, that was true, but he was also a little scared of him, as if he was in a cage with a tame tiger. Strawbones made you want to follow him, to dance with him, to fight for him. If Strawbones walked off a cliff, thought Ivo, then he would probably follow.

They left the room together and pounded down the stairs, Strawbones taking them three or four at a time, and Ivo behind him. They entered the kitchen to find that Christine had got everything ready for lunch, and nobody else was around.

Strawbones slid into a chair, and it looked almost as if the chair should be grateful that he was sitting in it. As Christine ladled out some stew, Strawbones made a ridiculous, hungry face. Strawbones's hands were very long, and the bones could be seen under the skin; his veins were quite prominent, and almost blue, like Chinese porcelain.

'How much?' said Christine, holding the ladle over Ivo's bowl, and Ivo, catching her eye, indicated that he wanted lots. Christine filled it up and placed it in front of him, smoothing down her apron. 'Have more, there is a whole vat, and I do not think there is anybody else who wants it. Have you seen Juniper? Are you looking forward to the kittens? I do not know who the father is, she is a very naughty cat.'

Ivo laughed and said he had seen her walking down the street this morning, but not since then.

'I will leave you to eat then,' she said, 'But you must find Juniper and feed her. *Au revoir*, Monsieur, *à bientôt*.' She smiled at Ivo, nodded at Strawbones, and Ivo watched her go, then turned his attention to Strawbones, who was scooping up the stew as if he hadn't eaten in months. He barely chewed each mouthful, and let the gravy run down his chin, but somehow in him it did not look unattractive.

When he finished, Strawbones looked absently out of the window, and Ivo was squirming in his seat. Ivo ate a particularly hot potato and, frantically blowing and waving his hand, quickly swallowed a glass of water; he noticed that Strawbones was looking directly at him with a skewed expression.

Strawbones leaned forward, picked up a decanter and poured himself a glass of wine; he filled Ivo's glass too, ignoring the fact that it had half an inch of water in it. Ivo picked it up hesitantly, and gulped at it.

'Where's the snake?' asked Ivo, emboldened a little.

'What snake?' said Strawbones, looking thoroughly confused.

Ivo spluttered.

'What are you laughing about?' said Strawbones, suddenly, and with such vehemence that Ivo nearly jumped out of his chair.

'Nothing! I wasn't laughing.'

'Are you *sure*?' said Strawbones.

'No . . . no . . . I wasn't!'

Strawbones paused and looked evilly at Ivo, before bursting into laughter again.

'Got you there!' he said, and Ivo found himself joining in with the laughter, it was so infectious.

Strawbones put his hand in his pocket, and out of it came the tiny, jewelled garter snake. Ivo watched the shining beast slither around on Strawbones's hand. He put the snake on the table gently, and it moved over towards Ivo. Ivo instinctively moved backwards. Strawbones regarded him keenly. Ivo didn't want to touch the animal; he felt repulsed by it.

'Do you want to touch him?'

Ivo shook his head. 'No way,' he said. 'Is it poisonous?'

'Hmm,' said Strawbones. 'I don't think that matters. I think you're restrained by something.'

The snake eased its way forwards over the white tiles of the kitchen table, its tiny, dart-like tongue shimmering in and out. Ivo didn't want to seem cowardly in front of Strawbones, so without waiting for him to say anything, he put his hand on to the table and let the snake slither on to him. He couldn't help shuddering, but managed to repress the thought. He felt the creature on his skin, cool and alive. He held his hand out, as Strawbones had done, and let the snake weave in and out of his fingers. He was surprised to find he loved the sensation of the animal, wild and free, connecting with him in this way, and he gazed at it, mesmerised. It coiled off his hand and dropped elegantly to the table top, sliding back across to

Strawbones, who scooped it up and stowed it away. There was no need for him to say anything; he merely caught Ivo's eye, and a deep understanding flashed between them. Ivo knew that he had proved something to Strawbones.

Strawbones poured Ivo another glass of wine. Ivo was feeling giddy, his cheeks were getting red, and his mind was getting fuzzy. The ruby, warm liquid looked almost like oil as it slid into his glass.

'Wine, Ivo, nectar of the gods, ambrosia even. It's a strange business, wine, and an even stranger thing to want to do – to *intoxicate* oneself, to be out of control, to lose your senses, don't you think?'

Sleepily, Ivo nodded, the warm, yellow walls of the kitchen cocooning him.

'Let me ask you something, Ivo,' said Strawbones, his long teeth gleaming in the light. 'Do you think you're happy? Do you think that you have everything?'

'Well . . . yes,' answered Ivo. 'I mean . . . I'm pretty lucky, don't you think?'

'Yes, Ivo, you are. But even if you have everything, even if you lack for nothing, are you then truly happy, truly free?'

Strawbones leaned back, rocking on two legs of his chair, pushing his bowl carelessly away, holding the wine glass to his cheek.

'A long, long time ago, Ivo, there were two men who thought they had everything. They were rich – richer than your Uncle Jago, richer than the richest man in England, richer than Croesus. They lived in a country thousands of miles from here, in a haunted, freezing castle on top of a mountain.'

Strawbones rocked forward on his chair, making a sharp crack on the stone floor of the kitchen, and leaned his elbows on the table. His voice was soft, and it soothed Ivo, as if he were much, much younger, and being read a story by his parents.

'They thought that they had everything. All the barons in the lands around sent them tributes, they had silks, horses, furs, maidens. They could *kill* a peasant,' he said, his voice rising, gripping the edge of the table, the wine glass forgotten now, 'if he failed to pay due obeisance, and nothing would happen to them. Sometimes they would kill for fun, sometimes out of pity, sometimes out of duty. You don't believe me?'

Ivo shrugged, moving his glass from side to side upon the table top. 'I don't know what to say. It sounds like a fairy story.'

Strawbones shook with laughter, banging his fist upon the table, shaking his glass so that his wine was spilled, looking for all the world like spilled blood. He stopped laughing, his teeth bared, his eyes soft. He twisted his scarf around his neck, and breathed deeply, heartily, his chest expanding.

'They became bored. They felt that their life was meaningless. What were they doing, spinning endlessly on this rock? Was there a God? Was there *anything*? They began to search, everywhere. And it was pure chance that brought them meaning, Ivo. Can you imagine? Chance! It made them think that there *was* some authority in the world. For they found something that gave them ultimate power. It was a remnant, Ivo, something left over from the days of the gods; and it still had some power within it, stronger and stranger than anything they had ever felt before. They used it, and were filled with new life . . .'

His words were loud now, echoing in Ivo's skull, battling for possession of his brain, some repeating themselves, some fading. *Left over from the days of the gods* . . . Ivo was feeling dizzy. Strawbones's outline was blurred, now it looked as if he were growing, expanding, until that alabaster face was larger than a giant's, and the whole room curved around him. And then his voice drifted off, and immediately, almost shockingly, Strawbones was sitting there, thin and nervy, dangling his glass between his fingers.

'And what happened to them?' said Ivo slowly, as if in a dream.

Strawbones was silent for ten, maybe fifteen seconds. Then he leaned forwards, grinned, and said, *'They lived happily ever after.'*

The rest of the meal was in silence.

When they had finished, Strawbones said, 'Shall we go and look at my portrait?'

'Do you think Lydia will mind?' replied Ivo, struggling to say something normal.

'Oh, *she* won't mind,' said Strawbones, and leaped off his chair as if he were a deer, and scampered out of the room, with Ivo trailing behind him.

'Oh wait,' said Ivo. 'I was meant to feed the cat.' He went to the French window, which led into a small garden, in which was a little stone fountain surrounded by grumpy looking statues of nymphs. The only things that inhabited the garden were rats and a noisy dog fox.

'Puss!' he shouted. 'Here, puss! Where are you? Juniper!'

Strawbones came and stood by him and joined in with his shouts. They searched round the garden, but could find no sign of her.

'I saw her going up the road earlier. God knows where she's got to,' said Ivo.

'I'm sure she'll return. They always do,' said Strawbones.

*

97

Lydia's studio was empty of Lydia – she had gone to consult with Julius about the party. Long, low and open to the world, it was full of washy light. Spatterings of drizzle on the windows made a not unpleasant sound. There were relatively few paintings hung here – some abstract ones of which Lydia was particularly proud, which she enjoyed having around her.

The easel was set up near the door, and there was a stool perched in front of it; behind the easel was the chair, draped in cloth, in which Strawbones sat for the portrait. Ivo didn't expect to see anything in it, he'd managed to banish the hallucinations from his mind, and he was feeling brave with Strawbones and the wine.

'Do you know much about art?' said Strawbones softly.

Ivo didn't, and said so.

'I don't either, although I have seen a lot of it. So many paintings, so many . . . I wonder what it is that they all want to say – what do *you* think the point of it is?'

He went towards the easel. 'I mean, come and look at this. This is Lydia's portrait of me. She's been doing it for, I don't know, a week now. Come, look.'

His voice was low and hypnotic, and warm, and Ivo drifted over to where he was standing, his body shielding the painting from him.

'I mean, is a portrait meant to capture one's *essence*?'

'I think so,' said Ivo. 'Isn't it meant to show your personality? Painters are meant to see your soul, aren't they?'

'They are . . . so what, Ivo, do you make of this?'

Strawbones stood aside and revealed what stood on the easel.

A mass of colour, light and shade, all swirling together; the strokes seemed to be shifting, vying for dominance. Ivo squinted at it, but he could not make out a figure.

'I can't . . . I can't see you,' said Ivo.

'Try harder,' whispered Strawbones.

Ivo moved nearer. The colours of the painting were clashing together, they seemed to move as he looked at them – and yes, he could see a figure, although it changed: now it was a man, with bloody hands and black hair; now it was a deer, rushing through forests wild with fire; now it was a youth, throwing stones into a savage sea.

What am I seeing? thought Ivo, as he came closer to the painting.

'You can see,' whispered Strawbones, and Ivo was aware of menace clawing down his side, his senses were suddenly as keen as a hound's on the trail when it finds blood. The weft and warp of the world had been pulled tight and something was about to break; somebody was whispering madness into his ear, madness that was sweet, knowable, enticing.

'Ivo. Ivo?' came a voice from downstairs, and Ivo turned round, pale. He was alone in the room and Strawbones was nowhere to be seen.

'Ivo! Come down here. I want you to come here, now.' Lydia's voice sounded terrible, a biting edge of authority in it which made Ivo rush downstairs.

'What is it, Aunt Lydia?' he said when he'd reached the hall.

'Look.' Lydia's stern face puzzled Ivo. The front door was open, and Christine was hanging out of it. It sounded as though she was sobbing.

'*Mon dieu*,' she was saying. '*Mon dieu. C'est un diable . . .*'

'Do you know anything about this?' asked Lydia. She wasn't accusing, but puzzled. Ivo looked at his aunt, and shrugged. Tenderly, Lydia pulled Christine aside, revealing what she had been weeping over.

There, lying on the front doorstep, was Juniper, the cat, and somebody had taken a knife to her, and slit her from end to end. And not content with this, where her tail had been there was nothing but a raw, bloody stump.

Chapter Seven

Ivo padded down the stairs later that afternoon, still reeling with shock from seeing Juniper dead. No one in the house had seen or heard anything. Two policemen came to take statements, but left without anything useful to say. Christine had been given the rest of the day off and was recuperating in her flat.

Ivo passed the drawing room, and paused to look in at the painting of Bacchus and Ariadne. He was about to enter, when he saw Strawbones, sitting on top of the piano. He'd swept away everything that was on top of it. Ivo nearly said something, but Strawbones was staring straight up at the ceiling, mouthing something; so, without disturbing him, and greatly puzzled, Ivo went out of the room. He had arranged to meet Felix and Miranda at the bus stop, as Perkins was having one of his afternoons off and so they were free. Felix was wearing a black jacket, which fitted him very smartly; he dug his hands into the pockets and had put his collar up, in what he thought was an extremely cool way. Miranda was huddled up in a fleece. She blew some strands of hair away from her face as Ivo came up, and grinned at him; Felix nodded curtly. Ivo told them about Strawbones sitting on the piano, and about the cat, and then the bus came.

They found seats on the top deck, right at the front. Ivo loved the crazy feeling that you were floating high above the busy streets, and everybody below looking so small, and the shops and houses looking unreal. Despite the weather, and the general mood of financial gloom, Oxford Street was pulsing with crowds, all bent on buying. Buses snarled up the street, letting out hoots and honks as they filled up with passengers and dodged pedestrians.

The journey didn't take long, down Park Lane and round Hyde Park Corner, and along Sloane Street on to the King's Road. They jumped off the bus quite far down the King's Road, and walked on a bit further; soon they were standing at the end of the mews where Blackwood had lived. It was a tiny road, hidden in between a jeweller's shop and an expensive restaurant. The houses were very small, but well cared for, window boxes enlivening the facades.

Number 17 was squat and painted an incongruous

peach colour. The doorknocker was shaped like a heraldic fish, a spiky dorsal fin sticking out of it.

'Well, there's your fin,' said Felix.

'Should we knock?' asked Miranda.

'Why? No one's there. Blackwood's dead, remember.'

'Shh,' said Ivo. 'So how do we get in?'

But Miranda had already pushed in front of him. 'Come on, Flixter,' she said commandingly. 'Show him the goods.'

'Right.' Felix rubbed his hands together and blew sharply on them. 'Card please.'

Miranda dug into her pockets and pulled out a cash card. Felix, looking from right to left, went casually up to the door, and jammed the card into the gap between the lock and the wall. He fiddled for a few seconds, and then appeared to be satisfied. 'Gentlemen,' he said, and pushed at the door.

To Ivo's surprise it opened. He turned to Miranda. 'Where did he . . .'

Miranda shrugged. 'Don't ask. Too much time on our hands.'

'In quick, guys,' said Felix, and they followed him. Felix pulled the door to behind them.

The entrance hall was narrow and crammed with objects, all of which were disappointingly ordinary. A telephone table was piled high with books. A flight of stairs led straight up to what must be a bedroom, whilst a cramped passageway led into a room which served as kitchen, sitting room and dining room.

It was oddly baronial, with panelled walls and a large fireplace. The mantelpiece was marble, and the pillars holding it up were fluted, carved with intricate fish. A large oak table stood in the centre. The room was ridiculously messy – a chaos of ashtrays in which cigarette butts and olive stones jostled for space, fragments of quails' eggs, candles long burned down to the end, photographs scattered aimlessly, as if Blackwood had had no real interest in them, jumpers cast across sofas, a bike helmet on a hatstand, a toothbrush on a bookshelf, every kind of book imaginable, in every kind of language, and the papers – piles, reams, acres, of papers, all towering and spilling from box files, arch files, folders and filing cabinets.

'Sheesh,' said Felix. 'Where do we start?' He put both hands on top of his head, revealing his skinny wrists, and kicked at a pile. It tottered for a second, and then slid over. The movement caused a minor avalanche; the three of them watched, helpless, as stack after stack fell. Clouds of dust poured up.

'What?' said Felix, in response to baleful glares from Ivo and Miranda.

'There must be something here, some clue somewhere, that explains why Blackwood was killed,' Ivo said, prodding a collapsed stack with his toe. Nothing happened. 'OK,' he said, sighing, 'we'll do this systematically.' They split the room up into thirds and began searching.

Fifteen, maybe twenty minutes went by. Felix began to grow restless. He flung down a file. 'I give up,' he said, stretching his long body and giving an almighty yawn. 'There's nothing here, and if there is we'll never find it. It's a mare's nest. A wild goose chase.'

'Don't be like that,' said Miranda, and they began to bicker.

Ivo looked up. 'You don't have to help me if you don't want to,' he said, somewhat snappily, and then regretted it, and then they all started arguing.

'Look,' said Felix, 'I know it's important to you but I'm not going to spend my free time trawling through papers. I don't even know what I'm looking for. I want to go to the cinema. I want to go swimming. I want to hang out. I want to play on my PS2. I want to do *loads* of things. I mean really. What do you think, we really believe you, that some weird object told you to come here? FIN!' He went to the mantelpiece. 'Or did you expect something else? Did you think you'd push one of these and then something would happen?' He pushed and pulled at the fish on the mantelpiece, angrily. 'See. Nothing.'

'Well, it was your stupid idea anyway,' Ivo snapped back.

Silence enveloped the room, and Ivo felt the hugeness of the exercise bearing down on him. Maybe Felix was right – there was no point. Whatever mystery Blackwood had entrusted him with would have to remain that. There was no way he could find out. He put down the folder he was looking at. He would never uncover what had caused his death, never put a stop to the dreams that haunted him.

'You're right,' he said quietly. 'It's no use. Let's go.' He got up without looking at Felix.

'Oh Ivo . . .' said Felix.

Miranda, meanwhile, had been fiddling with the mantelpiece. 'Wait!' she said, looking at the fireplace again. She frowned. 'Have you still got that thing – what was it, that said FIN on it?'

Ivo took it out of his pocket and held it out.

'Look!' Miranda grabbed Ivo by the sleeve and pulled him to the fireplace. She felt carefully over the fish again, and then her forehead creased, she took the object and fitted it neatly into a small depression on the underside of the mantelpiece. It clicked in, quite satisfyingly, and three letters, F I N, began to glow on it. Miranda turned to Ivo with a widening grin. 'Listen!' she said, and stood back; there was a groaning sound, and a crack appeared in the mantle; the two huge heraldic fish on either side of it moved in opposite directions. The crack widened and opened to reveal a television screen.

Letters appeared on it:

FIN

Which slowly morphed into:

FREEDOM
IS
NOTHING

The screen coalesced into a uniform white, and then images began to play on it. A young man appeared, gaunt, angular, tired.

'Blackwood!' exclaimed Ivo.

'Freedom is Nothing,' said Blackwood, as if it were an incantation, or a greeting. 'You have the Koptor.' His voice was haunted, his eyes wide. 'We are FIN. We exist to stop the Liberators,' said Blackwood. 'Use the Koptor. If you have found this message, give the Koptor to Hunter. Stop them. We are the force of control.

They are the force of chaos. You must stop them.' Blackwood's face vanished and was replaced by a series of confused images.

A band of soldiers wielding swords charged across a plain. 'They inspire madness,' came Blackwood's voice over the top. There were shots of villages, smoke pouring out of the houses, and of a crazed-looking man holding a meat cleaver dripping with blood. 'Madness, loss of control. Throughout the centuries they have worked to sow chaos.' The scene changed to one of tanks rumbling across battlefields, and war-ravaged towns, and bombs; screams echoed from the speakers; a woman ran across, blood pouring down her face, mouth open in pain. 'Excess is their watchword. The end of everything is their goal.' Felix, Miranda and Ivo each shivered with horror; Miranda put her hand to her face, and Felix held her by the shoulders; Ivo stood a little aloof, almost transfixed by the screen.

'Freedom is Nothing,' said Blackwood again, and disappeared; the two carved fish glided back into their places in the mantelpiece, where they looked as if they were nothing but ornamentation, not strange messengers from a stranger world.

Felix, Miranda and Ivo all sat down at once, speechless.

'So that's it,' said Ivo. 'That's who killed Blackwood. They were on to him. The Liberators. The Koptor. That's what we heard, in the tunnel. It all fits. So now . . . Now we have to stop them. Unless you want . . .'

Felix said, 'Hey, look, Ivo –' But Ivo spoke over him. 'It's OK, don't worry, there's no way I could have expected you to . . .' He stopped, unsure how to continue, and Felix moved in awkwardly, and hugged him.

Miranda made a gagging sound. 'God, honestly, you boys are worse than girls.'

'So we're OK?' said Ivo. There were sounds of assent from Miranda, and Felix drew his brows together, pursed his mouth and made the slightest of nods.

They resumed their search vigorously, a clear aim in mind. 'Hunter. He said find Hunter. An address book,' Ivo said, 'a letter, something, there must be something.' They continued their search until the clock rang out three times, and Felix said, 'I'm so hungry.'

'Is that all you ever think about?' said Ivo.

'Well, I am!' he said, plaintively. 'I think I've got a tapeworm or something . . .'

'Shall we go and get something to eat? Maybe there'll be something in the kitchen . . .'

'No need. Got it!' said Miranda, tossing her elegant head back, brushing her hair behind her ear, from which some small earrings jangled and clanked. 'It's a letter from one Alice Hunter. Her address is at the top. It's in Kensal Rise.'

'God – that's miles away,' said Felix. 'We can't go now – we've got to get back or Ma'll be furious. Perkins has got his day off, after all. He's probably off slinking in some rank hole somewhere.'

'Don't,' said Miranda. 'You're making me feel ill.'

'That man is *evil*, I swear,' said Felix.

So clutching the letter from Hunter, they let themselves out of Blackwood's house and got back on the bus in the opposite direction.

'Can you remember what Blackwood said to you on the platform?' asked Miranda when they were on it.

'Yeah,' said Ivo. 'But I don't really understand it. He said "*koptay thurson*", whatever that means.'

Felix's eyes glittered with excitement, and, balancing his bony face on his hand, he said, 'That's Greek. It must be. Can you write it down?'

'Felix loves Greek,' said Miranda.

'Shut *up*,' Felix said, poking her in the ribs.

'He does!'

'OK, I do,' said Felix, smiling a little. 'Go on, write down what the syllables were.'

Ivo searched in his pockets, found a receipt, and Miranda found a pen in her bag; Ivo wrote, in big letters:

'You know what I think that is?' said Felix. 'It's this.' Underneath he added some squiggles in the Greek alphabet:

κοπτε θυρσον

'But what does it mean?' asked Ivo. 'I've only done a bit of Greek.'

Felix stared at it for a while. 'I think,' he said, 'that the second word is a noun – it's got a noun ending. And the first word is a verb. I think it's from the verb *kopto*. That means "I cut" or "I break". And *kopte* means "cut" or "break" – it's an order, a command, like when you're telling somebody to do something. And a *thyrson* – or *thyrsos* it would be called, you know the endings change in Greek? – it's a kind of, stick I guess, that the maenads carried.'

'What are maenads?' asked Miranda.

'Followers of the god Bacchus,' replied her brother, 'idiot. Women who went into frenzies in his honour. They tore things apart – animals, even humans. Did you not know?'

'Break *thyrsos*,' said Miranda, ignoring him. 'It sounds even more confusing in English. Well done

111

though, old brother of mine, you've done well there.' She patted him somewhat condescendingly on the head.

'Cool. So the Koptor . . . that would mean, something that breaks things?'

Felix nodded. 'Yeah, I guess so. It doesn't sound proper Greek, but it could be a kind of slang or short-hand or something – maybe a nickname for something that breaks.' They were reaching Park Lane, the bus was crowded. Music blared from somebody's head-phones, and some schoolchildren pushed their way down the stairs.

'Break the staff?' said Ivo. 'But what on earth does that mean?'

Felix shrugged. 'I just don't know,' he said, and turned to look out of the window.

Chapter Eight

They parted at Charmsford Square, arranging to meet the next day to go to Hunter's house in Kensal Rise, and Ivo made his way back to his aunt's, where he managed to sneak in without being seen. He spent the rest of the afternoon lying on his bed, staring at the ceiling, twisting what he now knew to be the Koptor around in his hands. Wind rustled leaves outside in swirls of black and brown. The sun that day had tinged the clouds with an edge of crimson, as if the sky itself had been pierced. *Koptor . . . koptay thurson*. His spirits were heavy and his brain slow. His dreams had been haunted by the images from the tube playing like a stuck video; now they were endless, shifting, formless masses. Later, he shambled along the corridors and asked Lydia for a sleeping pill; she gave him one, reluctantly, and soon Ivo had fallen gratefully into oblivion.

When he eventually loomed out of sleep the next

morning, it was nearly twelve o'clock. He noticed a pattering at the window, steady, cold and relentless; he had forgotten to close the curtains, and grudgingly he got out of bed and pulled them together, then managed to get himself down to the kitchen.

Ivo was wondering how people coped in war zones. How could you deal with seeing somebody torn apart? The human brain wasn't equipped for that sort of thing, he thought. Although it must have been once; in early times, when men crawled out of caves and hunted ferociously and ruthlessly, then we must have been programmed for blood, he thought. Maybe what they had seen on the video was what everyone wanted – to be liberated from themselves. He could see that it was a seductive thought and shuddered.

As Ivo made his way down to the kitchen, his thoughts turned to his peaceful first term at school, so safe, so untouched, hidden in its fortified turrets, ancient and calm, like a benevolent giant. It perched in the middle of a valley, near to a river, and cast a glow over all the surrounding countryside. But now his memories seemed unreal, as if he had dreamed them, and he had a sudden longing for his tiny cubicle with its posters and books and music. He remembered Ballard, the boy who had the room next to his, and how he'd played cricket in the corridors, and all the slow, comfortable ritual he'd grown used to.

Ivo found Lydia in the breakfast room in a state of some excitement. She was standing – she never seemed to sit these days – with her mobile pressed to one ear, a landline held dangling from the other; her laptop, humming along on its wireless connection, displayed several open emails, whilst roosting next to it was a pile of important – and rather boring-looking – correspondence.

'Hold on,' she said into the mobile, and gestured at Ivo, pointing with her elbow to a large envelope on the table. 'When you've eaten something, dear Ivo, take that to Julius, will you? It's the proof of the menu. I want to make sure he likes it. He lives on South Audley Street, or is it South Molton Street? You can walk there, I think, or there might be a bus or something, don't you think?'

Ivo nodded, and Lydia resumed her conversation into both telephones and began tapping at the laptop. Ivo remembered Olivia Rocksavage's message about the party, and wrote it down on a piece of paper, putting it on top of Lydia's pile of correspondence, and then he pondered. Deliver something to Julius – Ivo wasn't sure if he wanted to come into contact with that man again, who seemed to have such power – real, tangible power. It seemed as if reality was, somehow, affected by Julius, in a way that was not entirely pleasant, and Ivo felt that he would be afraid to be alone with him. He plucked up the courage to speak.

'Do I have to?' he said when Lydia was between calls, his voice a little more dejected than usual. He knew that he was bound, whilst he stayed with his aunt and uncle, to be as polite as possible to them; but Lydia directed a glance past him which showed that she was pretending she had not heard what he'd said and dialled another number.

Christine came in with tea and toast, and put it down in front of Ivo. He consumed it swiftly, allowing Lydia's chatter to buzz around him. 'Do we want the nymphs to pour drinks? . . . What about the living statues? . . . How much security will we have? . . . Do we have Charles and Camilla? . . . Our guests will want a little freedom, after all . . . Well you know, darling, I've found all this so *liberating*, I mean I love the studio, but it's so *limiting*, don't you think, and dear Julius has given me such a new slant on things . . .'

Ivo looked at Christine, who was taking away some plates.

'Are you all right?' he asked quietly.

She half turned to him. She looked as if she hadn't slept, and her eyes were puffy and red.

'Yes . . . yes, I am. Do not worry about me. It was a

shock, that is all. It was horrible . . . a madman . . . Who could have done such a thing?' She trembled and the plates shook; Ivo leaped up, offering to help, but she shook her head, eyes downcast, and left the room.

Lydia glanced at Ivo in a disapproving manner, which he took to mean that she wanted him to clear off, so he got up grudgingly, found an A–Z, and set out in the rain. Luckily the envelope was inscribed with Julius's address, and he found it on the map without any difficulty.

It wasn't so bad, and he enjoyed feeling the coolness of drizzle on his skin. He sent a text message to Felix, and walked slowly down towards Oxford Street. Julius lived on the other side of it, on South Audley Street, and it didn't take Ivo long to get there, dodging as he did through the dawdling tourists and the frantic Christmas shoppers on their lunch hours. He sought gaps, sliding past women with shopping bags and on to the relative calm of Julius's street.

When he arrived at the address, he saw a flight of stone steps leading up to a huge double door, which was painted black. The doorknocker was in the shape of a lion, and there was a shoe-scraper set into the wall by the side of the doorstep. Ivy grew up around the door, and there were hanging baskets spilling over with abundant greenery. Hesitantly, he buzzed the bell, and it was a few seconds, as Ivo stood uncomfortably, head bent into the speaker, before its strange crackle announced a voice, which said simply, 'Who?'

'Er . . . Ivo . . . Ivo Moncrieff,' said Ivo. 'For Julius,' he added, as an afterthought.

There was no reply, and for a moment Ivo thought that he wouldn't be admitted; a police car rushed past, some raucous teenage girls sashayed by; then the door clicked and swung inwards at his touch.

He was in a large entrance hall, which had a sofa in it and a semicircular table next to the wall, on which stood an imposing vase of flowers. There were plants everywhere, so many that it looked as if they were growing out of the ground. A great marble staircase was directly ahead of him.

Ivo set foot on the bottom stair and cautiously climbed up, holding the banisters for support. Wreaths of ivy leaves grew up and around. It was unpleasant to the touch, so he took his hand off and continued to walk unaided.

At the top of the staircase there was a door which opened straight on to the top stairs. As he came nearer, it was flung open to reveal in the frame Julius – so still, so like a mannequin, his hewn features set in that civilised face; he looked to Ivo like some god who'd taken the wrong turning and appeared in the wrong century. He was encased in a three-piece suit, his hair artfully disarranged, his eyes – those changing, liquid eyes – seeming purple, almost as if they were not a part of Julius, but some remnant from the wild and savage past.

Ivo was transfixed, and unable to speak; when Julius opened the door wider and made the slightest of gestures to allow him in, Ivo scampered past like a frightened goat.

Standing in the middle of the room, Ivo could not prevent himself making a sound of appreciation. Hearing the door shut behind him, he turned to see Julius, immobile, arms folded.

'Well, what did you expect?' said Julius.

The room was huge, cave-like, almost domed; large windows at either side let in the grey light, which seemed, upon entering, to take on a different, more magical hue; this was a room of shadows, of gold, of hidden wonders and luxuriant riches.

Carpets of Persian design caressed the polished wooden floors, their muted colours playing like a kaleidoscope. Furniture crowded and jostled, each piece holding some object – a horse's hoof mounted, some horrifying long-nosed Venetian masks, a statue of a woman, frozen in mid-flight, invitation cards, some gilded little jewelled boxes that whispered 'Open me', vases made of china so thin it was almost translucent; there were books bound in every colour conceivable, paintings, exquisite clocks, jars of pickled embryos, a tiny, winged skeleton, of no species that Ivo had ever seen or heard of.

'So, Ivo Moncrieff,' said Julius, very carefully, and Ivo started, for he was at his elbow, 'what brings you to the house of Julius Luther-Ross?' Ivo thought, for a moment, that he had heard an edge of the foreign in Julius's voice, but when he spoke again, it had gone.

Ivo thought about Strawbones and the snake. I proved myself to him, he thought. I can do the same with Julius. He tensed his back and raised his chin, saying stiffly, 'Lydia sent me.' He held out the envelope. Julius took it without saying thank you, without even looking at it, and tossed it so that it landed on a desk beside some writing things. Julius walked behind Ivo, and towards a set of shelves, on which the horse's hoof stood. He made no noise when he moved.

'I saw you looking at this. What do you think it is?'

Ivo shook his head.

'I suppose you think it's rather beautiful.'

Ivo nodded.

'It is, isn't it?'

It *was* beautiful – it had been mounted on a gold

plinth, and seemed still to look as glossy as when it had been alive.

'Any guesses?' said Julius.

'Maybe . . . it was a favourite horse of yours and you cut off its hoof when it died as a memento?'

'There speaks the country boy,' said Julius, allowing his lips to curve slightly. 'It is touching, that you would ascribe such charming motives to what is such a ghastly object.' He moved closer to Ivo, so close that Ivo sensed his hot breath on his cheek. Julius was oddly free of any smell – no hint of sweat, or food, and certainly no cologne. 'Can't you *feel* the violence?'

Ivo shook his head. What on earth was he talking about? he wondered. He wanted to leave the room.

'Look around you,' Julius said expansively. 'Look at all these *exquisite*, ancient objects. That painting –' he pointed to a picture of a girl being led up to an altar – 'that's Iphigenia at Aulis. And we all know what's about to happen to her, don't we? She's going to be sacrificed. By her father. So that the ships can sail to Troy. They lied to her, said she was going to marry Achilles. She was only young.

'Sacrificed, for selfish motives. Or, sacrificed for the greater good of Greece. What do you think? A wonderful father Agamemnon was.' Julius laughed, loudly this time, the sound pealing like a bell into the corners of the room, filling Ivo with a curious desire to join in.

'Look at all these things! Such beauty, such crafts-manship, and what do they all have in common? What is it that these paintings all share?' His voice now fell, and he whispered one word: 'Violence.' He continued, looking very closely at Ivo, 'What is it that man glorifies above all else? Has anything ever been achieved, Ivo, without sacrifice? Violence, Ivo! Think of Alexander the Great, think of Caesar, Napoleon, Churchill – every single one of them bathed in blood. Man would be nothing without it! We would be nothing without excess. Every day we carry on with our little lives, being nice to people, giving up our seats, chatting, endlessly, pointlessly. And we make these scribblings, these works of *art*, and what lies behind it? *Darkness*. Fear. Violence. We must embrace the dark-ness in ourselves, we must acknowledge it. We must release it.'

There was silence in the room, and Ivo was afraid to break it. He wanted to go, but felt that moving would somehow disturb the balance, that Julius might fly at him, hurt him, maybe even kill him. The only way out was the door, and Julius was between him and it. He shifted his eyes to the left, seeking escape, and saw a window, but it was too high up for him to reach. The only safe thing to do was to move away from Julius, and so he stepped backwards.

'You seem frightened, Ivo,' said Julius, saying his name with peculiar emphasis.

'No,' Ivo replied, in a way which would have suggested to even the least perceptive observer that he was.

'It is good to be frightened,' said Julius. 'There is a lot to be frightened of.'

A door in the far vastness of the room opened, and a figure walked in; Ivo saw, with some relief, that it was Strawbones. Julius's younger brother came loping forwards, a grin on his face. He was holding a bottle of wine, and had three glasses, held between his fingers carelessly. He approached without saying anything, set the glasses on a table and filled them; with a faintly supercilious gesture he held one out to Ivo and bowed, indicating to him that he should sit down.

When Ivo had sat in a tapestried armchair, both brothers sat too, on either side of the fireplace, facing Ivo. He took the opportunity to study them. How different they were, he thought: Julius with his studied calm, and Strawbones with his crazy charm. Both were smiling now, but still Ivo did not feel quite safe. He looked around the room. As well as the paintings filled with classical and biblical images, there were several portraits, hung high up on the walls. He saw one, nearest to him, of a man in an Elizabethan ruff, an earring hanging from his ear. The face was pale, the eyes prominent. He wanted to ask who it was, but his thoughts were interrupted by Julius leaning forwards and saying quietly, 'Do you ever feel constrained, Ivo?' Julius took a sip of wine, and placed it back carefully on the table, and then put his arms behind his head. Strawbones shifted a little and crossed his legs.

Ivo nodded. 'Well – yes, I suppose so.' He gulped at his wine glass, allowing the warm, fruity liquid to roll down his throat. His hand was shaking slightly. Come on, he said to himself, stop being ridiculous.

'You're a bright boy,' said Julius. 'Strawbones here has told me a lot about you.'

Ivo turned to Strawbones, who, flopping back into his chair, blew hair out of his eyes and said, 'Yes, I have.' Ivo took another gulp; without asking, Julius reached over and poured him a little more. Ivo's mind was beginning to feel sharper and focused, and yet at the same time, whilst he felt he could do anything in the world, his grasp of physical reality seemed to be slipping. When he moved in his chair, he found that he almost knocked his glass over; he looked up shyly at Julius, who smiled. Ivo glanced round the room again, and his eyes alighted on another painting: a man in a wig, wearing a tricorn hat and a long, brocaded blue coat, slumping in a chair, his hands in his pockets.

It had stopped raining, and now the sharp winter sun was beaming in through the tall windows, striping light across the floor. Both Julius's and Strawbones's faces were half in and half out of shadow.

'We think you have a very great future ahead of you,' said Julius. Ivo considered this.

'How do you mean?' he asked.

Strawbones lifted his glass quickly and drained it, his long, white neck flashing in the light, his blond hair streaming back. 'We mean,' said Strawbones, 'that we think that you're going to go far. Do you remember what I said, about the two great forces in this world?'

Ivo was looking at another portrait, a man in a red soldier's uniform, his hair tied back, standing in front of a pile of classical ruins.

Julius had, almost without Ivo noticing, refilled Ivo's glass again. Ivo picked up the crystal goblet, and held it in his hands, then took a large sip. The red wine was like velvet on his lips. 'Tastes like strawberries,' he said. Ivo's mind was pleasantly fuzzy now. It seemed to him that Julius and Strawbones were both the friendliest people in the world. The room around him was taking on colours of extraordinary vitality, shimmering and rippling as he looked. He wanted, all of a sudden, to get up and dance. Though there was no music he felt an internal rhythm that wanted to burst out of him; he wanted to embrace Julius and Strawbones.

He noticed that Strawbones was looking at him and smiling, his long canines bared, and said, mistily, 'Oh – yeah, I do remember. You said there were two . . . things in the world. Remember that. Whawassit?' He laughed gently and slumped back in his chair. 'Nice pictures,' he said. As he looked at one of two men dressed like dandies from the 1920s, he said, 'They look like you guys. Cool!'

Julius and Strawbones glanced at each other. Julius spoke, his soft, powerful voice creeping into Ivo's cranium. 'One force: the force of reasoning, of man's intellect. The shadow in the picture in your aunt's room.'

'The other force,' said Strawbones, 'the force of will, of ecstasy.' Ivo, as he looked at him, saw his eyes glisten. His limbs were limp and langorous, eyes green and wide.

'We've seen your instincts, Ivo,' said Julius quietly. Ivo laughed. 'You respond to things in an interesting way. You have emotion, power, imagination.' The Persian carpets on the floor started to shiver, their bright hues undulating, and the objects in the room took on some inner, demonic vitality. Now all the room became animated; the statue of a woman in flowing robes seemed to be opening and shutting its mouth in silent screams, and then it seemed to be saying, 'It's OK, you don't need to be yourself, you don't need to carry around all that bundle of worries and anxieties and hang-ups that make you into the weak person you are. You can transcend that, you can join us.'

Ivo sensed that Julius and Strawbones were reaching out to him: their arms were extended, and they were clasping hands. Mentally, too, he felt that some great, intent force was focused upon him. It was an enormous opening up of his will; he felt the beginnings of ecstasy. Was it his imagination, or were vines and grapes springing from the ground around their feet? The two brothers got up, and walked towards a cupboard, opened it, and when they turned round, they were clutching a staff, which was glowing brightly. How can this be happening? thought Ivo. He felt inert, like a rag doll.

'Come here, *Ivo*,' said Julius, and held out the staff, which was radiating some strange light. It had all the warmth of the sun on a summer afternoon. It expanded, coming towards him, and Ivo knew that to be immersed in that light would be the greatest, most joyful moment of his life. He felt as if he had grown wings and could fly. Heat was concentrating itself in his stomach, seeping up into his heart, spreading out through his veins and arteries, sliding into his brain.

He was alive to everything: to the shimmer of Julius's wristwatch, to the glow of his polished shoes, to the deep blue of Strawbones's shirt, the many colours of his plaited belt.

'We can show you,' whispered Strawbones, 'what it would be like. To be totally free.'

Ivo was flushed; he was breathing heavily. He managed to pull himself up from the chair. 'I . . . I . . .' he slurred. Some part of him that was still conscious was flashing warning signals at him. The portraits: the man in the ruff, the man in the red soldier's uniform, the tricorn hat, the dandies: they were all the same people. They were all either Julius or Strawbones. He turned his attention to the door, and saw that on the hatstand was hanging the multicoloured jacket of the man on the tube. That's funny, he thought. That red embroidered jacket. The man on the tube, walking away from the death of Blackwood. A sudden burst of awareness came upon him; it was Strawbones.

He put his hands in his pockets, and felt the smooth bulk of the Koptor. His mind cleared, as if a veil had been taken away. He breathed deeply. The room stopped flashing and swimming around him. He saw the two brothers holding the staff, and his impulse was not to join them, but to run. They were facing him; the door was behind him. He made a sudden and desperate dash towards the entrance; he scrabbled for the handle, flung it open and leaped down the stairs and out on to the street and whizzed around the corner. Ivo wasn't sure if he was being pursued, but he sprinted all the way up South Audley Street, and across Oxford Street, nearly being crushed between two huge red buses, and it wasn't until he got to Charmsford Square that he stopped, panting and hot, feeling the sweat prickle down his neck. A kind of disbelief had shrouded his mind. He refused to accept that Strawbones was the man on the tube train, that Strawbones was at the centre of this insanity, that it all emanated from him. It was Julius, Julius who was the one, not Strawbones. It had to be. Ivo was devastated.

In the flat, Julius turned to Strawbones. Strawbones had flung himself into an armchair, mimicking the pose of his eighteenth-century counterpart. He pulled a handkerchief out of his pocket, and blew his nose loudly.

'You were right,' Julius said to his brother. 'There is power there.'

Strawbones shrugged. 'Aren't I always right?'

The sun went back behind a cloud; the room was still; the staff they had been holding had been returned to its secret place; Julius sat down.

'Don't worry,' said Strawbones to his brother. 'He'll come round.'

'Even so.' Julius stretched and yawned languidly, his teeth showing white. He gripped the arms of his chair. 'There will always be someone watching.'

Chapter Nine

I vo called Felix immediately: he answered, after a few agonisingly long rings. 'What's up?' he said lazily.

'Now. We have to go to see Hunter now. Are you working?'

'No, we're off till five. Perky's away. Mate, are you OK?'

'Weirdness. Meet me outside your house, now!' He hung up, hoping that the urgency in his voice was obvious. He paced up and down in front of the Rocksavages' house, and eventually the door swung open. Felix slouched out, zipping up his jacket, and Miranda followed. They pulled the door shut and stood at the top of the stairs. Ivo started walking. Miranda turned to her brother, shrugged, and chased after Ivo; Felix came a little more slowly at first, and then ran to catch them up.

Ivo told Felix and Miranda what had happened,

stumbling slightly as he tried to find words for what he had experienced when he'd been in Julius's flat. A negation of the self, a feeling of total and extreme power, that one could do anything, in a frightening, brutal sense. It was, he imagined, like the feelings of those first tribes who reared their low forheads out of the stinking swamps and the fly-filled jungles.

Not, he said, that he had seen God, or even a god, but he had felt a powerful attraction which was not natural. He described the staff which Julius had brandished. He didn't mention Strawbones. He still couldn't believe it.

Felix chimed in: 'The Thyrsos! That must be what Blackwood was talking about! The staff of the maenads.'

'I saw it! I saw it in Julius's flat.' Ivo was suddenly sure that this was what the Koptor had been entrusted to him for. Its purpose was destructive. The breaker, the cutter.

They took the Bakerloo line to Kensal Green. It was dirty, grey and empty; they hardly saw anyone as they trudged along the dull streets, full of rows and rows of dingy Victorian houses. They eventually found Hunter's street. A dog snuffled past them, ownerless. They stood on the doorstep, banging the fish-shaped doorknocker as hard as they could, and after what seemed like the longest time imaginable, it opened to reveal a short, frumpy middle-aged woman wearing a brown cardigan and a flowery dress, her dark eyes, as black as shoe polish, peering at them from under a careless fringe of hair, coarse and black, as black as the sky at night.

'Alice Hunter?' said Ivo.

'Yes?' she said.

'FIN?' said Ivo expectantly.

She shut the door in their faces.

The three looked at each other. 'I think I know what to do,' said Miranda. She took the doorknocker confidently and rapped three times. It opened a crack and they saw Alice Hunter's eyes peering at them suspiciously.

'Freedom is nothing,' said Miranda quietly.

Felix took the cue, and repeated the phrase; Ivo followed him.

Alice Hunter looked intently behind them, opened the door wider and they crushed in, Alice banging it shut behind them. Still reeling from the alcohol and his encounter with the Luther-Rosses, suddenly Ivo was confused, cornered in the passageway, by this pudding-shaped lady who pressed down upon him, sparks in her eyes.

'What do you know about FIN?' she demanded, eyes

narrowing, hands fluttering plumply as she waved the three of them into a tiny sitting room. It was the opposite of Blackwood's flat: scrupulously neat, with everything looking as if it knew its place and would never dare to leave it. But, despite the neatness, everything else was a riot of colour. The four walls of her sitting room were each painted a slightly different colour, as if she had tried each one out and then never got round to choosing one. A wooden table, painted dark green, sat in the middle, and the armchairs and sofas were covered in multicoloured cloths. The walls were crowded with photographs of Hunter and several other people, as well as a print of a dog poking its paw into a bath.

'Sit, sit, all of you, so many of you, go on, sit. Did anyone follow you?'

'No – well, I don't think so,' said Ivo, for in truth he hadn't expected anyone to do so.

'What do you mean, you don't think so? That's not good enough, is it? They could be swarming all over the place. Here, wait. *Acolytes*,' she hissed behind her.

She popped into the corridor like a champagne cork, Ivo heard the door being opened, and after a few moments shut again, and the sound of chains being drawn across the door.

She appeared again, looking rather martial.

'Well then. Can't be too careful. What's your story then, eh? Who's the leader? This one?' She pointed at Miranda, who shook her head dumbly. 'This one?' pointing at Felix, who also shook his head, and indicated Ivo with his index finger.

'You . . . what's your name?'

'Ivo Moncrieff, ma'am,' said Ivo, and he felt as if 'ma'am' was the right thing to say, although she laughed at that, showing her teeth, which were mottled and pied.

'So, Ivo Moncrieff, what brings you here?'

'Blackwood – he gave me this before he was killed – he told us to find you.' Ivo showed her the Koptor.

'He gave you this?' she snatched it from him and held it up to what little light came from a lamp in the ceiling.

'But this is the Koptor!' She looked at them suspiciously. 'When did Blackwood give you this?'

Ivo explained what had happened to him on the tube platform; suddenly he was overwhelmed by the memory, its sharp, bright, fierceness, and he felt dizzy, limp and exhausted.

'Here, you look like you're about to keel over! Restoratives, that's what you need,' said Hunter, and all but pushed him back into a big, squashy sofa that smelled of dog and biscuits. She went briefly out of the room and came back with a glass of water. 'Drink this,' she said briskly, 'and I'll make you some tea.'

Without thinking, Ivo gulped down the water; he suddenly realised that, even though she looked completely innocuous, they had no idea whether they could trust this Hunter woman, and decided to be on his guard.

Five minutes later Alice Hunter had brought in a delicate teapot and four china cups with blue figures on them, and some biscuits arranged in a pattern on a plate. Ivo, Felix and Miranda were sitting crushed together on the sofa whilst Hunter occupied the only armchair.

Ivo had to admit to himself, he hadn't thought that Alice Hunter would look like this. He'd imagined a dashing young lady, athletic, brave and beautiful, not somebody who spoke with their mouth full of crumbs and wore clothes that came from charity shops. Maybe she is an impostor, he thought, but that seemed preposterous. He resolved not to drink the tea, but it was too late to communicate this to Miranda and Felix, who were gulping it down and already stuffing themselves with biscuits.

'And what are your names?'

'Felix.' He looked up, blinking, running his hand through his dark hair.

'It means lucky. Are you?'

'Well . . . yes, I suppose . . . I mean, I don't always get caught, if that's what you mean –' Miranda elbowed him and he stopped.

'Good,' said Hunter, ignoring him. 'And you?'

'Miranda.' She put on her best grown-up grin.

'A girl to be marvelled at . . . Well, I won't ask you if you think you are.'

Miranda widened her eyes at Ivo behind her hand.

'And Blackwood gave the Koptor to Ivo . . .' she said, glaring at Ivo intensely. She was appraising his qualities, assessing him like a horse before a race. 'Bright eyes, springy step, good muscles,' he imagined her saying to herself.

'Thank the lord *they* didn't get hold of it,' she said. 'Though from what you say, they were close enough. Blackwood, Blackwood dead . . . I am the only one left. And you witnessed it. My poor dear,' she said, her voice changing suddenly.

'Who are the Liberators?' asked Ivo.

'They are not human like us – I'm human, don't you worry about that,' she said as the three of them started, Felix letting out a 'No way!' and Miranda squawking in disbelief.

'What do they want?' Ivo asked. 'The Liberators, I mean.'

'Freedom,' said Alice, brushing crumbs from her flowery skirt, her voice deep and full. 'Unconditional freedom. They believe in a world without rules, without boundaries. They call themselves the Liberators, believing that our poor, human, mortal world is bound in chains, that our so-called "free will" is a lie. You can't call them insane, because they're not human, but they are definitely dangerously psychopathic. They believe that what they want to do is, how can I put this, *good*.'

'*Good*?' Ivo said.

Alice Hunter sat up in her chair, and folded her arms across her chest. Her feet tapped out a rhythm on the bare floorboards. She thought for a while before responding. 'They think that our consciences are prisons. They believe that we are prevented from becoming the people that we should be. They wish to liberate us from our consciences.'

'So you mean – when I see something I want, and it's in a shop, and there's a little voice in my head saying "Take it, take it", and there's another voice saying "No, don't", they want to get rid of the voice telling me not to?' asked Miranda.

'Yes. That's it exactly.' Hunter stood up and went to rummage in a cupboard; she pulled out a plain blue file, and brought it over, yanking out a picture. It was an engraving of two men with long black hair. Their faces were fairly indistinguishable; the most remarkable feature was that they wore tiny bones and skulls tied ornamentally into their hair. 'This is the oldest picture we have of them. They can assume other guises, of course. Now they are walking around as –'

Ivo interrupted, knowledge burning in him painfully. 'As Julius and Strawbones Luther-Ross?'

Hunter took the picture back from him and said quizzically, 'You've met them?'

'Yes,' said Ivo. 'A few times . . .'

'Oh lord,' said Hunter. She patted her knees.

To break the silence, Miranda asked: 'So what does FIN do?'

Hunter turned to gaze at her, her brow creased. She got up to replace the file, continuing to talk as she did so. 'FIN was set up to stop the Liberators, after the Second World War. Through our research we followed their movements across the centuries. Whenever the world threatened to descend into anarchy, you could bet that they were behind it. We noticed a pattern: at times of great change, the Liberators would re-emerge. Communism, the Napoleonic Wars – we could trace their influence there. But until now they have never been able to put their full plan – Liberation – now the time is right. The global situation suits them.

Communication is so much easier, their message can be spread across the world in an instant; and so they have come back.' She stopped.

'Why are you looking at me like that, young man?' she asked Ivo.

Ivo realised he had been staring at her open-mouthed. 'I . . . I don't know.'

'You're thinking, who is this silly old woman and how on earth did she become a member of FIN? Don't deny it, I know you are. Well,' she said, looking at Miranda, 'many of us were recruited from the secret services. And yes, we are very highly trained.' As she said this she leaped across the room and had a knife at Ivo's throat; panicked, he sat absolutely still, and she brought it down and slopped back over to her arm-chair, sitting down and refilling her cup.

'There we are,' she said, ignoring the astonishment of the three. Miranda and Felix became very tense. Ivo touched his hand to his throat.

'Right, where was I? Oh yes. Some of us thought they were behind the Second World War; unfortunately that was just human nature. But they've been around now for a year or so, gathering Acolytes. As soon as we knew they were back, ten of us set out to stop them. But they've got rid of nearly all of us now. Their Acolytes are bound to them by their lives, and they will do anything to achieve total Liberation. What they offer is very appealing to many people.' Ivo saw that she was controlling herself with difficulty. 'There must be rules. Not petty rules – there can be too much of that. But there has to be order, there have to be limits, otherwise there is nothing. There cannot be just chaos. There is a pattern to everything, from the smallest flower to the largest star. You are up against something evil – something that kills and maims at the whim of a moment. And we must stop it.'

Ivo held out the Koptor. 'And this is the key?' he said.

Hunter looked at him appraisingly. 'You're right,' she said. 'The Koptor is the only thing in the world that can destroy the Thyrsos which gives the Liberators their power. Break the Thyrsos, break their power.'

Ivo gulped, feeling very insignificant. 'But it's so small,' he said.

'And yet,' Hunter continued, 'it contains within it the opposing power of Apollo. The Thyrsos belongs to Dionysus, the Koptor to Apollo: with order you can negate chaos. Chaos doesn't have to win.'

'I want to help,' said Ivo.

'And so you will. You have to keep the Koptor. It's safer with you. They'll get it off me if they can and kill me. They don't know you have it – yet.'

'I think they're moving already,' said Ivo. 'Julius is planning a party at the National Gallery.'

Hunter raised her head and sniffed, like a dog. 'That sounds like them,' she said. 'Right,' she continued, sweeping to her feet, knocking her teacup over and ignoring the splash, 'I must go. I must see what we can do. We will meet again. Now, out, you lot. Your presence here is dangerous. They might be coming any minute. We don't want them to know you have contacted me.'

'Wait – how do we find you?'

'Hold the Koptor and think of me,' she said. 'It operates at the most basic, atomic level of matter. If you hold it and think of me, very hard, quantum particles in it will be activated and influence those in me. And I will be transported to wherever you are, as quick as a shaft from the bow of Apollo himself.'

It was at that moment that the room started to shake. It felt as if something very strong was battering at the door.

'Oh my godfathers,' said Alice. 'Quick, out the back, all of you.'

They rushed into the passageway and saw the door buckling on its hinges. 'Come on! Through here!' she hissed. They went through a back room and Alice fiddled with the lock, and then flung the door open.

'Climb over the wall, you'll be in the next road down. Run as fast as you can, jump on a bus, any bus, just run.'

She slammed the back door in their faces and pulled down the blind. Ivo half turned to go back, but Felix pulled at his shoulder. Miranda had already run to the back of the garden and was scrambling over the low wall. Felix took it at one leap, and Ivo, looking back over his shoulder, dragged himself over it, and the three of them sprinted down the alley.

They came out on to the Chamberlayne Road and saw a bus stop ahead.

'Is there anyone behind us?'

'Don't know. Don't look. Just run!'

A bus was approaching, and they dodged across the traffic, avoiding cars; they just made it as the bus pulled up.

Panting, they flung themselves into the back seats. Ivo turned and gazed out of the back window – there didn't seem to be anybody after them.

'I think we're all right,' he said.

'Sure,' said Felix. 'All right. That's just the way I'd put it. All right.'

'I hope Hunter's OK. Do you think we should go back there?'

'I think she can probably cope,' said Miranda.

'There's more to her than you might realise.'

'But she looked so . . . so *rubbish*,' said Ivo. 'She didn't look like she could hold off a rabbit, let alone whatever it was that was after her. I mean, even that trick with the knife –'

'After her? Or were they after us? Don't you think it's odd that she would be attacked when we were there?' said Felix.

'I don't know,' answered Ivo. 'Let's just hope they don't find us.' Ivo breathed on the window and drew symbols in the mist. Felix glared down at the ground, his ankles crossed over each other, and Miranda pretended to text. The bus continued its way down the gloomy streets and the three of them huddled in silence.

Felix was fiddling with a piece of paper in his pocket, and eventually he sighed and brought it out. 'Look,' he said. 'I found this.' He spread it out on his knees. Miranda and Ivo crowded round him. It was a printout, old and faint, of a plan.

'It's a map,' he said. 'Of the underground tunnels.'

Miranda kissed him.

'You know, old brother of mine, sometimes you really do come up with the goods.'

Felix brushed her off. 'Look,' he said. 'Here. There seems to be a large chamber in Marylebone – that's where we first saw Perkins going. And then another one in Mayfair, here.' He pointed to a large square, with two tunnels branching off it, one going west, which came out in Hyde Park, and one going east, which ended in the back streets of Soho. There were several smaller rooms off the eastern tunnel. There were three or four clusters of chambers, including one under the National Gallery. There was an exit in Mayfair too.

'It's on South Audley Street,' said Ivo. 'It must go up into Julius's house.'

He took the map and pored over it until they got off the bus.

When they reached Charmsford Square, Miranda said, 'We've got two hours with Perky now. It's five o'clock.'

'And then what?' said Ivo. 'We have to move quickly . . . and Perkins is our only lead.'

Felix, looking serious, said, 'I think we should follow him again. All of us. See where he takes us. We'll find out how deeply he's involved.'

Chapter Ten

The two hours stomped by, punctuated by Perkins marching smartly up and down the dining room where Felix and Miranda had their lessons. When, eventually, he looked at his watch and said, 'Hand them in, please,' the siblings did so with the barest acknowledgement. Outside, the blackness of evening showed in the squares of the windows. Electric light reflected back from Perkins' spectacles.

'All the fight gone out of you?' said Perkins. 'Good. Then we're getting somewhere.' He hitched up his unpleasant trousers, rose, and, nodding curtly, left the room.

They hung back in the doorway of the dining room and watched him go to the front door. He opened it, said loudly, 'Goodbye,' and slammed it shut. Exchanging a glance with Miranda, Felix put a bony finger to his lips, and they crept after him, their hearts beating quickly and their stomachs tightening. They slipped out on to the street and in the glow of a lamp post saw him turn the corner ahead of them. Ivo emerged from behind a large dustbin where he'd been hiding and joined them in silence.

They followed Perkins all the way down Baker Street, keeping muffled up in their scarves and hats in case he turned around, but he was resolute, striding ahead. At the end of Baker Street he turned right and walked straight across Oxford Street; they nearly lost him as four buses passed at the same time, but they glimpsed him nip down a side street and enter the Mayfair streets. They had trouble keeping up with him – there were a lot of people around.

'This is near where Julius lives,' Ivo whispered. They were in the warren of streets around Grosvenor Square.

About a hundred feet behind Perkins, they saw him vault straight over some railings into a garden square, without looking either right or left. They paused.

'Guys,' said Miranda, 'I don't like this. Let's go home.'

'No,' said Ivo, his face tight and drawn; he felt as if he had a hard case around him like a shell spiralling outwards. 'We have to do this. Come on.' He sprinted across the road and leaped over the railings in one bound.

Felix shrugged and loped behind, and Miranda, shaking her head, went too. They joined Ivo on the other side. Ivo pointed. Perkins was striding towards the centre of the garden. There was a large statue of what looked from a distance like a tiger, baring its teeth, overshadowed by a tall tree spreading its branches out.

Perkins disappeared behind the statue, and then did not come out again. Ivo pressed on, the two siblings trailing behind him. Ivo's mind had become colder, harder. He came up to the plinth on which the statue loomed. It was clean, and new, an inscription bearing a date not two years ago: '*This statue was erected by the generosity of Julius Luther-Ross*'.

A sliver entered Ivo's heart. He went round the corner of the statue. Felix was at his elbow now, Miranda a little behind.

'I like the statue,' Felix said, under his breath. 'Cool tiger.'

The back of the plinth presented a blank face to them. Ivo passed his hand in a businesslike manner over it, and then his face contracted into creases of concentration. Aha, he thought. He traced his finger around until he found what he was looking for – a small crack which indicated the presence of an entrance.

'Can we go now?' asked Miranda.

Ivo ignored her. He was taken up with the force of his mission. He felt the Koptor in his pocket and took it out.

Let's see if you do what you say you do, thought Ivo, and held it tightly. He inched around it for a button or a groove or something, but found nothing. Undeterred, he continued to squeeze it, thinking hard all the time. We have to stop them, he thought. He focused on thoughts of order, peace and serenity, remembering what Hunter had said about Apollo, all the time willing the blade to come out. And then, almost as if it had been there all the time, it was there, shining and sharp and deadly. Ivo stepped forward briskly and put the blade against the crack and moved it downwards: it passed through it as easily as if it were made of nothing more substantial than cloud. The stone panel shifted slightly forwards.

I did it, thought Ivo. I made it open. My own will caused it. Grimly and suddenly aware of the powers and possibilities that this entailed, he pushed against the side of the plinth. He felt it give, and as slowly as possible, he heaved it aside, trying not to make any noise, then entered the space. The others went after him, Felix closing the panel behind them.

The entrance opened into a corridor that headed

downwards. Stealthily, they felt their way down the passageway through the darkness; this time there was no carefree joking around. Soon a light appeared in front of them, and they saw that they had come to the end of the tunnel, where it opened out into a large room. Felix held out his hand, halting his sister and Ivo; they crouched in the entrance way, hidden by the shadows, and edged as far forward as they dared.

The room was enormous, far larger than the one they had been in before in Marylebone. There were two black statues of panthers on either side of the room, and the walls were hung with tapestries that showed hunting scenes. Fine carpets covered the floor. The atmosphere was dry. In the hall was a thin, languid young man with very long blond hair and a finely chiselled face; his features were so symmetrical as to be almost unreal, and he had a wispy, ethereal face that was devoid of any expression, as if he were posing for a photograph in a fashion magazine. It was Strawbones, and he was slouching in a velvet chair.

Perkins was standing as if to attention in front of him.

'Well, Perkins?' said Strawbones. 'What news?'

'I hate my pupils,' was Perkins' response, enunciating every word with suppressed rage. Miranda squeezed Felix's hand.

'I've said before, Perkins, that you should not

question me. It is a means to an end, that is all. Their parents are very useful. They know the right people. They're bringing a table to the National Gallery.'

Lydia's party, thought Ivo.

Perkins threw himself on to the ground, so that he was kneeling, with his head bent before Strawbones. Ivo thought for one horrible moment that Strawbones was going to tear Perkins' head off. But instead he stretched, and yawned, and said, 'We are all set for Liberation.' Something scuttled across the floor, and the three friends watched a large rat skitter away. A gust of air howled through the hall; Felix shivered next to Miranda, who pulled her jacket closer around her. Ivo ignored it.

Strawbones raised himself from the chair, standing up straight. A change came over his face – his eyes appeared to be turning completely green, and when he spoke his voice was stronger. 'Yes . . . we, Julius and Strawbones Luther-Ross, the Eleutheroi, the legends, the Liberators, will rise to power. Long have we waited in the dark places, long have we hidden ourselves from the light of the world, this corrupt, filthy, *heaving* world of barbarians. We will make them see what it is to be untrammelled by restraints, to act on every impulse, every desire, without fear, without consequence.'

The friends watched Strawbones lift his arms out as if he were crucified, or flying, and Perkins remained kneeling, mumbling something, some kind of chant. His chant rose higher and he threw his head up and Strawbones was lit by strange fire. Then Perkins' voice dropped, and Strawbones, relaxing, sat back in his chair. Perkins got quietly to his feet.

'There is no obstacle,' said Strawbones gently, and then he said, even more quietly, 'except the Koptor. Did you find the Koptor?'

Miranda gently nudged her brother. Ivo tensed, its coldness in his hand. They are so close to it, he thought, and they don't know. This made him feel strong, and powerful.

Perkins muttered inaudibly.

'I'm sorry, I didn't hear you. I asked you if you had found the Koptor. Did you?'

'No.' Perkins said no more.

'Well, that is *depressing*. Honestly, Perkins. We charge you with one easy little task like finding the Koptor and you can't perform it. What will we do with you?'

There was a pause. Felix, Miranda and Ivo held their breath, sure that any sound they made would be picked up.

'Find it,' barked Strawbones, and suddenly his voice

was old, and full of blackness, and then he began to laugh. He picked up a long walking stick that had lain by his side, and banged it three times on the ground. The knocks echoed, and as if in immediate answer a tapestry was flung off one of the walls to reveal a doorway, out of which poured a riot of people. Felix, Miranda and Ivo drew further back into the shadows, watching the throng flowing in, rushing like a stream, gurgling and foaming. There were thirty or forty of them, and Ivo could see that they ranged in age from the teenage to the elderly. Some were clapping cymbals together, some were pounding sticks on the floor, some were shouting. They surged around the chair where Strawbones was reclining, and formed an unruly circle, baying and hooting like animals. Strawbones stood up suddenly, quick as a salmon leaping. He basked in the Acolytes' attention, and as Ivo watched him he felt Strawbones's charisma boil outwards from him like a stellar force.

Don't give in to it, he thought. He hoped Miranda and Felix would be able to resist too. He turned to look at them, and saw the swift spark of interest in Felix's eyes. Perturbed, but unable to do anything about it, he turned his gaze back to Strawbones.

'Do we have another recruit?' shouted Strawbones above the din.

There was raucous laughter; a murmuring of voices, and then one came out louder than the rest: 'Yes, O Liberator, we do.'

'Good. Where is he? Or she?' Strawbones's voice was cold, thought Ivo, but somehow deeply attractive: it made you want to please him.

'Here!' said a woman's voice, strong and clear. Somebody stepped into Ivo's line of vision, and he saw that she was about forty, very well dressed, in a business suit, with hair impeccably arranged, and diamonds shining in her ears.

'Ah, excellent!' said Strawbones. 'Now what is your name?'

'Jennifer Brook,' said the woman brightly.

'And are you committed to our cause?'

There was no pause, indeed his words were barely finished as she shouted, 'Yes!'

'She has performed the test?' asked the Liberator. 'Show me the proof!'

Jennifer Brook opened her handbag and rummaged in it, and then pulled out something which looked to Ivo from a distance like a long, thick piece of string. Except that it wasn't. Ivo realised what it was just before Jennifer said, 'The tail of a cat! Slaughtered for you, O Liberator!'

She flung it into the air and Strawbones caught it,

and held it high above his head. Every mouth in the room was open, revealing crimson, cavernous throats and pinkish, worm-like tongues hollering.

Juniper, thought Ivo. She killed Juniper.

'Then we shall begin. Acolytes!' Strawbones's voice now was full of richness, of enticing undertones. There was a roar from the rabble. Felix and Miranda, Ivo noticed, had exchanged a glance at the mention of Jennifer Brook. Taking advantage of the noise, Felix leaned into Ivo's ear, and whispered, 'She knows our mother!'

They watched as the herd of people danced round in a circle with Jennifer Brook in the centre of it.

Then a voice cried out, 'Eeyoh! Eeyoh!' It was filled with elation, with joy, with the vibrant, bursting, chaotic sensation of life. It was intoxicating, and it promised freedom. Ivo felt as if he were part of the world itself, as if he could feel things growing, and he felt as if he understood everything about the universe. But Ivo recognised it – he felt, on the edges of perception, what he'd felt on the underground. Glancing at Miranda and Felix, he saw their mouths trembling, laughter threatening to spill out. Controlling himself fiercely, he clamped his hands over their mouths and stuffed a huge amount of his jumper into his own, biting down like an animal.

'Eeyoh! Eeyoh!' came the cry again, and the Acolytes danced more wildly.

Ivo could see Jennifer Brook standing in the middle of the circle, and he saw the bliss in her eyes. She undid her hair, which tumbled around her shoulders, and tore off her shoes, flinging them out, not caring where they landed.

The Acolytes began to chant: 'O Eleutheros. O Liberator. Swallow-Feather, Nightfall, Abandoner. Clash of Cymbal, Prince of Deer, Stone Eater.' Jennifer Brook joined in, screaming over the top of them: 'I will join! I will join! Free me, O Liberator, free me, Prince of Deer!' Round and round the Acolytes danced, faster and faster and faster, and Ivo was sorely tempted to run out and join them. But he held on to Miranda and Felix, feeling them strain.

'I am Eleutheros!' proclaimed Strawbones. 'I am freedom!'

The crowd pounded the floor with their feet. A haze of dust flew up from the carpets.

'I am Liberator!' he shouted. 'I free you from your selves!' Again they beat the floor, twirling round and round, like dervishes whirling.

'I am the swallow's feather! I am the bringer of night!'

Incessant, his followers spun in a vortex around him.

'I make you abandoned! I am the clash of cymbal! Swift as deer, destroyer of stone! I am the Liberator!' His voice rocketed around the hall.

'I will join!' Jennifer Brook yowled.

'Eeeyoh! Eeeyoh!' Strawbones gave voice and then a very bright light enveloped the room and seemed to Ivo to become part of everything. He watched the light descend upon Jennifer Brook, and she was lifted up into the air, her mouth open in ecstasy.

The cry was reverberating around them, cannoning around the room like a living creature. The air smelled rich, everything was sharper. Ivo pressed his jaw fiercely closed, feeling Felix and Miranda shaking beneath him, tensing and shivering. The Acolytes slowed now, and some stopped entirely; Jennifer Brook stood in the centre, her eyes shining.

'So near!' she cried. 'So near!' Her voice was thrilling with energy.

'You see,' came the voice of Strawbones, the Liberator, 'what will be yours! You are now an Acolyte, bound to the Liberators! Swear to me!'

'I swear to you, O Liberator! My life is yours!' Jennifer Brook stood, ecstatic, her arms out wide, as if she wanted to embrace the universe; and then she bowed, and dropped to her knees, her head almost touching the ground. A figure came and stood before

157

her – Ivo thought that it was a man, and that he was wearing a long fur coat, and that bones were hung all over it – and placed his hand on her head; he was holding a staff, which Ivo saw was glowing. The figure held his hand on Jennifer Brook's head for a second, and then she screamed, and he released her. She stood up, and even from a distance Ivo could see that she had been transfigured, and that her eyes were empty.

The other Acolytes let out a clamour of approval, clapping and jumping.

'Follow me!' yelled the Liberator, and they all, dancing, stamping, some making sounds like animals, some singing, some shouting 'Eleutheros! Eleutheros!' went in a clamorous rout out of the room through the door behind the tapestry. Perkins, luckily, went with them.

Ivo noticed that Jennifer Brook's discarded shoe lay near to them; for some reason it appalled him. He removed his hands from Felix and Miranda's mouths. They were gasping furiously for breath. Felix's face was in an angry snarl of rage.

The roar died away as the Liberator and his followers clanked further away from the room. Ivo, Miranda and Felix slipped out in silence, back up the corridor to the statue of the tiger, and they did not stop until they had cleared the park gates and had the width of

Oxford Street between them and it.

They fled through the streets to Charmsford Square, bounded up the stairs of the Rocksavages' house, and went to Miranda's room and collapsed on her sofa.

'There's an invitation on the mantelpiece in the drawing room, shaped like a vine leaf. It's to the National Gallery party. We've all been invited,' Miranda said.

'Yeah, I was really looking forward to it,' said Felix.

'I keep thinking about Perkins . . .' said Miranda, rubbing her arms as if she were shivering. 'He looked *mad*.'

'Yeah, he's not even like that when I haven't done my Greek,' said Felix, trying to make a joke out of it. He didn't laugh.

'Liberation,' said Miranda, and the word hung, strange and fiery, between them. Felix was as white as Ivo. Miranda was curled into the sofa, heavy blankets around her, despite the central heating being on full blast.

Ivo was thinking about Strawbones. He had dismembered Blackwood on the tube. Strawbones had murdered somebody in the most savage way possible, in broad daylight, he'd dulled the passengers on the tube with madness. It made him feel nauseous.

Felix suddenly said, 'You know I was enjoying that.'

He held his head up, as if expecting to be shouted down.

'What do you mean?' Ivo said. 'How?'

'Didn't you feel it? Couldn't you feel what it would be like? It would be amazing.' He flung his head back on to the sofa. 'To be totally free –'

'How can you say that?' interjected Ivo. 'Didn't you see what they did to Juniper – and they killed Blackwood.'

'So what do we do?' moaned Miranda, from inside her protective shell of blankets, her head peeking out like a tortoise. 'They've got some plan about the National Gallery, it sounds like they're going to . . . to *liberate* everybody who's been invited . . . and we've seen what that means. Did you see Jennifer Brook? What are we going to do?'

'We can't tell anyone. Ma and Pa would never believe us. Police wouldn't either.' Felix was matter of fact, decisive.

'And I can't tell Lydia and Jago – I mean, Lydia's *painting* Strawbones, for Christ's sake, she's actually arranging the whole shebang with Julius!' Ivo made a gesture of despair, and there was a silence in which nothing could be heard but the rumble of the outside world.

A thought struck them all at the same time, and Felix

said carefully, 'Do you . . . do you think that she knows about it? Lydia, I mean. Do you think she's involved?'

Ivo considered for a moment, letting the silence fill the room, and said, blowing his cheeks out, 'No. I think Lydia just enjoys this sort of thing. She loves parties. She'd never believe anything against Julius, anyway. She's completely in love with him. And with Strawbones, I think.'

'Does Jago mind?'

'I don't think he notices. What about your parents? Do you think they know?'

'I don't think they know about it,' Miranda replied. 'Honestly, I really don't. I mean, Ma's an interior *decorator*. She's not likely to be part of some, like, terrorist thing, is she? And Pa – well, Pa is Pa.'

'The thing is, are you sure?' said Ivo.

'Well, are *you* sure about Lydia?' asked Felix angrily.

'What are you suggesting?' Ivo too was in a temper, and it felt as if everything that had happened to him was now suddenly boiling up in him, all ready to blow up.

'Just that your aunt might have more to do with it than you think! I mean, she has Julius and Strawbones over all the time. Don't you think that they might be, like, influencing her? They might have made her into an Acolyte.'

'She can't be! And what about your parents – your

mother's friend was initiated, we saw her, why can't your mother be too?'

'Don't you dare say that about my mother!' Felix stood up. He was much taller than Ivo, but Ivo didn't care and threw a punch at him; he heard the impact, and Felix was knocked back but quickly jumped to his feet and lunged at Ivo, thumping him in the stomach and winding him; Felix had him in a headlock, and Ivo was being crushed; he summoned up all his strength and broke free, and aimed his fist at Felix's nose; Felix yelled out, blood spurting from his face, and kicked Ivo savagely in the shins; they knocked over a table and a vase of roses came crashing down to the floor. The deep crimson flowers lay splayed on the ground, soaking in wetness, and still the boys fought each other among the shards.

'Guys! Guys! Stop it! Stop it!' Miranda's voice rose high above the melee. 'Stop it, you idiots – what the hell are you doing? Stop it!'

The door swung open and Olivia Rocksavage came bursting in. She surveyed the scene of destruction, and tightened her lips. Miranda ran to her; Felix released Ivo and snarled at him, a pure, animal noise. Ivo put his hand to his lip and tasted blood. They looked, all of them, at Olivia, expecting a tirade of anger; but she merely said, 'That's enough. Clear this up, you two.

And don't be late for dinner. Ivo, you won't be staying?'

'No,' he said, in a subdued manner.

'Well then,' said Olivia Rocksavage, and departed.

Felix and Ivo sat staring at each other glumly. Miranda rushed to her brother to give him some tissues, which he took roughly and pressed to his nose.

'I've got an idea,' said Miranda.

'What?' asked Felix, in a depressed lilt. He had lost the burst of anger that had overtaken him, and now felt like a deflated balloon. He also felt ashamed.

'Hunter. Tomorrow we'll use the Koptor to call her. We should tell her about Perkins' plans and the National Gallery.'

Felix and Ivo looked at each other, and, despite themselves, they both smiled.

'You got me pretty badly,' said Felix, touching his nose with care.

'Yeah . . . sorry . . . my father taught me how to throw a punch once, he needed to learn how to fight when he was going around Central Asia and stuff.'

'Cool!'

'Yeah, pretty cool,' said Ivo.

'Good,' said Miranda.

Having shaken Felix by the hand, and hugged Miranda, Ivo slipped downstairs and out of the house, and went back across to the Moncrieffs'. It had stopped raining, and he was feeling stronger in his heart, now that he was aware of the dangers he faced. The rest of the city, he thought, was moving blindly towards Christmas, the festival of light in the darkness, the shining beacon fire in the black wilderness of winter. Lights went up everywhere; trees appeared and presents were laid out; and all were unaware of the madness that lurked beneath the very streets they trod.

Chapter Eleven

Above the three of them a helicopter hovered, its blades slicing through the air, splitting the dim rays of light as they fell to the ground. An alarm was ringing in the distance, agitating the air with its high-pitched screams. It was a crisp day, winter sunlight washing the world, the day after Ivo had punched Felix.

'Felix,' said Ivo dreamily, '*kopto* means break, doesn't it? Or cut? In Greek, I mean.'

'Yes,' Felix replied, looking at him from over a newspaper. They were sitting on some swings in a deserted playground, somewhere near Holland Park. They'd gone there on the grounds that it was far enough away from Marylebone and Mayfair, and nearer to Kensal Rise.

'And *helios* – it means sun? You know, like Helios the sun god,' Ivo continued.

Felix pushed back on his swing, nodding, the rusting chains making a not unpleasant creak. He twisted round and round, until he could twist no further, and then suddenly let go, spinning quickly, mimicking the movement of the helicopter's blades, letting out a yelp of excitement. He came to a breathless stop facing Ivo, and grinned at him wolfishly.

'So does helicopter mean a sun-cutter?' said Ivo, watching the machine's blades as they cut through the sunlight, making stripy shadows in his eyes, the chugging, constant sound filling his ears. He was still a little wary of Felix, of the energy coursing in those skinny limbs.

'That's a nice idea,' said Felix, coming to rest next to Ivo. 'But it means something different – winged screw, I think. *Pteros* means wing, and *helix* means screw. Like in DNA, you know, double helix. Double screw.' He stretched his legs out, thin as wires, and scraped the soles of his shoes across the ground.

'Oh,' said Ivo, swinging back gently. Sun-cutter. It had seemed a beautiful way of naming a machine – to give this ugly, unnatural monster that tore through the skies a poetic label would have been somehow glorious; to find out it was just as bland as anything else was disappointing.

'I'll always think of it as a sun-cutter,' he said quietly, and watched as the helicopter juddered away into the distance.

Ivo was about to continue, when he noticed a figure moving towards them, swaying from side to side, mumbling and wailing. As the figure approached, its features became more defined. What had seemed to be a mass of dark, bearish hair showed itself as a wrinkled face, bounded by black matted locks and a beard which looked capable of supporting several life forms. The man was almost circular, he was wearing so many coats. He carried a black plastic bag, and he shuffled towards them.

The man was muttering and sputtering to himself; as he came nearer, words became distinguishable. 'Mr Bumblebee . . . hello . . . what have you done with my clock?'

Ivo realised the question was being addressed to them. Without speaking, they all got off the swings and backed away. The tramp came nearer to them. A dense stink of alcohol and dirt came off him. His skin was broken and red veins stood out on his cheeks, his nose was as purple as a bunch of grapes.

'*What have you done with my clock?*' His voice was deep and gravelly.

Ivo, Miranda and Felix continued to walk backwards, and when they were several metres from him, Ivo said, 'OK, now run,' and they sped away, up a slight rise until they had enough distance between them and the tramp to stop. They were now on the southern side of Holland Park, near to Kensington High Street, in the quiet, hidden groves of trees and shrubs. They concealed themselves behind a clump of bushes.

'Does it look like he's following us?' asked Miranda, panting.

'No.' Ivo watched as the vagabond spiralled away. He caught his breath, unnerved.

'Shall we call Hunter then?' said Felix.

'All right. Do you think it will work?'

Ivo shrugged. 'I'll have a go.'

Ivo felt in his pocket for the Koptor, and pulled it out. He held it rather self-consciously.

'Remember – you have to think very hard of her, and the quantum particles will be activated,' Felix reminded him.

Ivo did, trying to bring up in his mind a picture of Alice Hunter; but she kept being overlayed by other people, by his parents, by Julius, by Strawbones with the snake hissing out of his mouth, and Ivo knew he hadn't done it.

'It's no good,' he said. 'It's impossible. I can't concentrate on her. It's like when you say don't think of orange dogs and then all you can think of is orange dogs.' Despondent, he drew away from the others. Felix bounced up and down on his feet.

Miranda, who had been thinking carefully, uncreased her forehead and said, 'Wait! What if we all do it? If we all join forces. Maybe we can do it then.'

'Might as well.' Ivo came back to them, and Felix and Miranda grabbed hold of the Koptor, and all three closed their eyes in concentration.

'Just picture her as we saw her when she opened the door,' Miranda said. 'Think only of her. Only of Alice Hunter. There, can you see her? I can see her, standing there, with her cardigan on. She's here, standing in front of us, now.'

Nothing happened. They could hear the calling of birds, the whisper of the wind in the trees; a dog barked far in the distance; a jogger pounded past, music blaring from his headphones. Once more Ivo felt the weight of the future upon him, feeling that these ordinary things were somehow massing together to spell out some truth. He shook his head and looked at Miranda. He was about to speak, when there was a subtle change in the quality of the air, and Hunter appeared.

She was wearing a brown mackintosh and a dress with red polka dots on it, as well as what looked to Ivo rather like bedroom slippers; from her left hand dangled a ladle, smeared with soup.

'Phew! That really takes you apart. Hah!' Following

Ivo's quizzical glance, she said, 'I was making my lunch.'

'Sorry,' said Ivo. 'It's just . . . you know, it's quite hard to believe that you've just . . .' He tailed off.

'So,' she said, ignoring him, 'what have you got to tell me?' She was agitated, looking around, her eyes shifting quickly over them. They told her about Strawbones's plans for the National Gallery. Her eyes became more and more alarmed. 'This is it,' she muttered. 'Liberation. The moment when the Eleutheroi will rule the earth, when all conscience will be gone.' She lifted the hand holding the ladle to her forehead; thick red tomato soup dripped on to the ground.

'What will you do?' asked Miranda.

'We must go to Julius's flat and find the Thyrsos. We'll have to go by normal ways,' she replied, striding off, the three friends scampering behind her to keep up. 'You can only materialise like that with the Koptor, and it isn't nice. I'm not, unfortunately, like the Liberators. They can move quickly – very quickly – like the gods coming down from Mount Olympus. That's why,' she said, 'no one saw Strawbones on the tube. He was too fast for them.' She was breathing very heavily, her face grey and drawn, and she looked to Ivo almost insubstantial.

They were coming to the playground where they had been earlier, and Ivo was discomfited to see that the tramp had not left, but was now sitting on one of the swings, gently rocking to and fro, his feet just touching the ground, the tips of his toes poking through his rotting boots, showing his disgusting nails. He felt the tramp's eyes upon them as they sailed past him, and as they reached a safe distance Ivo was filled with relief. The creaking of the swing stopped, and Ivo heard the tramp getting off. He consciously sped up, and motioned to the others that they should do so too. They made towards the car park that spread its grey tarmac nearby, Hunter powering on ahead of them.

'What? What is it, Ivo?' asked Felix, noticing the anxiety in Ivo.

'Just . . . I don't know, come on, quickly!'

A voice cracked the air. 'Hunter! Hunter! I have seen you. Come back here!'

Hunter reacted quickly, leaping round like a kangaroo and facing the sound. It was the tramp. 'Hide!' she whispered urgently. 'Quick, behind that car. And listen – to stop them, you have to become like them. Remember that.'

'Hunter! What is the point of resisting! You know you're powerless!' The tramp's voice was unfeasibly loud, rolling and cannoning around them.

Ivo, Miranda and Felix hurried behind the car, peering awkwardly through the windows. They saw that another car was drawing up, and in it were two men. One of them was Perkins. The engine's throbbing filled their ears; the car came to a slow, menacing halt. The radio was on and music spilled out into the air. The doors opened, and Perkins got out followed by another Acolyte.

'Hunter,' he shouted, as Alice began to back away from him. 'I could make a joke here,' he continued. 'What does it feel like to be hunted?' He guffawed.

Alice turned and began to run, away from Ivo and the Rocksavages.

'It's no use,' shouted Perkins, pushing his glasses back on his nose, his eyes magnified threefold.

The Acolyte advanced upon Hunter, a grin on his face, as Perkins stood by, laughing. The tramp, meanwhile, had discarded his overcoats and ripped off his beard; now he looked lean and tall, heading directly to Hunter.

'She's *toast*,' Felix whispered to Ivo.

There was the sound of a fist connecting with flesh, and Ivo was surprised to see that Hunter had taken on one of the Acolytes. He stumbled back, putting his hands up in a defensive position. The other Acolyte wheeled round to the back of Hunter. Her skirts flapped in the wind. She swung the soup ladle round and round and struck him on the head with it; he retreated. The first came forwards again and tried to rugby tackle her, but she evaded him, kicking him in the stomach with her slippered feet; one of the tartan slippers came off and she nearly fell. 'Dammit!' she said; but she'd winded him, and he was bent double, and she took the opportunity to kick him again, and then brought the ladle down on his neck. The other Acolyte advanced once more, and Hunter turned round, and appeared to collect herself; then in a whirlwind of speed she spun on her heels and karate-chopped him in the shoulder.

Perkins all the while stood by the side, a smirk on his face; Hunter advanced upon him and he held his hands up, in a slightly mocking gesture.

'Hunter. Where is it?'

One of the men raised himself up from the ground and lunged at Hunter, but without looking she kicked him in the face and he fell again.

'I will never give it up,' she said. She crossed her arms.

'But you're the only one left, Hunter. You might as well give up now.' Perkins' voice was wheedling; he glared. Hunter backed away as he began to approach, and then turned and ran.

A jogger appeared over the brow of a hill, head-phones on, focused on his running. Perkins stopped, seeming to calculate, and then called to his Acolytes, 'In the car, quick,' and, staggering, the two followed him, one holding his shoulder, the other pressing both hands to his ears; they tumbled into the car and drove off.

After a few moments, Hunter reappeared over the rise, panting, her cardigan flapping open. The jogger, when he reached her, saw only a mad old bag lady muttering to herself. She picked up her slipper and put it on ruefully.

She went round to the side of the car where Ivo and the others were hiding. 'Get home, as quickly as you can,' she said. 'Go on, home. We'll meet again soon. Home!' She shooed them away, and, startled, they ran off back to the bus stop. Ivo turned back to see her running away in the opposite direction, head bent, cardigan clutched tightly round her, her breath making little clouds as she went.

Chapter Twelve

Ivo, Miranda and Felix jumped on a bus on Holland Park Road, taking them eastwards in the direction of Marble Arch and Oxford Circus. Soon they were going past Lancaster Gate. Felix was twisting his hands together, twitching and jittering, Miranda was staring blankly out of the window, Ivo sat with his knees pressed close, chin down on his chest. Even for Christmas the streets were unusually thronged. There seemed to be hardly an inch of space on the pavements; people were bustling and knocking each other off into the road, where motorists crawled slowly by. A couple started an angry argument, causing the stream of pedestrians to break around them; some boys in tracksuits ran, laughing, in the opposite direction to the flow; a policeman muttered into his walkie-talkie. The bus lurched onwards, and then stopped at a traffic light for what seemed like ages. Ivo tapped his knees, Felix and Miranda fidgeted; eventually Ivo said, 'Shall we just jump out here?' and they all scampered down, pleaded with the driver to open the doors, which he did (somewhat grumpily), and spilled out just in front of the cinema. The white bulk of Marble Arch squatted on their right.

'Do you think we've been followed?' Miranda asked, her voice trembling a little.

Ivo nodded. 'Almost certainly.'

He looked around at the crowds of people. A prickling sense of fear began to tickle his throat. 'I think we should just try to get home, as soon as we can. I think that's where we're safest. Come on!' He led the way, dodging through a crowd of Spanish tourists dawdling outside the tube station. Felix dug his hands into his jacket pockets, and Miranda, shaking her head slightly, trotted after him.

There was a much louder background level of noise than usual; there were more shouts, more laughter, more buses honking. Outside Selfridges it was almost impossible to move in the crush. The three slowed down to a walk. Ivo kept a careful eye behind him, but it was impossible to tell who was an Acolyte and who wasn't. His frustration was building up. He wanted to release it all in a huge burst of rage. But he repressed the feeling. Felix put the collar of his jacket up. Miranda, perplexed, trudged just next to him.

A group of girls ran past them, shouting with glee, almost knocking Ivo over. He was getting frustrated. They weren't making much headway against the streams of shoppers. They crept down Oxford Street towards Oxford Circus. The shops were pulsing with light and music, each doorway disgorging crowds of people, massing together like ants.

Ivo hopped on to the road, checking on the others behind him. Felix was looking distinctly grumpy, thought Ivo. Distracted, Ivo almost walked straight into a lampost; he righted himself, and carried on.

'Let's try and go up a side street,' came Miranda's voice from behind. But there was a tumultuous horde to their left; it was impossible to break through them. Ivo was swept on ahead, towards Oxford Circus, past the road they should have gone down. He was helpless; he tried to turn but couldn't. He was now separated from the others. Frightened, he scanned the crowds, but could not see either of their faces.

He was pushed on ahead, to the junction of Oxford Street and Regent Street. Traffic lights held the buses in check; they groaned like dragons. People spilled across the roads, ignoring the system, dodging in between cars, risking their lives. Ivo jumped on to the pavement and held on to the black iron barrier just next to the entrance to the tube station. The surge of bodies around him was disorientating; he closed his eyes, and tried to calm himself. The air was cold and piercing; a flurry of sleet passed over them.

He pulled out his phone and tried both Miranda and Felix's numbers; but a network busy signal came on. He saw a man walk out into the middle of the street, seemingly unaware of the commotion around him, or of the traffic. A bus was approaching, its horn sounding long and loud; the man stood still in the centre of the junction, and lifted his arms wide. He had long black hair. The sky darkened, the clouds taking on a black, wine-like tinge. The man threw his head back and let out a scream: it thrilled Ivo to the very core. Then the man threw off his overcoat. Underneath he was wearing a long fur; was he also wearing a sword-belt? Ivo couldn't quite see. Ivo held on to the cold railings as some people pushed past him. Traffic had stopped. A policeman was making his way across to the man. People paused and looked.

The man, as the policeman approached, paid no attention to him, but instead started to yell, two syllables, 'Ee-yoh, ee-yoh,' which held in them the vibrancy of madness. There was such power in those sounds that Ivo felt his marrow burning with desire. He recognised the call of the Liberators. Ivo began, despite the cold, to sweat. He climbed up on to the railing, holding on to it as if he were drowning.

He surveyed the scene. The policeman had stopped in his tracks, and Ivo could see the look of puzzlement on his face changing, first into joy, and then into wildness; the policeman threw down his notebook, ripped off his walkie-talkie and flung it away. There was a loud smash behind Ivo, and he turned to see that somebody had thrown a brick into the window of a nearby shop; some other people joined in, kicking the hole until the whole window smashed, fragments of glass falling and clattering to the ground, and then they poured in; alarms went off, shrieking above the din, but nobody took any notice. There were more smashing sounds. Ivo felt his heart thrum; he desperately wanted to join in. But he held the Koptor and struggled to keep his mind clear.

Now the rain was black, and Ivo let a drop fall on his tongue, and it tasted like wine. A surge of people poured out of the stationary buses and there was a melee in the middle of Oxford Circus. There were Christmas hampers, and food was being thrown out to everybody; Ivo saw two women fighting over a turkey, a man stuffing himself with mince pies; brandy bottles, champagne bottles were being passed round. A thousand people, abandoning themselves, foaming and surging like the sea upon the shore, and standing in the middle was the tall man with the long black hair. His skin looked parched to Ivo, yellow and old, his eyes were green – wholly green – the green of leaves, of deep grass in summer. Ivo was reminded of the strange apparition he had seen sitting in the armchair in Lydia's studio. Julius had been downstairs ... so this was Strawbones.

Ivo could feel the pure pleasure of release – girls running out of a clothes shop, bedecked in jewellery and new fashion, a mother, swathed in bed linen, bursting through the crowds, mouth gaping open, a boy howling like a wolf, men tearing off their ties – and now, as he watched, were there cracks in the pavement? A snake of ivy was growing out of the tarmac, and creeping its way over a bus, its green shocking against the metallic red. The black clouds above shifted, and split apart, revealing the cold blue of a winter sky, through which a pale yellow sun shot its rays. Helicopters swarmed overhead; sirens sounded; but nothing could get through to the centre.

And now the ivy was growing up everything: it turned the railings into living masses of greenery; Ivo felt it sneaking its tendrils up his body and tore them off. The rioting people were ripping up the vegetation, placing crowns of leaves upon their heads. The ivy grew with such speed that soon barely an inch of concrete, tarmac or shopfront could be seen. Ivo saw a man heading towards him, a knife in his hand; Ivo, quicker than he thought he'd be able to, leaped up on to a bin, and then scrabbled on top of a telephone box; there he stood, feet entwined amongst ivy, immune and terrified. Where were Felix and Miranda? He could see no sign of them. He wondered if this time they too were taken up by this frenzy. A rock sailed past his ear; somebody on the ground screamed. There were more screams now, of pain and fear; fights had broken out and people were ferociously scrapping over what they had looted.

Ivo saw, slowly, moving northwards up Regent Street, a phalanx of riot police, shields held out in front of them, truncheons bristling. People were trying to clamber up the telephone box now; not sure what to do, Ivo tore off the ivy to give them less purchase. He felt the phone box rocking, and held on.

Looking back to the centre of the riot, Ivo saw the man in the fur coat turn round to face the advancing riot force. He spread his arms out wide, as if to greet them, laughing; and then he vanished. One moment, he was there, the next he was not; although Ivo thought he could see a blur of movement, as of something moving very fast. The ivy receded, as suddenly as if it were water and a plug had been torn out of the bath.

The scene it revealed was devastating. The clouds rolled back across the sky. Everywhere, as far as Ivo could see, lay injured, groaning people. Smoke gushed out of windows, the constant sound of sirens pierced his eardrums, shattered glass lay everywhere.

Ambulances began to make their way in; the buses were moved on; Ivo saw people on stretchers, policemen corralling rioters. Television crews were already on the scene; a man whose ear had been bitten off was giving an interview, the sky above was buzzing with police helicopters. Someone helped Ivo down off the phone box, and, somehow, he found himself heading back to Charmsford Square.

Chapter Thirteen

RIOT IN OXFORD CIRCUS screamed the boards of the London papers that night. Ivo had phoned Felix the moment he got reception, and found that both Felix and Miranda had fled into a shop and slipped out of the back just as the riot was beginning. Felix sounded a little upset about this. 'I had to protect Miranda,' he said, although Ivo felt there was a deeper current there. As soon as he could, he'd gone over to the Rocksavages', and they were now sitting in Miranda's room. Felix went out to get a newspaper, and came back exclaiming, 'The papers are flying off the stands. Everyone's rushing home. Look outside!'

They went to the window and saw, down towards the Marylebone Road, streams of people, looking neither to the right nor the left, hurrying off in the direction of tubes, buses, cars, swarming and foaming, umbrellas shooting up like hideous black mushrooms.

'I'm hungry,' said Felix, to break the silence. His chin was tucked into his jumper. Miranda lay on her front on a rug. Ivo was curled into the corner of Miranda's sofa, feeling the plush red under his fingers.

'Ma and Pa are out to dinner. Something's been left for us if we want it.'

'Let's look at the article,' said Ivo, getting up and drawing the curtains, feeling a shade of anxiety creeping up his spine. They settled on the sofa, and Felix read out loud: '*Oxford Circus was today the scene of horrors not witnessed since the Blitz. A riot broke out in the afternoon.*' Journalists suggested that terrorist groups were involved, and connected the idea of laughing gas with the murder of Blackwood. The London Stock Exchange had taken an enormous fall that afternoon, dropping over two thousand points; the paper was illustrated with pictures of mournful bankers, phones clamped to their ears, and graphs diving downwards. A large investment bank had collapsed; many jobs were on the line. The London Mayor was called to account; the police chief besieged.

'Julius and Strawbones. They're behind it, I know. All of this,' said Ivo, remembering the man with black hair. He had looked exactly like the man in the picture Hunter had shown them. But Ivo was sure it wasn't Julius. This smacked of Strawbones – extravagant, provocative. 'What can we do?'

'I don't know why you're so set on stopping them,' said Felix, mooching towards Ivo. 'Didn't you feel the riot? It was wonderful.' His face shone. His fingers were twisting, nervously; he unzipped and zipped up his top. Miranda whacked him with the rolled up *Evening Standard*.

'Idiot. We should do something, now,' she snapped.

'What can we do? There's three of us. And what, like, supernatural powers have we got? None.'

'There's this.' Ivo showed them the Koptor, sleek and dark.

Felix scoffed. 'And we don't even know where the Thyrsos is. What good will that do for us?'

Ivo felt the hotness of anger burn in his stomach. He felt as if his brain were suddenly blocked, and he wanted to shout; but he controlled himself. 'Felix – don't you understand? This is chaos.'

'But what's wrong with chaos?' said Felix testily. 'What's so good about order? Just think,' he said. 'What kind of a world is this, anyway? Wars, famines, dictators, floods – there's a disaster every time you turn on the news. And where does it come from? Order! Without order, there's no one at the top. Without order, you haven't got dictators, you have no wars. You just have the freedom of yourself. And that,' he continued, his voice growing more urgent, 'is electrifying.'

Ivo couldn't believe it. Was Felix being converted? He struggled to reply. 'You're wrong!'

'How?' said Felix, his voice nasty.

Miranda sat up suddenly, her eyes glistening with tears. 'If you can't see that, you're no brother of mine!'

It evidently hurt Felix, for he swiftly turned around, and bent his head, placing his forehead against the wall; Ivo saw his back rising slowly up and down. He was collecting himself, thought Ivo. He'll turn around again in a minute, and be the same old Felix. The silence in the room was thick.

The sound of the front door being opened interrupted the silence. 'Hang on – didn't you say that your parents were away?' asked Ivo.

'Yeah, out for supper. Why?' Miranda sank back into the sofa. Felix turned around, and stood with his back angled against the wall, not looking at either of them.

Ivo motioned to them both to keep silent. They listened, intently, and there was the unmistakable sound of a door being shut. And of footsteps in the hallway.

'Perkins!' mouthed Felix. The three glanced at each other in sudden terror. 'In the linen cupboard!'

Miranda scuttled across the room and waved the

two boys after her. She opened a nondescript-looking cupboard door. In it were slats on which piles of white and blue linen reposed innocently. Miranda crouched down and slipped under the bottom one. 'Come on!' she whispered urgently. 'Quick!'

The other two scurried after her, and squirmed under, Felix finding it hardest. There was about two foot of space at the back of the cupboard, which was about the width of a man's armspan. The mountains of linen, falling down, concealed them, and Miranda managed to pull the door to.

They heard rumbles and murmurs coming from downstairs, and then the feet headed upwards. The steps were pounding quickly. Perkins must have been leaping two or three at a time, and now it sounded as if there were more people coming up after him. Sharply and brutally, the bedroom door was flung open.

'Felix!' Perkins said, in a wheedling voice. 'Miranda! It's time for your Latin!'

The three held their breath. They could hear Perkins stamping around the room.

'Come on, you two,' he barked. More clomping feet entered.

'They're not here. They must be out, the little pests. Probably with that Ivo Moncrieff. It's time we did something about them. I have a feeling they

187

know a little too much about us.'

Perkins came closer to the door, and they shrank back as they felt pressure on it. Without warning it was whipped open.

Never had Ivo been more frightened. He was so scared he closed his eyes as tightly as possible, wishing it was all a nightmare and that when he opened his eyes they would be drinking tea in a café somewhere. A shiver of cold, liquid terror washed over his body, his dry lips chafed, his heart beat slowly, one, two, three . . . and the cupboard door closed again. They were well hidden by the blankets.

'Yes . . . those irritating mites must be got rid of. *Eliminated.*' They heard him pacing up and down, the floorboards protesting, and they heard the sound of chairs being knocked over, and the mattress on the bed being pushed away. 'They're getting too close.'

There was another pause, during which Ivo was sure that if he even so much as opened his eyes he'd give away their hiding place. 'We'll come back later, when they're in bed. And then . . . well, you know the drill.' The way he said 'drill' drove right through Ivo's brain like a sliver of glass. 'Right. Let's go.'

Clomp clomp clomp . . . the heavy boots of the Acolytes went out first, followed by Perkins' lighter steps, and the door to the bedroom closed. Felix immediately made to move, but Ivo restrained him; he waited, counting to a full sixty seconds, until they heard the front door slam shut, before signalling that they could go out. Felix kicked open the door with relief and they all tumbled out.

They spoke in hurried undertones.

'We have to go after them,' said Ivo. 'We have to now. We'll follow them, we'll find out what to do, we'll find their weak points, we'll do it.'

'No, *we'll* follow them,' repeated Miranda, her voice, though a little shaky, full of conviction. 'You've got the Koptor. You've got to keep it safe. You go home. There's a back way out, a fire escape that takes you into the area, go out there and you'll be in Charmsford Square.'

It was true, thought Ivo. If he was caught by Perkins now, then it would be all over. He had to keep the Koptor safe until he knew what to do. 'It's dangerous out there!' Ivo said, worried. 'You should stay here!'

'What, and risk being a sitting duck for Perkins when he comes back up? No thanks. I'd rather die fighting than in my sleep,' Miranda said.

Slightly more muted, Felix said, 'Yeah, me too.'

Ivo felt a surge of admiration for his two friends, as they stood in front of him, surrounded by the chaos of their upturned lives, but strong and firm, with the blaze of battle burning within them. He glanced thankfully at them. 'OK. But keep in touch. Don't do anything stupid. Stay out of sight. Where will you sleep?'

'We'll think of something,' said Miranda, and kissed him on the cheek. 'See you tomorrow.'

Ivo crept out into the corridor, and, first checking to see if there was anyone around, carefully opened the window that led on to the iron fire escape. Worried that it would make a lot of noise, he was pleased when he found that if he trod lightly it made no sound at all; he tripped down it as lightly as a squirrel down a tree, and shot across Charmsford Square to the Moncrieffs' house.

After Ivo had gone, Felix turned to look at his sister.

'Are you ready?' he said.

Without pausing, and without speaking, Miranda nodded. A grim kind of certainty had gripped them. Felix opened the door to Miranda's room, and they stepped out on to the landing. Down below in the stair-well he could see the faint blue glow that came from the fish tank. There was no sign of anyone. He turned and beckoned to his sister. The siblings smiled at each other, a smile of love and apprehension, of under-standing and fear. Felix was excited; the knowledge that Perkins could be involved with something as dangerous as the Liberators had almost given him a touch of glamour. Miranda too was filled with a strange kind of emotion, almost glee, that thrummed and bounced within her, as boiling and bright as the rays of the sun. They crept out and down the stairs. 'How can we find him?' asked Miranda.

'We'll try the alleyway.'

They ran down the stairs into the hallway. Their faces looked strange in the blue light, unreal and ghostly. Miranda stepped forwards and reached for the door. 'How far do you think they've gone?'

Felix didn't reply. Miranda lowered her arm slowly. 'Felix?' she said. 'How far do you think they've gone?'

'Not far at all,' said a voice, and Miranda turned round to see Perkins holding her brother by the neck. Perkins, standing tall and full of rage. He gleamed, and opened his mouth wide, but Felix wrestled free from his grip; Miranda wrenched open the door, and they ran outside, banging it shut. They ran fast, heading by instinct towards the bright lights and cars of the Marylebone Road; Perkins came behind them, two Acolytes with him.

'You! Come back here!' he shouted.

Perhaps it would have been more sensible to go to him, to say that they had no idea what was going on, but it was too late, and Perkins' enraged, maniacal face was enough to send them bolting.

'Maybe we can lose him over the road,' Felix shouted to Miranda breathlessly, as they reached the wide expanse of the Marylebone Road. The lights were on green and the traffic was fast. Miranda and Felix teetered on the edge of the kerb. Perkins and the Acolytes were fast approaching. A lorry zoomed past them. Miranda stepped into the road, but Felix pulled her back.

'Now!' said Miranda, seeing a space in the cars. 'Let's go! Now!' She sprinted across, darting between the cars; one honked at her; she made it across to the island and looked back. Felix was dithering – the traffic had speeded up. The Acolytes were a few metres away from him, and closing in.

'Come on! Move!' shouted Miranda.

Felix judged the cars, and their speed, and jumped off the kerb; then he let out a yell, and Miranda saw Perkins catching him by the back of his jacket.

'Go!' shouted Felix. Without looking back, Miranda went. She ran and ran through the streets of Marylebone; but the Acolytes were behind her; lost and confused, she fell and scraped her knee. Lying there, on her front, she allowed herself a second of rest, as the tears sprang unheeded to her eyes.

'Get up,' she said to herself, 'get up.' She managed to force herself, and, hobbling, almost toppling over, shrill animal noises coming from her mouth, she ran on again, ignoring her bleeding knee, her torn jumper, her broken bracelet, which shed pieces as she sprinted, wildly, blindly, as quickly as she could, as far away as she could, until she found a main road. The dirty London buildings, shops lit with Christmas lights, glowered down on either side. Repelled, she turned back and went down a side street.

'Are you OK?' It was an old man, concerned; she shook him off, and walked further, until the bustle of people absorbed her in its anonymity.

What could she do? She had lost her brother. Perhaps even now they were murdering him, ripping him apart, sacrificing him in some strange and dreadful ritual, to that creature, that monster. She felt as if a wedge had been driven into her brain and somebody was splitting it in half. She needed Felix, as he needed her. She saw ahead of her a large building looming, and recognised it as the Wallace Collection; she sat – almost collapsed – on the pavement in front of it, feeling the rough cold stone beneath her. Her foot was in a puddle but she didn't notice.

Ivo. She must talk to Ivo. His face came back to her, and she felt in her pockets for the bump of her mobile phone. It looked alien to her when she took it out, and she stared at it, unable to remember how to make it work. Then a wave came over her, she pressed the buttons hurriedly, and held the phone to her ear, breathing more slowly now, but lips quivering.

It rang, the beeping in her ear seeming unbearably slow. When she heard a click, and Ivo's voice softly saying 'Hello?' she could barely suppress a yelp. But she did and, biting her lip, she said, 'Ivo.' And then left a pause, long enough for Ivo to say, now sounding impossibly far away, 'Miranda? Is that you? Hey, Miranda, are you OK?'

The tears came now, and Miranda couldn't stop them; she let the phone fall to her side, Ivo's voice calling in vain, and she lowered her head into her hands and wept.

Julius stood in the half-light, the dim orange glow from the electric lamp illuminating him only feebly. Strawbones was standing with his back slightly facing his brother; he was looking away. Julius was looking right at Strawbones's neck. His hands were held together, and he was leaning against the wall; this, somehow, made him look menacing, like a tall praying mantis. There was silence between them, and then Strawbones shifted around.

'I'm sorry, guv'nor,' he said in a Cockney accent. 'I couldn't 'elp it.'

Julius, when he spoke, measured his words carefully. 'You are really the limit.' He moved his face further into the light, suddenly, and Strawbones drew back. 'I have laid my plans – *our* plans – so carefully these last few years. The tunnels, the National Gallery – everything is in place now. And *you* –' he moved forwards, as swiftly as a hare, and pulled his brother close to him, so close that Strawbones could feel Julius's spittle on his face – '*you* cause a riot in Oxford Circus!'

'It was *fun*, brother,' said Strawbones, in a composed voice. 'Nobody knows it was *us*.'

'Still,' said Julius, releasing him, 'I want you to stay quiet. It's not long now. A riot!' he smiled at his brother. 'There will be time enough for that soon. Time enough.'

Chapter Fourteen

Ivo heard the dial tone go. Immediately he rang Miranda's phone back, but received no reply; he rang Felix, and nothing; he rang the house phone, but nobody answered, and he hung up before it reached the answerphone.

Ivo's stomach was swirling with fear. He was sitting on the end of his bed. He put down his phone slowly, and then suddenly kicked it away, as if it were something distasteful. A sickening thought had come into his head, and he could not shake it from his mind: that the Acolytes had got Felix and Miranda, and that they had already killed them. He thought, I'll wait. I'll wait for an hour and see what happens.

At the end of the hour, he decided to go over, risking being seen himself. Without stopping to put on a jumper, he made his way down the stairs quickly and quietly, and then turning a corner, backed up in terror as he saw Julius coming out of the studio with Lydia.

He heard them laughing, and Julius muttering thanks. 'It's really wonderful, Lydia, my brother will, I'm sure, absolutely love it.' Lydia murmured some self-deprecatory phrase, and then waved Julius off down the stairs, before going back into her studio.

Ivo crept past her door and paused at the top of the last flight, and watched Julius slide out of the house. Ivo's heart was thumping. He went down into the hall, jumping the last four steps, and was just about to reach the front door, when Jago stepped out of the drawing room.

'Ah, Ivo, how are you, old horse? Haven't seen you in a while. Come in here.'

Ignoring Ivo's protests, Jago dragged him into the sitting room for backgammon. The radio was on, a gas fire threw shapes on the walls with its dancing flames. Ivo felt in his pockets and realised he'd left his phone upstairs. He swore softly. Jago, flexing his thick fingers, opened the wooden backgammon board, which shone in the soft light. They played. Ivo lost every time. Jago regarded him with his hawk-like eyes.

'Something worrying you, old horse?'

'Oh . . . no,' said Ivo. What could he tell Jago? That his own life was in danger, that his friends might be dead? He managed to push his feelings into a corner of his mind, but only a tiny part of his brain engaged with his uncle. He might as well have been an automaton.

'You're staying for dinner, Ivo?'

Ivo jumped at the chance. 'No! I'm going out to see . . . I mean I'm meeting some friends – I said I'd meet some friends from school, down at the Odeon, we're going to see a film.'

Jago's face darkened. 'But you are staying to dinner, Ivo. We discussed this. Your cousins are coming.'

'Oh . . . but . . .' Ivo knew that arguing was futile. He was dependent upon Jago and Lydia; his parents had instilled that in him – while he stayed with them, he must obey them.

Unable to control himself, he was clumsy and knocked over his glass; apologising, he left the backgammon board and ran upstairs to check his phone. There was nothing.

He heard his name being called, and powered down the stairs again; panting, he arrived in the hall to greet his cousins.

At dinner he spoke to no one unless spoken to; his girl cousins, who were about the same age as him, giggled and joked; his boy cousin, three years older, maintained an aloof presence and spoke only to the adults. Ivo ate, his mind only on one thing.

After dinner, he checked his phone once more, but nothing. They played a game, called 'Who's in the hat?', in which everyone put names of people in a hat, and then one person acted out the name they pulled from the hat, and everyone else had to guess; Ivo was roundly voted the worst player of the night. He endured a film which he had seen before. Before bed he tried calling, first Felix, then Miranda, and then the house phone again, but got no reply; in desperation he checked every available means of electronic communication on his computer, but there was nothing, except for an email from his parents, which, in his anxious state, he ignored.

Having said goodbye to his cousins, he tried to get ready for sleep, but it was impossible; his head was buzzing and, though he longed for oblivion, he could not reach it, and Lydia would not give him another sleeping pill.

Eventually, some time around five, in the blackness of early morning, which had become to him another, strange world of muted colour and sounds that echoed for miles; eventually, as he lay muffled, wondering how many other people in England were lying awake, staring manically at the ceiling, he fell asleep, although when he woke at eight thirty it did not feel like he had been sleeping at all. He looked at himself in the mirror – eyes bloodshot, bags under his eyes, and wondered ruefully what Jago and Lydia would think he'd been up to.

The first thing he did after a breakfast of salmon and scrambled eggs – which, though delicious, he ate absent-mindedly, concentrating instead on three glasses of orange juice, causing Christine to tease him a little – was pull on his coat and run round to the Rocksavages.

He knocked on the door, expecting it to be opened by a tearful Olivia Rocksavage; but when she did open it, she looked remarkably composed.

'Oh, it's you, Ivo. They're busy. Working. They have lessons till one. Why don't you come back then?'

They! She had said 'they'. Ivo's heart burst with relief. A glowing, tumbling hotness of joy bubbled in him, expanding all over his body. But why hadn't Miranda called him to let him know that they were OK? He felt a creeping sense of unease at the thought that they might even now be with Perkins, who had pursued them only the day before.

After Ivo had agreed to return at lunch time, smiling at him, Olivia Rocksavage shut the door. He knew that Felix and Miranda had lessons in the dining room, which was on the ground floor and faced on to the street. Ivo nimbly leaped on to the wrought-iron shoe-scraper, from which vantage point, if he stretched far enough, he could see right into the dining room.

Usually Felix would be staring, frog-like, into the square, and Ivo, as Perkins had his back to it, would be able to attract his attention, while Miranda would keep Perkins diverted.

But they were sitting, perfectly naturally, both very neat and tidy, almost demure; Felix was wearing a shirt – and it was buttoned almost to the top; Miranda was wearing a very preppy-looking jumper. Both of them were looking attentively at Perkins.

Miranda was reading aloud from a book, and occasionally would stop and Felix would take over. Perkins paced up and down. Ivo ducked as Perkins swung past him, eyes glaring out on to the street, and then slowly rose up to peer at his friends when Perkins' back was turned again.

Ivo waved at them, trying to catch their eyes, but they did not see him, or pretended not to; he considered throwing a stone but did not want to risk alerting Perkins to his presence. Eventually Miranda said something and marched to the window, and without even looking at Ivo, she pulled down the blind. Ivo, crestfallen, slipped off his perch and stood, mind buzzing, alone in the street.

Chapter Fifteen

Stretched out on his bed, Ivo listened to the sounds below him. Miranda and Felix were dead to him – they were frozen, somehow. He would never be able to forget the look in Miranda's eyes as she had come to window – was it hatred, or distrust, or just simple blankness? He doubted whether he would ever be able to see them again. Seeing his friends whose jokes and warmth had made cold London so welcoming behaving like robots, as if some hostile, alien intelligence had taken over their minds, was crushing.

There was bustle and movement in almost every room of Lydia and Jago's house. People were constantly walking in and out of doors, bearing flowers, boxes, materials for Lydia's dress; Christine was always making something that smelled delicious, and streams of wellwishers, helpers, hangers-on and sycophants were always to be found huddling in the drawing room, subsisting on Christine's excellent sand-wiches and cakes.

Ivo moved, rolling off his bed with great effort, and slouched towards his desk. He put the mysterious Koptor on the desk in front of him. The thought had occurred to him that he should try to enter Julius's flat in order to find the Thyrsos. It was a decision he had been playing with, turning over and over in his mind. Julius and Strawbones, he knew, were somewhere downstairs. He had seen Strawbones sliding into the studio, and Julius was in the drawing room being courted by half a dozen eager socialites. Their presence in the house unnerved him. Strawbones hadn't come up to his room, for which he was grateful.

And there was also Blackwood's house, Ivo thought. He could return there, find some information. Maybe there would be something that could help him.

He hoped that the Rocksavages, in their newly docile state, had not confessed everything to Perkins. Ivo couldn't know what Perkins had done to them – had he enslaved them, or hypnotised them, or even somehow lobotomised them permanently? It was too horrible to think about.

He had managed to avoid the two brothers. Neither had attempted to spend any time with him since he had seen them on South Audley Street. Ivo was hoping that they were now too occupied with their larger plan to worry about him.

It was ten thirty, and raining, on the Monday of the week of the party. Outside, muddy swirls of water gurgled down drains, sucked into the mysterious underground, and bent pedestrians scuttled by under glistening umbrellas, like beetles. Ivo pulled on a coat and stomped downstairs without saying anything. He slipped outside, narrowly avoided a collision with someone bearing a huge bouquet, and made his way to Chelsea.

When he got to Blackwood's house, he remembered how Felix had opened the door. He jiggled his cash card in the lock, not really knowing what he was doing, and to his surprise it opened. The house was as he had left it – a mess of papers. First he went to the mantelpiece and put the Koptor into the small depression, and clicked it into place. Nothing happened. He sighed and began leafing through the files. Rain stippled the windowpanes. It seemed as if someone had been through all the papers and removed anything that had to do with the Liberators.

About to give up, he found, amongst a mess of what looked like party invitations, a small book which had simply the letters FIN on the front. It was heavy, despite its size, bound in leather with gilt edges.

was written, in neat handwriting, on the first page. He flicked through to the back and saw on the last page:

8th December 2009

It was initialled by two sets of hands: A.H. and G.B. Hunter and Blackwood. He turned back to the first page and read.

> *The members were sworn in. 'Freedom is Nothing' is our motto. We have set up the group to monitor and prevent the activities of the two brothers who call themselves the Liberators. They have become active once more. Jamie Lovat and Constance Mantel have been despatched to the Balkans to carry out our research.*

There was now a lot of what looked like administrative stuff, so Ivo skipped on to a later date where he saw the names Lovat and Mantel again.

> *Lovat and Mantel have voyaged to the village in the Balkans, at great peril and personal risk, where it had been rumoured that the Liberators were*

born. They report that the brothers were of ancient nobility, sprung from a family which had inhabited the same hill fort for generations, ruling the lands around them with despotic cruelty. A rugged, desolate place, where no priest found a convert, no conqueror dared tread. The last of the dynasty to live in the castle, Dragan and Milan, were by far the cruellest and maddest. Deep in the mountains of Montenegro, the expedition found peasants who still related garbled folk tales of the monstrous Dragon brothers, ten feet tall, with teeth made of diamonds, and hands made of knives.

Lovat, searching in the hidden archives of the one bleak monastery that clung to a hilltop, found a parchment which told the history of their savage rule. They were said to have slaughtered thousands of people and drunk the blood of their foes, even cannibalised their remains.

Lovat reported that at the peak of their violence, in the late thirteenth century, whilst marauding through Greece, the brothers discovered, buried deep in a cave on top of a frozen mountain in Arcadia, a staff.

This staff proved to be the Thyrsos, the staff of Bacchus, that holds within it the power of frenzy. This power can be a positive one. Bacchus is the

releaser, the liberator of tensions and hatreds,
enabling the order of Apollo to be restored. But the
brothers bent the Thyrsos to their will, using it for
unrestrained freedom, and the horror of insanity.
The Thyrsos gave them power, at the expense of
their humanity, for slowly they became immortal.
Beautiful, heartless and deadly.

Soon they drew hundreds of people to them, and
they called their followers 'Acolytes'. The name
they gave themselves was 'hoi tou eleutherou
adelphoi', or 'the Eleutheroi' – the Brothers of
Freedom. As they grew in power and strength they
also took one of the names of Bacchus – 'Liber' –
and labelled themselves 'The Liberators'. Those
who followed them were 'blessed' or 'liberated' in
stages until they became totally without restraint.

Prickles of fear ran down Ivo's back, his hands trembling, his heart fluttering. He had seen the Thyrsos, seen people killed for the greater glory of the Liberators: he was in the middle of something whose depths and strangenesses he could not guess at. The two brothers that Strawbones had told him about were Dragan and Milan, and they were Julius and Strawbones, he was sure. Strawbones hadn't told him his real name.

Ivo jumped at the sound of a mouse scuttling across the floor and continued to read. It appeared that most of the disturbances of the last decades had their roots in the activities of the Liberators. They were waiting for something, for a period when global chaos would be widespread enough for them to step in and take over. And that period was now: the financial market, the lifeblood of the world, was in ruins; wars devastated large swathes of territory; terrorists aimed at the destruction of Western civilisation.

The entry for 1st November 2009 read:

> *The Acolytes have eliminated several of our number. There are few left in FIN. Twenty souls remain. We must recruit more.*

Ivo read the last entry with growing unease.

> *Blackwood's whereabouts are unknown. He has the Koptor. The Liberators are strengthening.*

It was initialled simply A.H. Ivo closed the book and put it down gently. But Hunter had him to help her now. Ivo . . . the sound rolled in his mind. Ivy – the plant that could bring down huge buildings – that was him, he could do it; he was on his own, defenceless, but by clinging on, by plotting, by never giving up, he could stop them.

There was a loud crashing noise behind him. He spun around. The window was being smashed in. Slivers of glass exploded on to the carpet. Two men vaulted into the room and, without saying anything, advanced towards Ivo. The men were fast and one had immediately blocked off the door. Ivo wondered if they were going to kill him. The other came nearer to him, silent, and Ivo prepared to fight; he mustered up all the energy that was in him, but the man came at him and was too strong. He punched Ivo in the stomach whilst the other grabbed him from behind, and the last thing Ivo saw was a glaring face, grinning at him, showing perfect white teeth.

A low, buzzing hum. No air. A tiny room, cell-like, the light coming from a small lamp in the corner, which cast an orange circle upon the ground. A door, heavy, iron, impossible to break. All these things Ivo took in very quickly as he opened his eyes. If he stretched out, he could touch both walls.

I must be in the tunnels, he thought. He had been dumped in a corner. There was no furniture in the room, although somebody had rather thoughtfully left a glass of water by him. He surprised himself at how quickly he gulped it down. He had been dreaming of deserts, of water ever out of his reach.

He patted his pockets, slowly at first, and then feverishly, as he realised that he did not have the Koptor any more. He turfed out everything on to the ground – coins, front-door key, phone, wallet. There was nothing. It was in their hands. They had it. He was captured; he had failed. An emptiness opened in him, and he lay with his head on the cold floor, feeling the pounding of the blood in his veins.

He heard the sound of a lock being turned. He sat up in a corner, his knees held up to his chin. The door creaked and was pushed open. Two Acolytes entered: a woman, beautiful, whom he recognised as Jennifer Brook; she looked grim and calm; and the man who had attacked him in Blackwood's house. They were followed by Perkins, wearing a baggy red T-shirt and jeans, pushing his glasses up on his nose, and he was followed by Julius.

But this was not a Julius that Ivo recognised, who would fit in at cocktail parties, charity dinners and launches for one thing or another; whom you might see sipping champagne in the Royal Enclosure at Ascot.

He had a sword slung across his chest, the scabbard banging at his side. His face – so civilised, so clean, so pure – was pale, and his eyes were green, deep green, and his mouth was a crimson gash, and his hands, sinewy, strong, were those of a murderer.

'Ivo Moncrieff,' he said, his accent harsh and deep, 'you are a child. I do not understand. You have thought that you would be able to *break* us?' His English was slightly awkward, as if he were translating it a word at a time in his head.

He didn't laugh, but looked fiercely at Ivo.

Ivo was still thirsty, his mouth dry, his lips sticky. His vision was blurry.

'Do you even know what I am? What we are?' asked Julius.

'I've seen your vision of the future,' said Ivo, spitting slightly.

'Did you not feel its goodness?' said Julius, his eyes roaring.

'No! It's *evil*!' exclaimed Ivo.

'But freedom, Ivo, is all that mankind wants, is it not? Have we not always struggled to throw off the chains of our oppressors? To be enslaved, is that not the greatest of all sins? Surely to dissolve that enslavement must be good?'

'But not in the way you want,' said Ivo. 'It doesn't work like that. You have to have rules, otherwise the world breaks down.' He remembered dowdy Alice

211

Hunter. 'Dionysus and Apollo. Too much of either one is bad. You need both.'

'Foolish child. You should have joined us when we gave you the opportunity. I will kill you,' said Julius, lazily lifting up a finger. 'It will hurt, very much, but it will be over soon.' With that he began to laugh, a horrible, sing-song laugh, and he spun on his heel and left the room, followed by the Acolytes.

Time passed; Ivo didn't know how much, it could have been hours, it could have been minutes. He reached for the most pleasant memories he could – the smell of grass and the feel of the sun on his face; the sound of a cricket bat; plunging into cool waters; the song of a stream across pebbles; but they were all coloured with blood, all pulsating with the knowledge of horror.

Eventually the door clanged open again and Perkins scuttled in. He stood at the entrance, and threw a bottle of water at him. Ivo grabbed it from where it had fallen and drained it in one go.

Perkins then lobbed a paper bag at him. 'Eat this, it's all you'll get today.'

Perkins lingered a moment, glaring at Ivo, then he left.

Inside the bag was an energy bar, which Ivo stuffed into his mouth, barely taking time to chew it, and an apple, wrapped in paper, which he ripped off in a desultory way, throwing it aside. He savoured biting into the crisp surface of the fruit. He slumped back into the hard corner of the room, watching the orange light splash on the floor. He had to work out how to escape. But it was impossible. He was worried, too, about Lydia and Jago. He wondered how long he had been away. Would they be sending out search parties? Maybe they knew about all this?

He reached out to pick up the paper he'd thrown aside; fiddling with it he scrunched it up, and unfolded it, his mind elsewhere. Then he noticed, out of the corner of his eye, something written on it; it took him by surprise, so he smoothed out the paper properly and read it again. He shook his head. Yes, he had read it correctly.

'Do not be afraid,' it said. 'I am on your side. Wait and I will help you escape.'

Perkins – the vile Perkins, who had trapped Felix and Miranda – Perkins was on his side? It was unfeasible, he thought; it must be a trick, a sadistic trick, which even now Perkins was revelling over, probably with Julius or some of the Acolytes. If you spent time with someone as inhuman as Julius, then surely you would become inhuman yourself? How could Perkins possibly be on Ivo's side? It was inconceivable – and yet

213

the message was there, and now it burned in his brain.

It gave him hope, a twisted kind of hope, but enough to keep him going. He remembered the image of ivy crawling up a great house, slowly and surely destroying it. There was a way of stopping the Liberators. It was going to be hard, he knew, but he was ready for it. He clenched his fists together and beat the ground twice.

Many more hours passed. Later he heard the sound of the lock, and pulled himself into an upright position, ready to face whatever it might be. It was Perkins. He came in and closed the door behind him, and moving towards Ivo aimed a kick at him. 'Ow!' Ivo let out an exclamation. He had been hurt in the ribs.

'Where's the Koptor?' said Perkins loudly. He kicked Ivo again.

'I don't know!'

Perkins retreated to the door. 'You know we have many ways of torturing people. The brothers are old. They have done it many times before, and in more ways than you could imagine. I will leave you to think about that.'

Ivo kept his mind alert. He wasn't going to let himself be dulled into passivity. He focused on happy memories, and the prospect of escape, and the task which he must complete. Sometimes he could not help reliving the horrible events of the past few days, and they were all the more vivid for his isolation, but he managed to force them out of his mind. He pictured his parents, roaming around Mongolia on horseback, sitting in yurts, drinking fermented mare's milk, meeting shamans, watching the wolves as they tracked deer. He thought about school, and his friends, and walking through the draughty cloisters, clutching books, being late for lessons, all the humdrum school life. He tried to remember some poems, and was glad that he'd been made to memorise a few. He listed names of animals, plants, books, people. He was not going to be beaten.

A hollow *clang* drove him out of himself. He looked up, his eyes unaccustomed to focusing, and saw that it was Perkins. Ivo immediately stiffened, for he was still suspicious. Perkins changed nothing in his behaviour towards Ivo, acting as meanly as he had done before. Maybe they're watching him, thought Ivo.

'Do Lydia and Jago know where I am?' asked Ivo when he'd drunk some water. 'They'll come looking for me.'

'Your aunt and uncle think you're with the Rocksavages. I said you'd gone with them to their house in Scotland, where there's no phone reception or Internet. Lydia's hardly noticed and Jago's working very hard.' Perkins said all this with a malicious expression on his face.

'They'll find me. My parents will fly back when they realise they haven't heard from me. You can't keep me here. You'll be put in prison.' Ivo spat out the words.

'Don't be ridiculous,' snapped Perkins. 'In a few days' time, Liberation will come, and none of that will matter any more.' He removed a knife from his belt. 'But until then . . .' He went up to Ivo and grabbed his arm suddenly, and drew the tip of it down Ivo's forearm, making a long, bloody scratch. Perkins did not look Ivo in the eye. 'It's very easy to hurt people, you know, once you've started,' he said, and got up. 'Where's the Koptor?'

'I don't know!' shouted Ivo, trembling.

'We'll see about that.'

A thought had occurred to Ivo. He needed to get a look outside, see where he was. As Perkins was leaving, he ran right up to him and cannoned into him, faking sobs. 'I want my mother!' he said. 'You'll get sent to prison, you will, you will!' He was pretending so hard that he actually felt tears forming. 'Let me go, let me go!' he cried.

'Get off me! Rat!' Perkins yanked at him, but Ivo clung on. All the time he was hanging on to Perkins, his head half-buried into Perkins' side, he was looking carefully up and down the corridor behind. It was quite long and appeared to be deserted. There were doors at both ends.

'Please go and see the Liberators! Please, I want you to take me there! I want you to set me free!'

Perkins grabbed hold of him and propelled him back into the cell. 'Humph,' he exclaimed. He kicked Ivo for good measure, and marched out; Ivo quickly crawled to the door as Perkins shut it, and just glimpsed him turning to the right.

He remembered the map that Felix had found. He guessed that they were in the complex which lay underneath the tiger in the square near Julius's flat. That entrance hadn't been marked – he supposed it must have been constructed after the map had been made. So that left two exits. If Perkins had gone to the right in order to see the Liberators, that meant that he would surely be heading for the central chamber. And that meant he was in the corridor on the eastern side.

But the Koptor, he thought. He cast back furiously in his mind to when he'd last had it. Blackwood's house, in Chelsea, where he'd tried to see if there were any more messages left. His body stiffened, and he held his breath. He clenched his hands, and brought them together, and closed his eyes. Perhaps it was safe. For now, all his thoughts must be on escape. He could still resist. Hunter would want that, and he in himself knew that he could never see the Liberators win. He would rather die.

And so he scouted out the confines of his prison. He felt all around the door to see if there were any cracks. There was one air vent, high up in the corner. Too high to reach. He remembered his father and mother, out there in Mongolia. The wolves had found a way out, his father had said. People had escaped from worse prisons than this before. And, he thought with resolve, so would he.

Chapter Sixteen

Tapestries swung lazily in a breeze that couldn't possibly be there; there was a hint of fire, of roasting meat. Strawbones threw a chewed bone over his shoulder and burped loudly, stretching out to his full, elastic length, his long hair, now black and greasy, falling on to his shoulders in waves. His face, so white, was dissolving, or so it seemed, for rivulets of sweat were snaking their way down his cheeks. A long black fur dangled around his body. It glimmered and shone. Picked carcases gleamed on a plate in front of him. A dog snapped up a rib and retreated to a corner.

'Why is it so HOT in here?' drawled Strawbones, flinging off the coat. 'Somebody *do* something about it.'

An Acolyte scuttled to the corner of the room, and fiddled with a thermostat. They were in one of the underground chambers beneath Julius's flat. All around them were the sounds of trains, and mysterious, dark, underworld noises. But Strawbones did not fear them. Strawbones was fear. Strawbones was the shadow in your nightmares, Strawbones was the violence under the surface, Strawbones was the blood-dimmed tide, the thing of darkness that cannot be denied.

'I haven't noticed any difference,' said Strawbones, burping. 'Why can't anyone do anything I want?'

The doors to the chamber were flung open and Julius came marching in. 'We must go to see the boy.'

'Excellent,' said Strawbones, and he stood up and mooched after his brother.

They came bursting into the cell in which Ivo was kept. He was huddled in the corner, his knees drawn up in front of him. He tried not to shiver when they came in, especially when Strawbones leaned forward and grinned, not an inch from his face. Strawbones poked him. Ivo felt the tip of his nail press into him and shuddered.

'Do you know what pain is?' said Julius. Ivo did not move, or look at him. 'It is an extraordinary phenomenon, and I have studied it all my long years, and attempted to understand it – and, eventually, to overcome it. Although I don't suppose that you have learned such a thing. Well, we shall see. Strawbones?'

He motioned to his brother, who came forward, grinning in a lopsided way. He was holding a whip. Ivo thought, I can deal with this, I can transform the pain.

Strawbones, smiling almost tenderly, turned Ivo over. 'Kneel,' he commanded, and Ivo slumped into a kneeling position. He wondered whether it would be better to tense, or to relax, but he had no chance to decide, as a blow came down upon his back and he felt the whip searing into him. The pain was stinging. He tensed his body as another blow came down.

'Where is the Koptor?' asked Strawbones, in a quiet, gentle voice.

Ivo didn't answer. Strawbones brought down the whip again. Ivo felt fire spread across his shoulders. Tears sprang into his eyes and he blinked them away. Strawbones took a couple of paces back, and then whipped him with such force that Ivo's whole body rocked, and, against his will, he whimpered. Strawbones let out a ghastly yell of exultance, and did it once more. Each blow felt like a line of flame across his back, but Ivo clamped his teeth together and focused all his thoughts on other things.

Strawbones put down the whip, and Ivo breathed out; and then Strawbones came forwards, holding a cat-o'-nine-tails in his hand. Without saying anything, he cracked it down; and Ivo let out a scream of real pain.

Immediately Strawbones stopped and knelt down beside him.

'Ivo? Ivo, my boy, is it hurting? I am sorry, I'm so sorry, I don't know what came over me.'

Ivo's face was wet with tears. Strawbones leaned in to him and whispered, 'Here, don't worry, it'll be OK.' For a moment all Ivo wanted to do was collapse, but he shrank away from Strawbones, who put a hand on his shoulder and said, with a cloying sympathy that chilled Ivo to the marrow, 'I am sorry, Ivo.' And then he backed away, a look of grave apology on his face.

When they had gone, Ivo let his tears flow. The agony was overwhelming. He didn't know where the Koptor was. But he had to escape, and he had to stop the Liberators, and that was what was keeping him going. He lay on the ground, feeling the cold concrete, breathing heavily. He remembered Felix and Miranda, and wondered if they were trapped in another room somewhere, or if they were Acolytes by now.

He turned his thoughts to escape. The door to his cell was heavy and made of iron. He forced himself to stand up and tottered over towards it. There was a handle on the inside; he grabbed it, and jiggled it up and down with all the force he could, but it was solid, immovable. He looked around the room. There was, in the right-hand corner, above the level of the door, an air vent, which looked as if it might be just wide enough to crawl through. If only, he thought, he could get up there. Exhausted though he was, he moved to the corner and drew his energy together. OK, he thought, I can do this. One, two three . . . He jumped, but his hand just touched the bottom of the grille and he fell back down, feeling hopeless. The welts burned. He put his hand to them and brought it away wet, covered in his own blood.

At this point the door opened again, and Perkins came in. He was carrying bandages and iodine. Brusquely he said, 'Take your shirt off,' and Ivo did; Perkins dabbed his back with the iodine, which was unpleasantly stinging, and then taped some bandages on.

When he'd finished, Ivo turned to look at him. Perkins' T-shirt was damp with sweat, his spectacles slipping down his nose, his pasty face screwed up in a sneer. Ivo said nothing, but pulled his shirt back on.

'We don't have much time,' said Perkins quietly. 'Come with me and wait for my signal.'

'Why are you helping me?' Ivo asked suddenly.

Perkins, rocking back on his heels, looked sharply at Ivo. 'I was a secret service plant at the Home Office, reporting to MI6. I met Blackwood. He was working in the Defence Ministry. He'd noticed my CV and decided to induct me into FIN. My job was to infiltrate the Liberators. I've been successful, haven't I?' He flashed a smile at Ivo, who shuddered inwardly. 'I was the one who told them about the tunnels. I had to give them something big for them to trust me. As well as, of course . . .' he stopped. Ivo guessed he was remembering whatever he had had to do for his initiation. 'The party, of course,' went on Perkins, 'was their idea. They love spectacle, like all terrorists. Because that is what they are.' He spoke matter of factly.

'One more thing,' He continued in an undertone. He put his hand into Ivo's, and closed Ivo's fingers over something. Ivo uncurled his fingers slowly, and then gasped, biting his lip. It was the Koptor. Ivo was unable to believe what Perkins had done. If he was on the side of the Liberators, there was no way he'd have given him back the Koptor. 'You left it in Blackwood's house, in the mantelpiece,' said Perkins. 'Come on then.' Perkins pulled Ivo up roughly from the floor and motioned to him to follow. Ivo began to wonder whether he was being taken to his execution.

It was cold in the corridor. They turned left. That means, thought Ivo wonderingly, that we're going away from the central chamber. Why would that be? Perkins said nothing as they walked along, Ivo in front of Perkins. There was nothing pressed into his back, but he knew that if he moved or tried to run he would be dead instantly. They passed several open rooms, in which Ivo could see people gathered. One contained weapons, rows of grim black rifles, boxes of ammunition, even what appeared to be hand grenades.

A door appeared ahead of them at what Ivo supposed was the end of the corridor. Perkins said, 'Wait here,' and then went into a room on the left. Ivo, puzzled, stood where he was. He drew nearer to the door.

'The Acolytes will wait underneath the National Gallery.' Ivo recognised Perkins' voice and wondered who he was talking to. 'They will be armed, as a precaution. The party starts at seven thirty. Five hundred people have been invited. The Prince of Wales and the Duchess of Cornwall, the Prime Minister, the heads of all the banks, of all the galleries, newspaper editors, magazine editors, Russian oligarchs, singers, actors, socialites, philanthropists – all are coming to this party, which is being dressed up as the charity ball to end all charity balls. Which, I suppose, in a way, is what it will be,' said Perkins. Ivo heard a smirk in his tone.

'The Acolytes under your lead,' continued Perkins, 'will come up the tunnel into the gallery, and will secure it from the inside, ensuring that no one can escape. Julius will stand up to make a speech – but instead he will bless them with the Thyrsos, liberating them entirely, and they will be released into the night. Chaos will ensue and Julius will take over. And so will his reign begin . . . All the safe trappings of current civilisation will be overthrown. There will be breakdown.'

There were murmurings from the others. Ivo looked at the door at the end of the corridor. What if it was open? He shook the thought away. But no, it couldn't be. He inched towards it.

'But what about the boy? What's his name – Ivo?'

Perkins laughed. 'Oh,' he said, in a very clear voice, 'I think he knows what to do.' This was the sign, thought Ivo. *Knows what to do* . . . His heart thumping, he put a hand on the metal bar. The door was plastered with notices that said, '*ALARM*' and '*DO NOT OPEN*'. Gently, very gently, he pushed it.

And the door clicked open. Without stopping to think, Ivo pushed it just enough for him to slip through, and then was into the tunnel beyond. He was hungry, he was tired, he was in pain, but he was full of a fire that smouldered in the recesses of his body. Why had Perkins let him out? He didn't bother to question it for the moment. But where should he go? To get out, that was what he had to do first. He powered on. The tunnel was coming to an end. Curious humming underground noises were filling his ears. He imagined the world above him – icy pavements, pedestrians muffled up against the biting cold, the shimmering lights of Christmas, shops spilling over with produce, cars revving their engines at lights, indomitable rickshaw drivers bicycling in shorts. All so peaceful, so self-absorbed. People never thought anything would happen to them, he reflected. Typhoons, floods, earthquakes, famine, dictatorships – they all happened on the other side of the world, far away, never in London, never in the United Kingdom.

Well, they were wrong, he thought. And as he crawled, he felt that he, too, was dangerous, that he also was a ticking time bomb, waiting to explode.

He saw a ladder ahead of him. He reached it and struggled up it. It was rusty. He eventually reached the end, and guessed that it opened into a trapdoor. He pushed against it, hoping that it would be open. It didn't move. Come on, he thought. He pushed harder, feeling all of his weight and power, and there was a creak; slowly he tipped it open and then let it fall to the ground of its own momentum.

He was so excited about getting out that he almost tripped as he came into a cellar. It was gloomy, but his eyes had become accustomed to the dark. He was only wearing a shirt and it was cold. He had no idea where his coat was. He shivered, but it was a pleasurable shiver. Free . . . the word filled his mind and expanded. He was free. He charged up the cellar stairs into the hall.

And then he stopped dead. He recognised where he was: the vast entrance of Julius's house in Mayfair. Perkins had sent him here and given him the Koptor. That was why he'd done it. He felt a sudden admiration for Perkins, working under the very noses of the Liberators. And he'd break the Thyrsos now, and they could do nothing about it.

Winter light gave everything an eerie air, and Ivo was filled with a hot madness, as if rationality had deserted him, like a berserker in battle. The grand staircase was threatening, menacing, but he went up it. He was focused now upon his task. He went into the drawing room. Everything seemed to have gone silent as he entered, almost as if the rest of the world had disappeared as soon as he had crossed the threshold. Ivo was aware of the blood pounding in every part of his body. He could feel the swiftness of his heart's beating, his tongue dry, his stomach overturning queasily. He had envisaged everything closing in, eating him up until there was nothing of him left. A place like this, he thought, knows how to get rid of you.

The room appeared to be empty. He thought he

sensed movement in a corner, but it was only a curtain flapping in the wind. He looked around, gazing at the crowding treasures. He saw the hoof – Julius had never explained it. Suddenly taken by an enormous sense of curiosity, he moved to the cabinet where it stood and gingerly lifted it up. He turned it over. There was an inscription in very small writing, engraved into a silver plate.

THE HOOF OF THE HORSE OF VLADIMIR OF THE BULGARS. SLAIN BY DRAGAN, 1321

Killed by one of the brothers and kept as a ghastly souvenir for nearly seven hundred years. He noticed each hair, each bristle, and imagined the warhorse falling; then he replaced it where it had stood and returned to his task. He wondered where the Thyrsos might be. He could feel energy coming from the Koptor as if it knew the Thyrsos was nearby. The room was so large, and so full of cabinets, cupboards and boxes, that it could be anywhere. He'd seen Julius take it from somewhere though, he remembered. It was hard to sift through his memories of the last time he'd been here: everything was blurred by the wine. He went to the chair where he had been sitting and sat down in it once more. Where had Julius come from? He racked his brains. He looked around the fireplace. He sat in the chair in which Julius had sat, on the right-hand side of the fireplace, and reached out his hand.

There was a large mantelpiece, and on it was a box, long, thin, made of highly polished rosewood. It was chained to the fireplace, and there was a shining padlock upon it. The opulence of the box made Ivo almost dizzy with excitement. It was studded round with emeralds and amethysts, shimmering and flashing, catching the light that came from the tall windows. Inscribed upon the lid was a word, in Greek letters:

ELEUTHEROI

The Thyrsos must be in it: the godlike staff that contained the brothers' powers. He was here, and he was going to break it. Ivo touched the box, barely, waiting for something to happen, but nothing did. He took out the Koptor once more; the blade extended, and with one swift movement he sliced through the chains that bound the box to the mantelpiece. He pulled it off, as quickly as he could. It was remarkably heavy and he nearly dropped it, staggering under the weight. It was heavier than his school trunk. He let it down on to the carpeted floor quickly. It squatted innocently amid the blue and red swirls of the carpet. He knelt. It seemed appropriate.

The box had a clasp made of gold. Ivo's breath was now coming a little faster, he felt it, and, tinkering with the Koptor, he unfastened it easily, and then, without thinking, he flung back the lid.

Beautiful black silk lined the box, and it was studded with jewels the names of which Ivo did not know but which flashed and burned like stars reflected in water.

There it was – a staff, no longer than Ivo's arm, unadorned, clean and smooth. It did not look as if it were made of wood, but more like something carved out of granite, or even out of some substance found deep in the earth's crust, from some darker world, far distant.

Looking at it, Ivo began to feel the savage elation of the hysteria which preceded the murder and the riot, which possessed those who had been Liberated. How pleasant it was, how wonderful to feel so free, to feel so distant from life.

The Koptor's blade was shining, deadly. Ivo was moving very slowly now, as if he had been hypnotised, or as if his actions were being programmed by somebody else. He felt part of a current, a wave which was beyond his control, some mysterious sweeping tide in the universe that went ever on, bearing him along with it to this end.

A vision of his potential Liberated self flashed through his mind, wild-eyed, tearing through the streets, bloodied, maddened, but so wonderfully free.

Dreamlike, as if moving through water, he drew back his arm as though he were about to split open a log with an axe. The Thyrsos, the mystical object that held such godlike powers. All he had to do now was to cut it in half, and Julius and Strawbones would lose their powers, become human, frail, as vulnerable and mortal as any one of the people they had killed. Ivo felt as if he were the centre of everything, as if time itself flowed from him. There was no sound, and if there had been, he wouldn't have heard it, entranced as he was. And then he brought the Koptor down, swiftly, and missed.

He picked up the Thyrsos now. It was heavy. It was so smoothly cut, it almost had no edges, seeming instead to blur into the air around it. It oozed power, enticing, alluring. It was as if a veil had been lifted, and Ivo was more than human.

How funny and puny people were, he thought, scuttling around with their boring little lives . . . what was the point of it all? Why did they bother, rushing around, getting on trains, sitting at desks all day? Wouldn't it be better just to be free, to be allowed to have anything that you wanted, to do anything that you could do, to push yourself to the furthest limit of human experience.

He saw the world as an anthill, and all the people as ants, crazily rushing around, picking up leaves and putting them down again, dragging useless bits of paper, treading mindlessly over their fellow creatures, and he had a sudden desire to crush everything, and everyone.

'No!' came a voice in his head. It was his own self, pulling him back. 'You have to break it!' He thought of long-limbed Felix, putting his collar up and lifting his chin, of Miranda with her beautiful hands, tying a band around her long hair; he thought of hawk-like Uncle Jago, and vague but lovely Lydia; his school-friends, his teachers, and, finally, his parents, all passed before his eyes. How could he destroy the bonds that he had with these people? He had to break the Thyrsos.

He drew back the Koptor, enjoying its weighty feel. He imagined himself as a hero, some helmeted warrior fresh from spattering his enemies' blood over the unforgiving stones of Troy. How everybody would worship him, his tale told over and over . . . He was ready to strike.

OK, he thought. One . . . two . . . He aimed the Koptor at the staff. 'I will break you,' he said, and swung back.

'I wouldn't do that if I were you,' said a voice, soft, cold, recognisable.

He turned quickly, to see his Uncle Jago standing not three metres away from him. Ivo was so startled that he dropped the Koptor, and Jago picked it up. 'This looks like a very valuable sort of antique. *Not* the sort of thing that Julius would be pleased to know you'd been playing with.' He doesn't know what the Koptor is, thought Ivo. But did he know about Julius and Strawbones? He said, very politely, 'Uncle Jago, I was just looking at it – could you give it back to me and I'll put it back where I found it?'

Jago looked down its length. 'Looks rather nice. Very strange though. Can't think what period it's from. But Ivo, old boy,' he said, suddenly changing tack, and swinging the Koptor, 'you're an intelligent chap, aren't you? You've got both your parents' brains.' His eyes were shimmering. The sharp cut of his lapels, his carefully pressed trousers, his neat cuffs, all seemed familiar, normal, but his eyes were filmed and luminescent. 'There are many more things which we should be discussing, things which touch our immediate futures.'

'Like what?' said Ivo.

'I wish you would stop playing the innocent. Haven't you guessed yet?'

'Guessed what?' said Ivo.

'Why do you think I'm here?'

Ivo kept silent. Maybe, he thought, if he didn't give away too much, he could get out of here.

'I'm helping the Liberators,' said Jago casually.

When he said that, it was as if Ivo were a tall poppy, and the words a scythe that sliced through the stem, scattering the scarlet petals on the ground.

Ivo brought his hands to his mouth involuntarily.

'I've been so bored, Ivo. You have no idea . . . all those hours sitting in front of a computer screen, looking at rows and rows of figures . . . it can drive you *mad* . . . Julius and Strawbones. I met them at a party, and told them about what I did. I think they noticed I was bored. They just make everything so exciting! The markets are crashing, Ivo, and we've been behind it all . . . Financial chaos, global chaos – now is the time when the real heroes will be made.' He stopped. 'Now, would you like to explain what you're doing here?'

His voice was measured, slow, almost too slow, thought Ivo. 'Aren't you meant to be with the Rocksavages in Scotland?'

'They had to come back quickly today,' said Ivo, thinking very fast. 'We got a plane down, we've only just arrived, and Olivia sent me here with a message for Julius – some plans that she wanted him to look at for decorating his . . . bathroom.'

'Oh really. What were you doing with this then?' he said, casually holding out the Koptor. Ivo said nothing, letting it hang in the air between them, almost joining them with its sighing, fatal length.

'Really, Jago, I was just playing with it . . . I found this on the mantlepiece,' he said, pointing at the box, 'I'll put it back.' He inched towards it, and, trembling, shut it, almost staggering under the weight of the Thyrsos as he lifted it back up. 'Just don't . . . just don't tell Julius that I was here, please, Jago.'

'Well . . .' Jago seemed to be considering this, looking very carefully at the Koptor, and he seemed to be about to hand it back to Ivo, when the blade retracted. Jago dropped it in astonishment, and Ivo quickly caught it as it fell.

'What is it?' said Jago, suddenly alert.

'I don't know!' said Ivo. Jago came closer to him, and held Ivo by the shoulders.

'Ivo – what is going on here? You must tell me!'

With a quick movement, he elbowed his uncle in the stomach, causing Jago to release him, and Ivo moved away whilst Jago collected himself.

'There, you see, I told you.'

Ivo spun round, and what he saw made his throat tighten and his legs tremble. Coming through the door was Perkins.

What is this? thought Ivo.

Perkins advanced into the room and stood beside Jago. For a moment they stared at each other, and then Perkins smiled. 'This boy here is trying to sabotage everything we have been working for,' he said, looking directly at Ivo. 'And you must make him pay for it!' yelled Perkins. Jago glanced from Ivo to Perkins, and looked as if he was about to say something, but Perkins moved towards Ivo, and Ivo felt the Koptor in his hand, and extended its long, thin blade.

'Stay back!' he commanded.

'Get it from him!' yelled Perkins, mouth opening wide and ugly, spittle spraying from his lips. Jago stood still. Perkins sprang, but Ivo was too quick for him. He swung the Koptor in his direction, not caring if he slashed him.

'You were never on my side,' said Ivo, advancing towards Perkins – vile, maniacal Perkins. 'You brought me here to make Jago kill me! How could you be so . . . Did they know all the time? The Liberators – did they know about your little game? Is that why they left the Thyrsos undefended?'

'What . . . to make me kill him?' Jago said. Perkins ignored him.

'It was never "undefended", little Ivo. Acolytes!' screamed Perkins. There was a thundering noise, of many boots upon the stairs, and the door burst open and in came four armed men.

'Where are you going to go now, Ivo?' sneered Perkins. 'No escape for you. Can't go to Mummy and Daddy. Can't go to Uncle and Auntie. You have to stay here and meet your fate.'

Ivo glanced around. He was on the first floor. There was a window behind him, but it was too high. How could he reach it? He had to jump out of it. It was the only way. But how to distract them? He roared so loud it made the glass shiver. Then he threw himself behind a cabinet and pushed it over; he took advantage of the moment of confusion and jumped on top of it. From here he could reach the catch. He scrabbled at it, opening the window. He looked out and saw the cold pavement below. He turned round. The Acolytes were advancing. He had no choice. He tried to remember how to fall properly, took a deep breath and sprang out.

He fell so quickly he barely noticed it. He landed on all fours, and rolled over, and then he began to run. His wrists were aching.

Perkins appeared at the window. 'Ivo! Ivo! Damn you, Ivo!' but Ivo was not listening to his curses, as he was running as fast as he could.

His legs almost a blur, he sprinted down the road,

not knowing in which direction to go; as he crossed a road a car swerved to avoid him, he knocked into a passer-by, spilling her handbag. She shouted after him, but he kept on running, running, until he saw a church ahead of him, and memories of peace and goodness stirred him inside.

He clattered into the dark interior, and slipped into a pew, collapsing, kneeling, satisfied that there was no pursuit. There was a large piano in front of the altar where a girl was practising; an elderly lady was praying in the front pew. Ivo's heart was pounding, his limbs painful, sweating.

The music was soft and rippling, the pianist playing a phrase two or three times, then launching into a piece that was bright and pure. It made Ivo calm, and he sat up, looking around.

Now he had to consider his options. He couldn't go back to his house. Nor could he go to the Rocksavages'. Every avenue was closed, every door shut, and he was a stag at bay, waiting for the dogs to advance and tear into his flesh.

Chapter Seventeen

Hunter. He could use the Koptor to call her. He wondered if it would be too much for her to bear. She had looked so ill after they had last done it. But this was an emergency, if ever there was. So he held the black phone-like Koptor in his palm, squeezed it hard and concentrated as deeply as he could on the figure of Alice Hunter. The pianist stopped playing and gathered up her music; the old lady in the front pew pattered down the nave. And then, as if she had been there always, Hunter was sitting next to him. She was wearing a black sequinned dress that billowed around her, and a feather boa, which she flung around her neck. But she looked old and ill and tired, thought Ivo.

'Ready for the party? I was worried. Thought I should be ready for anything. Got into my gear this morning. Party's tonight,' she said grimly. 'Where have you been?' Her voice echoed in the church around them; a priest, coming in from the vestry, didn't seem to notice them. Hunter shifted. 'How are you, dear boy?' she continued. 'But look at you – what's happened? You're freezing! And you've . . . who did this to you?'

Ivo explained. Hunter stood up majestically. 'This has gone far enough,' she said. 'But Perkins . . . he said he was a member of FIN?'

'Yeah,' said Ivo.

'He was lying,' she said with decision. 'He was lying to trick you, so that he could make Jago kill you for the Liberators. It's all part of their twisted games.' She shuddered, and not from the cold. The light streaming in from the windows was grey. Dust motes filled the beams. The church was empty.

Ivo told Hunter about Felix and Miranda, and she tapped her fingers on the pew in front of her.

'Hmmm. It sounds like we should rescue them. We need their help. And your Uncle Jago . . . The first thing to do is go to get your friends. And then – well, I think you know what you will have to do.' Ivo nodded slowly. Butterfly to caterpillar, thought Ivo, that's what I am. I have to throw away my inhibitions. I have to become like the Liberators. He had felt the release of violence surging through him when he confronted Perkins, and was allowing it to course through him. He sensed its depth and power, and knew how the Liberators might feel.

They took a taxi to Charmsford Square. It was just before twelve. Hunter was visibly agitated, constantly looking out of the window. 'We don't know what we'll find when we get there,' she said. 'It sounds as if Perkins got to them somehow. You say they wouldn't look at you?'

'No, or answer their phones.'

They pulled up outside the Rocksavages' house and paid the driver. Hunter tottered up the stairs in front of Ivo and banged on the doorknocker. To Ivo's mild surprise, after a few seconds, the door opened a few inches. Hunter had her foot in the gap in a second and was inside; all Ivo could hear were some horrible-sounding choking noises, and then there was nothing. Hunter released whoever it was she was holding, patted down her dress, said, 'Well, *there* we are,' and they went into the house. Hunter stepped delicately over the prone, unconscious body of one of the Acolytes and, humming, went on into the hall, followed by Ivo, who glanced back at the Acolyte. A big, burly, man, Hunter had seemingly taken him out with one move. His muscles bulged from of his clothes, but he lay there like a sleeping lamb.

It was very quiet, which was unusual as Miranda and Felix, whenever they had any free time out of lessons, would usually be watching TV or listening to music. Hunter put her finger to her lips, and Ivo went first, heading up to where the bedrooms were. He climbed to the top of the stairs – and then stopped in his tracks. There was a man standing in front of Miranda's door. An Acolyte, thought Ivo. Hunter pushed straight past Ivo. The man looked up, startled. He reached for his pocket and pulled out a small pistol – but Hunter was on him already, and with a deft chop to his wrist disarmed him. They scuffled, and Hunter knocked him to the ground, pinning his arms back. She beat the man's head against the floor. Soon the man was insensible. Hunter did all this without even grunting. She quickly got up, dusted her hands and her dress, straightened herself, flung the boa around her neck and said, '*Well* then.'

Ivo tried the door to the room; they could hear noises on the other side of it. 'Felix? Miranda?' he called through the door.

They heard a muffled yell, and then saw the doorhandle being tried violently. 'Right, Ivo, you take over here,' said Hunter. Ivo nodded. He took the Koptor out of his pocket and felt along it, searching for the hidden switch, willing it to become a blade; the long sharpness of it extended into the air. Ivo tensed.

'Stand back!' he yelled, and with the tip of the

Koptor made a circle around the lock. It cut through it easily, as if it were a loaf of bread. He looked at Hunter and then he kicked the door open, and they went in to find Miranda huddled on her sofa at one end of the room, and Felix at the other looking very angry. Ivo stood, unsure. He'd been expecting them to greet him with relief. But Felix looked as though he might fly at Ivo, who had the presence of mind to hold the Koptor out in front of him. Felix held his hands up and moved backwards slowly. Miranda turned her face away from him. Sobbing, with her face averted, she said, 'If it wasn't for you this would never have happened.'

'We haven't much time,' said Hunter, hitching up her dress. 'What on earth is going on?'

Ivo went closer to Miranda, and sheathed the Koptor, confusion and fear clouding his mind. 'What's the matter?' He reached out a hand to comfort her.

'Stay away from my sister!' yelled Felix. Hunter moved in between Ivo and Felix; Ivo reached the sofa and knelt down. Miranda's sobs grew louder.

'What is it, Miranda? Come on! We've got to hurry, the party's tonight!'

'I know,' said Miranda, through her sobs. 'And they've . . . they've got our parents!'

This pierced Ivo like a sword. He sat down slowly, next to Miranda.

Miranda's shoulders heaved. 'They came . . . after they got Felix and me, after you came to see us – we saw you through the window but we couldn't say anything, Perkins was there, there was an Acolyte in the corridor with a gun. They locked us in here and took our parents. They said . . .' she rubbed her eyes, and said, clearly now, 'they said that if we tried to escape, or tried to get help, then they would kill them.'

'You see?' said Felix. 'You see what happened? If we'd only joined them, we wouldn't be in this mess.' He was screwed up into a ball of fury, tight lines on his forehead, hands taut.

'*Joined* them?' shouted Ivo, standing up quickly, his face reddening. 'You think . . . you think it's *fun*, what they're doing? You think it's, it's . . .' His anger overwhelmed him, making the words jumble and jostle in his mouth.

'Stop it!' Hunter interjected forcefully, and turned to Felix. 'We haven't got time for this. Come here, all of you.'

To Ivo's surprise, Miranda and Felix meekly came towards Hunter. 'Koptor, please,' she said. Ivo handed it to her. She continued, 'The Koptor has the power of Apollo in it – the power of reason. That's why it can negate the Thyrsos. But what was the other power of Apollo?'

Felix said gruffly, 'Prophecy.'

'Correct. Now hold it. You too, Miranda, Ivo.'

Ivo reached out to touch the Koptor in Hunter's hand. Ivo could not avoid touching the others, but Miranda resolutely turned her eyes away, whilst Felix glared at him with deep fury.

'There now,' said Hunter. 'Now relax . . .' Her voice was very soothing.

They were no longer in the Rocksavages' house. Ivo looked around him. They were standing in a peaceful town square – it could have been anywhere – a stone cross in the middle of it, teenagers sitting around on benches, mothers pushing toddlers, families wandering, looking into the bright windows of the shops, walking, eating, living. It was, in short, a normal afternoon. But it wasn't, thought Ivo. When he tried to move his hand, it didn't move normally. He looked at Hunter. There was no expression on her face. Miranda had stopped crying. Felix was protectively close to his sister. They watched the crowds, fearful.

There was a subtle shift in the activities of the people in the square, in the geometry of their movements. First it seemed as if they were grouping together, randomly, dropping their bags, abandoning their children. It looked as if there was an enormous spontaneous party sparking off. Bottles of wine and champagne appeared, and crates of beer. Cars drew up side on in the street and their drivers got out, turning their radios on, dancing on their roofs. People were dancing, singing, laughing, hugging each other. Ivo could feel the collective joy, and he could see again that Felix was enjoying it. His eyes were wide open and he was murmuring something. Miranda was more cautious. She understands, thought Ivo. She can see underneath the surface. He braced himself for what might come next.

The blissfully smiling faces began to be distorted by jealousy and anger. People squabbled over bottles and food. Disorder broke out, fights began between groups; a woman with a bleeding face ran, screaming, so close to them that Ivo flinched; three men were arguing and started punching each other, the fight rapidly became a brawl; there was looting, smashing of windows, fires sprang up; the square was a riot, an uproar of noise and violence.

Their movements speeded up, and Ivo realised that the scene was being fastforwarded in time: shadows lengthened and shortened, white clouds scudded, turned grey, burst; the buildings of the town square became dilapidated; hordes of people roamed, screaming, yelling, dancing; weeks and years went by and the town was a ruin, the haunt of rats, packs of wild cats, and mad-eyed groups of marauders dressed in stolen rags and chewing on plundered food; and through them all, collected, calm, shining, walked two figures, tall, bright and inhuman, the forms of Julius and Strawbones Luther-Ross.

Ivo saw himself limping, his clothes rent, long scars across his face, and in his eyes he saw nothing but the thoughts and feelings of an animal. He saw Felix with gore around his mouth, and Miranda with her lips bared and face snarled up in cruelty. He watched in helpless horror as his future self bore down upon a group of children, he waved a stick at them . . .

'Stop! Make it stop! Please! Stop it!' It was Miranda's voice, although the sound came from miles and years away.

The vision faded, leaving the three of them gasping for breath.

'What was that? That wasn't me, I would never do that – how could you show us that? – it's madness, it's awful, it's . . .' Miranda stopped, unable to convey her feelings.

'That is what you will become,' said Hunter. 'Whether your parents die or not, if the Liberators go through with their plans tonight, you will become like that – an animal, senseless, mindless, wallowing in your own sordid violence. That is what they want. That is what they call freedom.' Her voice, usually

248

that of a kindly aunt, had taken on a stern, steely quality.

Ivo looked at his friends. Felix's lips were trembling, whether with desire or sadness Ivo could not tell.

Felix said quietly, 'How do we know you're not lying to us?'

Hunter looked shocked, and then said, in a voice that filled the room, as if the god himself were speaking through her, 'Apollo never lies.'

Felix sighed deeply, and sat down on the sofa, a hand across his forehead. Miranda turned to Ivo. 'Ivo,' she said, 'what're we going to do? Our parents . . .' They stood in silence, with Hunter looking over them, her face calm; and then Felix brought his hand down, and there was an expression in his face that Ivo had never seen before. It was determined and resolute.

'We have to help you,' he said. He looked Ivo straight in the eyes.

Ivo separated himself from Miranda and looked at him in shock. 'Are you sure?'

'We do. We'll find a way. We have to. It's not . . . that's not what I want.' His face contorted briefly, and it looked as if he were holding back tears. With a great effort, he controlled himself. 'I thought . . . I thought they promised real freedom. I hate this stupid world, I really do. I hate having to go to school, and *doing*

things all the time. I just want to be left alone. But . . .
I didn't think it would be like that. I thought, I dunno,
I thought it would be like a utopia or something.' He
smiled awkwardly. 'You know, with everyone being
happy and nice to each other. Not . . . not *that*.' He
stopped. Ivo realised the immense effort Felix must
have put into resisting his impulses and he felt the
warmth of friendship rise up within him. But he said
nothing, only smiled at Felix, and when Felix smiled
back, he knew that he was telling the truth. Felix
coughed, and put his fist to his mouth, and then said,
briskly, 'Miranda?'

And Miranda, who feared the Liberators more than
anything she had ever met, who loved order, reason
and light, said softly, 'We have to. We'll help you, Ivo.'

Hunter nodded, but kept back. She looked discreetly
at her watch, and inclined her head towards Ivo.

'Good,' said Ivo. 'Then I think I've got an idea.'

And suddenly the three friends were hugging each
other.

'It's so good to see you,' Ivo said, his voice somewhat muffled by the fact that his mouth was in Felix's
shoulder.

'And you, old boy,' said Felix, and Miranda kissed
him on the cheek.

'Yes, yes,' said Hunter, hiding her own smile. 'Come

on chaps, let's get on with it.'

Ivo told them that Perkins had tried to trap him, but did not mention Jago.

'Are you hurt?' asked Miranda.

'No – I'm all right. But listen. We've got to move fast.' He broke off, and felt energy leaving him. He was almost a shell. He needed to eat. But he could do without it. He wrenched himself up. 'Olivia's an interior decorator, right?' He told them his plan, in a hurried whisper. Felix smiled. 'So what we'll need is, some silver spray paint, some plain white bedsheets and some ivy leaves. We can do that, right?'

Miranda nodded.

'We'll get into the gallery through the tunnels. You still got the map?'

'Yup,' said Felix, fumbling in his pockets and bringing it out with a flourish. 'Still got it.'

'There are two entrances,' continued Ivo, 'one that goes into the East wing, and one into the West. We'll take both, and then block them up afterwards to stop anyone else coming in.' And Ivo felt the Koptor responding to his emotion, felt it glowing with renewed energy. 'And Hunter . . .' She looked down at her dress, which was torn now, and dusty. Her boa was trailing on the ground, and she flung it flamboyantly around her neck.

'I get your meaning,' she said. 'I'll have to slip into something a little different.'

In Charmsford Square, in her dressing room, Lydia was sitting, a still rock whilst Jago rushed about her, hunting for his favourite cufflinks. Her face was calm, beautifully made up, her clothes perfect; she had been staring at her reflection, emptying her mind, ready, waiting for the car that had been ordered, waiting to make the entrance that she had been dreaming of, waiting for the adulation of thousands.

In houses all across London, from Wimbledon to Whitechapel, from Holland Park to Hampstead, women were having baths, getting their hair done, pulling on their dresses; men were squeezing into waistcoats, polishing shoes, fiddling with their ties. From houses in the counties, cars were setting out, their occupants late, excitement roiling in their stomachs.

The National Gallery glowed like a beacon, or a spaceship, decked with green lights. Trafalgar Square had been roped off, but there were still crowds of people waiting, drizzle splashing their faces, with anoraks and flasks and autograph books, mobile phones at the ready, and a bank of photographers, milling, chatting, waiting for the first cars to arrive.

And underneath it all the Acolytes were stirring.

Ivo slipped through the shadows in the tunnels beneath the gallery, a wraith now, a mole, the one who brings down the great from within, from below, silently and stealthily.

Quickly and lightly, he passed a room in which Strawbones and Julius sat, in beautifully cut tails, and Acolytes were gathered around them.

Ivo thought, You don't know what I'm doing, and he felt a surge of power, and he knew how it must feel to be like them, to think nothing of human life, to waste away for centuries, to have the ultimate key to freedom in their hands and to be so near completion.

He grinned to himself maniacally, the glint from the fire on his eyes making him look like a demon, and scampered on.

Outside the National Gallery, a swarm of elegant young men with umbrellas emerged, waiting in the portico. A long, lush red carpet had been laid out and the men lined the route. Inside the portico were a couple of hired actors, dressed in Roman costume; they paraded up and down, behaving as if they were not entirely in this century or this place, but rather some remnants of the past, wandering down what they thought was the colonnade of the temple of Jupiter.

Some jugglers were doing tricks, and some children came and danced round them.

The first car drove up – long and low, and the door was opened by a man in a bright yellow security jacket; one of the elegant young men, nimble as a racehorse, leaped forward and held the umbrella ready, the door opened, the crowd gasped and got out their mobile phones; but then put them away in disappointment, as out of it stepped Lydia, and behind her, neat, charming, smiling, Jago. 'Why is that man wearing a yellow jacket? I told them not to,' Lydia whispered to Jago. Her dress billowed in a gust of icy wind. A coal-black sable was curled around her throat, which gleamed whitely. Her eyes were wide. Jago's face was set. His hands were in his pockets. If you looked closely, you might have seen him clenching his jaw, very slightly, and unclenching it again. A muscle moved in his cheek. He took Lydia's arm.

They paused for the *Tatler* photographer, and then went in, Lydia floating in a wide, green gown, a tiara sparkling on her head, Jago in white tie. They stood at the bottom of the stairs, ready to greet the guests. Behind them rose the marble steps, and the echoing halls of the galleries spread into the distance, carpeted in crimson. Huge electric chandeliers dripped with light. Green lamps had been set all the way along the edges of the entrance hall. It looked like a forest, sun tinged and in leaf, and Lydia and Jago stood arm in arm. The actors in Roman costume walked sedately around them, as if they weren't there at all.

'Where are the nymphs? Why aren't the drinks ready? Why are the ornamental young men drunk already?' Lydia looked around her, the questions coming out almost automatically, her face retaining its smile.

'There's not much you can do about it now, Lydia,' said Jago under his breath. 'Where are the Luther-Ross brothers?'

But he did not have to wait long for an answer, because it was as if a fanfare had been blown; suddenly the entrance hall was alive with nymphs, rushing, dancing and playing, running away from men dressed as satyrs, throwing leafy crowns to each other, calling and laughing and singing as if they were in some forest glade in Arcadia, not in a cold building in the capital of a foggy little island.

Julius and Strawbones entered. There was a rustling sound and a train of women followed them. Both brothers were as far from their demonic selves as possible, both walking very tall and smart, their clothes sharp. In Julius's right hand he held a staff; it was the first thing everybody noticed about him. A lot of the elegant young men thought that they should probably get hold of one too, it looked so appealing. The brothers approached the Moncrieffs, shook Jago's hand, and, having kissed Lydia on both cheeks, took their positions at the other side of the flight of stairs.

Back in the underground tunnels, Ivo was heading towards the eastern end of the National Gallery. Now he was set for the final push. He was hungry, and tired, but his body did not care; his brain was pulsing with excitement, his limbs twitching with energy; it was as if he were an athlete on the night of a competition and he'd been training for years to get to this one moment.

Ivo's mind was flashing with thoughts; he felt wild, free, a savage. He could do anything; there was no stopping him: he was the hunter, he was the terrorist, the freedom fighter, the one who could save everything.

The tunnel this side was empty. His knees were grazed and his elbows were bleeding, his hair was dishevelled and crazy. He knew it was not far now. The passage came out into a dusty back corridor of the gallery, where paintings hung that nobody wanted to see and a few busts languished uncared for. He saw light ahead of him. He reached the exit and crouched, listening. There were no sounds. He pushed on the grille and entered the gallery, and, on the other side of the building, Felix and Miranda slipped through as well.

Chapter Eighteen

The guests were pouring up the steps now, a river of diamonds and flowers and laughter. In and amongst them darted the nymphs and the satyrs. Sometimes a nymph would run up to a guest and throw a girdle of laurel leaves around their neck. Sometimes two satyrs would take a woman by the hands and lead her away, whispering into her ears. Everybody was excited. Jago watched them all as they flowed upwards. Shouts came from the photographers outside; endless bulbs flashed like lightning. A film crew trailed its wires over everything. A starlet shivered in the cold as she gave an interview.

The Prince of Wales and his Duchess arrived last. Silence and reverence descended as the pair made their way, followed by a train of people, Lydia and Jago among them, into the main gallery, where tables had been laid out. Jago left Lydia talking with the Prince, and slipped away and grabbed a drink off a waiter's tray. He watched the throng.

Beneath paintings hundreds of years old, the rich and the famous, the beautiful, the lucky and the charmed sipped their champagne. Everybody was in a raucous mood, everybody had been looking forward to this for months, not least Lydia, who was surrounded by people she loved and admired, and was having an absolutely terrible time. Her necklace felt like a noose around her neck. Conversation was stilted, she thought the cocktails were too strong, and she had seen one of the guests smoking next to a Titian. She was pleased with the living statues though, who stood around the edges of the room, painted in gold and silver. They did look incredibly imposing, although some of them weren't quite as good at staying still as she had hoped. She looked for her husband and saw Jago leaning against a pillar; she lifted a finger. He saw her movement and, bowing his head slightly, slipped back to her side.

'Stop fretting, Lydia,' Jago whispered to her. He turned to the group in which Lydia stood, and said something that made them all roar with laughter. 'Here, have a drink,' he said to his wife. He motioned to a waiter, who sprang forward and filled Lydia's glass with wine; she absent-mindedly lifted it to her lips and drank it down in one gulp.

'Hey, I didn't mean that quickly,' said Jago, but Lydia glared at him and he lapsed into silence. Lydia, emboldened by the wine, began to enjoy herself rather more, managing to make a witty remark after a professor of history said something which required one.

Jago kept glancing over at the Luther-Ross brothers, wondering what their next move was going to be; in truth, he knew very little about them, or about what the Thyrsos was or even what Liberation meant; he half believed it was going to be like a sort of mass religious experience, and half feared that it was just some ghastly publicity stunt.

He hadn't been entirely sure what had happened in Julius's flat, when he had stumbled upon the boy. At first he thought it was a prank. Perkins had told him to go there. He was a little troubled. The things he'd been doing in the financial markets – that was fun, it tested his brain. But when it came to Ivo – he liked the boy, dammit. After all, he and Lydia had never been able to have children and he liked having Ivo around. He was beginning to feel unsure about the Liberators. Yes, he was bored of his life, and yes, he wanted an escape; but if it involved massacring innocents, he wanted absolutely nothing to do with it. He remembered Perkins in the flat, and shuddered.

*

Ivo looked out over the scene in front of him – a whirling kaleidoscope of colour, sound and movement. Men in white tie and tails, women in beautiful long balldresses, some with tiaras glistening on their heads, many with heavy jewelled necklaces. But he could not enjoy the bustling crowd. He was standing discreetly, in a small alcove, from where he could see the top table. He was wearing a toga made out of sheets from the Rocksavages' linen cupboard, and he was covered in silver paint, and there was a wreath of silver ivy leaves on his head. It was impossible to tell him apart from any of the other statues, aside from the fact that he was a little smaller, a little thinner. Felix and Miranda were positioned on the other side, and Hunter was milling amongst the guests, a leopard-skin around her shoulders, and a matching mask on her face. They had changed at the Rocksavages' house, and taken a taxi that had deposited them in the back streets behind the gallery.

Ivo was planning to wait until Julius gave his speech, and then he was going to slip around to the table. From there he hadn't really thought about it, but he knew that he might even have to kill Julius. After that . . . he couldn't tell. Nymphs and fauns danced amongst the guests, asking them politely to sit down for supper. Many more wandered around the edges,

261

pausing to look at the guests, smiling at each other; some ignored the party completely, as if somehow our world had merged with that of the ancients. Wine bottles were opened, the beautiful red liquid poured into crystal glasses, the noise of the guests like a hive of bees.

Julius and Strawbones strode down the centre of the gallery, followed by a procession of people: two men in leopard-skins, a man with a snake – a living, long snake – wrapped around him, a small boy dressed as a faun, and women in long robes clashing tambourines. A hush fell over the room. Julius stood behind his chair, smiled, raised his staff. Ivo tensed, ready to spring forwards, but Julius banged the Thyrsos on the floor.

There was a silence – or at least something approximating a silence. Julius held out his arms and smiled. He said, his voice bouncing and echoing off the gallery walls, 'Welcome!' That was all. He smiled once more, then he sat, and everyone followed, their chairs scraping and shuffling on the floor. The light from the chandeliers was dimmed, and candles were lit on the tables. People's faces flickered in the half-light.

Ivo shivered. He watched Julius and Strawbones carefully. Julius was sitting at the main table, on which the Prince of Wales was the guest of honour. Strawbones was on a more lively table, in between two very beautiful young actresses, who were shrieking with laughter. Strawbones, Ivo noticed, was exceptionally pale, and was not eating anything. His eyes were greener than ever.

The dim green light seeped in from the entrance hall. Cymbals clashed as the nymphs and satyrs continued to dance around the edges of the room. Ivo looked across and saw that Hunter had gone to her pre-arranged hiding place. Felix and Miranda were still in their positions. He saw Lydia laughing, and Jago, his fingers around the stem of his wine glass, leaning intently into his neighbour. I can do it, he thought. I can destroy them. Just as he was steeling himself with this thought, he heard a voice at his feet.

'And what have we got here?' said the voice, and Ivo looked down to see a woman. It was Jennifer Brook. He could see the tip of a pistol pointing out of her robe. 'You're not on my list. There are only meant to be ten living statues. Why are there suddenly thirteen? And you're an awful lot skinnier than the rest of them. Get down.' She spoke in an undertone. 'Oh, Strawbones will be so thrilled.'

Ivo saw that it was useless to make a scene. All his highly strung energy seemed to flow out of him.

'You'd better come with me,' said Jennifer. 'And don't worry, we've got the other two as well.' Ivo stepped down from the alcove. Nobody noticed the exchange.

'I will have to take you in front of the Liberators,' said Jennifer Brook. 'They won't like it. They won't like it one bit. I don't suppose you'll live to see the new dawn tomorrow . . .' Her voice was soft and bright, the voice of authority, the woman who tells you to report anything suspicious, or to wait because your call is important to her. Ivo hated it.

'Come on, this way,' she said, and poked the gun into his back. Ivo walked, or rather stumbled, ahead of her, cursing himself inwardly. He saw Felix and Miranda with another nymph. He caught Felix's eye, but the nymph pushed him on. He felt the hardness of the gun in his back. He saw the light glinting off the silver skin of his friends. Ivo wanted to speak, to shout, but held his tongue.

They were all led down one of the side corridors. Waiters swanned past them. They tramped down the long passage, and came to a small room.

It was clearly an office of some sort. In it were two more nymphs. Jennifer Brook pushed Ivo inside, and Felix and Miranda came with him. Jennifer closed the door. The other two nymphs stood up. They were smiling. One, delicately, took Felix's arm, so that he was restrained by two; the other took Ivo's.

'So . . .' said Jennifer. 'Three little rats. Three, little, silver-skinned rats. You two . . .' She put her face close to Miranda's. 'I know your parents. And do you know where your parents are?'

Miranda said nothing. Her eyes were tightly closed. Ivo saw bright globes of tears shivering at the edges of her eyelashes. The tears fell and streaked a white path through her silver make-up.

'Your parents,' said Jennifer, 'are downstairs. Bound, drugged, incapable.'

Miranda's tears poured forth, her face dissolved into a crush of pain. Ivo struggled against his captors; he saw Felix straining against his own, but Jennifer had put the gun to Miranda's forehead, and Ivo knew that she would pull the trigger. 'Felix!' he said sharply, and Felix caught his eye, and went limp. He closed his eyes, his silver head fell limply forwards on to his chest. Don't go, Felix, thought Ivo. Stay with me.

'And you.' Jennifer removed the gun, and pointed it at Ivo's heart. 'We know all about you, Ivo. We've been watching you for some time.' Her face was lit by a wide, toothy grin. Ivo tensed.

'You,' said Jennifer, pointing at a fellow fanatic, 'go and get Strawbones. Tell him it's important.' One of the nymphs, dressed in trailing vine leaves, got up and slunk out of the room.

'Why do you keep looking at Julius?' whispered Lydia into her husband's ear. 'His speech isn't until after pudding.'

'I know, dearest, I know,' said Jago. 'But I want to make sure I don't miss it.'

'How can you miss it, darling?' said Lydia. She had now had three large glasses of wine, and was not at all nervous. In fact, she was positively enjoying herself, and hadn't, as she kept announcing to anybody who would listen, enjoyed herself quite so much since her student years.

Jago noticed that one of the nymphs had sidled up behind Strawbones's chair, and was bending unobtrusively down to whisper in his ear. He saw Strawbones, very carefully and very slowly, break a glass with his hand, making a noise loud enough for the tables around him to stop talking and look in his direction.

'It's nothing,' said Strawbones, loudly and clearly and got up. His hand was bleeding. Jago saw the thick, blood spill black on to the white tablecloth. The actresses on either side of Strawbones didn't seem to mind. Strawbones bowed, and left, led by the nymph.

What is going on? thought Jago. What had made

Strawbones break the glass? Jago decided that he would get up and follow. He whispered to his wife, 'Just popping out for a sec.'

'Not for a ciggy, darling, please,' came Lydia's voice, raucous now.

Jago pushed his chair in and went in the direction of Strawbones. The dining room erupted in laughter as the pudding was brought.

'What can you possibly have to drag me away from my *dinner*?' came Strawbones's drawling voice as the door to the room swung open. The nymph came in first, followed by the Liberator.

When he saw the three children standing, huddled but firm, against the wall, he pushed the door to behind him, very softly, without taking his eyes off them. Blood was spilling down his arm but he didn't seem to notice. His civilised clothes, the white tie and the waistcoat, suddenly looked out of place on him. His skin had become very, very pale, and his eyes were changing colour, becoming green, his hair was growing; before their eyes he morphed into the inhuman despot that Ivo had seen before, lank fronds trailing the ground, beads and bones and skulls twisted into the locks of his hair, his mouth a gash of redness, his teeth long and animal-like.

Stone Eater, Swallow Feather, Prince of Deer, thought Ivo, remembering the chants. Strawbones came forward, and inclined his head, almost politely. Ivo saw Felix, standing to his left, tall and skinny and angry, containing himself, his breaths coming very slow, very deep; and Miranda, to his right, like a frightened fawn, shivering in the breeze.

'Hello, my little chicks,' said Strawbones, his voice suddenly rasping. He took one step closer towards them, and all three tried to stand further back. 'All my pretty chicks – all of them? Three, all lined up, ready for the *plucking*.' His voice had taken on a guttural quality, as if he were speaking a language foreign to him.

'Where did you find them?' he said to Jennifer abruptly.

'Pretending to be statues,' she said.

'Well done. You shall be *rewarded*,' said Strawbones, dripping with venom. Jennifer affected indifference, but Ivo could see something like passion blazing behind her eyes, her black-rimmed eyelids fluttering.

Strawbones now seemed to take up much more space than he should have done. The bones and skulls entwined as ornaments in his hair clattered when he shook his head from side to side. Ivo could smell him – the reeking smell of animal, of hot horseflesh. Strawbones waved at one of the nymphs, who brought him a cloth. He pressed it to the gash in his palm, and then turned to Ivo.

'I'd forgotten about you, Ivo. Don't think that you were ever important. It is wonderful to have you here, with me, with us, at our final hour – it almost disappoints me that I shall have to kill you before Liberation takes place,' said Strawbones, licking his lips. His tongue, thought Ivo, was too red, too bright.

Ivo saw Felix straighten up.

'And you.' Strawbones came forwards, step by step, towards Felix. Ivo could see Felix was trembling. Strawbones came within an inch of Felix, and put his long white fingers under Felix's chin. Felix turned his head away. Strawbones slapped Felix suddenly and stood back. Felix said nothing. 'You,' continued Strawbones. 'What do you think about all this?'

He's sensed it, thought Ivo. He can feel Felix's need. He knows what Felix thinks. Stay with me, Felix.

As if in answer, Felix snapped his head up and shouted, 'I hate it! And I hate you!' Phlegm joined his lips together. He scrunched up his eyes.

Mocking laughter engulfed the children, and they shrank back into the wall, feeling it cold and unresponsive behind them.

'What black fates have you allowed to control your lives?' said Strawbones. 'What Furies have you set loose upon your souls? You who were so innocent, so happy, so *free* . . .'

'What are you going to do to us?' said Miranda shakily.

'I think I've said that before!' said Strawbones. 'Oh, what was it again, will you remind me? Er . . .'

He pointed at Jennifer, who said, slowly and langorously, 'Wasn't it something about killing them?'

'Oh, Ivo, do you hear that sound?' Strawbones exulted.

It was the sound of tramping feet, and he flung the door open into the corridor, and Ivo saw trooping past the figures of the Acolytes. They were in the building, and they were going to surround the guests; at that moment Ivo knew it was over.

'It is nearly time, Ivo, nearly time. It's a long time since I've had such *fun*,' yelped Strawbones, giving a little jump in the air and kicking his heels together, his whole long body shaking with excitement. 'Not since I massacred a village in Switzerland in, when was it . . .' He gestured towards Jennifer. She shrugged her shoulders.

'When was it?' he said again, more forcefully.

She stood up a little, and raised her hands. 'I . . . I don't know,' she said.

'When *was it*?' he screamed, and Jennifer quailed.

270

'Oh, I forget these things, don't you know,' he said more quietly. Without warning he reached out a hand and grabbed Felix by the neck and began to throttle him. Ivo ran to Strawbones and tried to force his hands off Felix, but Strawbones lifted him up above the ground and flung him aside as if he were a doll. The Acolytes didn't need to do anything. Electricity crackled in the air, and there was a sound like the wind rushing around them; it smelled of battles and flames, the beacon fires of beseiged cities, of infected corpses thrown over walls.

Ivo watched in horror as Felix struggled and gasped, his face going purple, his veins popping out on his forehead like thick ropes. Felix is going to die, he thought, and it is all my fault, and there is nothing that I can do to save him.

Something bashed into Strawbones, and the shock made him release Felix, who collapsed panting on the floor. Miranda immediately pulled him towards her and stood over him protectively.

'How . . . how could you do that?' said a voice, and Ivo looked in amazement at Jago, who had stormed into the room, disarmed the nymph and, having knocked her over, was now pointing her pistol at Strawbones. The other Acolytes stood at bay. Hunter was behind him, the leopard mask off her face. Then there was a bang, and smoke, and silence. Ivo saw Jago stand over Strawbones, still pointing the pistol at him.

Strawbones lay on the floor, his long body jerking, blood flowing freely from his wrist and from his mouth. Then he sat up, his eyes totally green now – his body all red, caked in coagulate gore – and spat, collapsing into juddering laughter.

'You . . . are just . . . all . . . so . . . *funny*,' he said, the words coming between gasps. 'I don't know why you even bother.'

'*What are you?*' said Jago, his voice curiously edgy now. 'Tell me what you are. What do you want? What were you doing to that poor boy?'

'That would take too long to explain,' said Strawbones, reaching out a hand and clutching Miranda by the hem of her dress, drawing her towards him. 'If you won't let me kill that one, then I guess it will have to be *this* one first.'

'No!' said Jago; there was an exploding sound, and it seemed to Ivo as if everything had gone very quiet, and very slow, and he watched in awe as a bullet flew from the pistol Jago was holding. A star-shaped, bloody hole appeared in Strawbones's chest. As Strawbones collapsed on to the floor.

Jago took command. Strawbones's body lay limp. The nymphs were petrified by the gun. 'Quick,' said

Jago, and Miranda, Felix and Ivo tore off strips from the sheets around them, and gagged and bound the three nymph and Jennifer.

'Come on,' said Jago. They ran towards the main galleries.

Chapter Nineteen

'What are you doing?' shouted Ivo as they ran down the echoing passage. Jago was slightly ahead, Felix to his right; Miranda was by Ivo, Hunter behind them.

Jago replied, 'I saw what he was doing to Felix . . . it was evil. I thought . . . I don't know what I thought, I was seduced, I can't believe I was taken in by them. They're monsters.' They sprinted down a red-carpeted corridor, old masters flashing by them.

'Is Strawbones dead?'

'No. He won't be out for long,' said Hunter suddenly. 'Here. Wait here.' They turned a corner. They were in a quiet antechamber, a hundred feet or so away from where the main dinner was taking place. Ivo could hear the noise. Hunter shepherded them into a group. Ivo could feel the heat coming off them all. He was panting. Sweat rolled down his cheeks.

'How did you find us?' Ivo asked Hunter.

'I was watching Strawbones, and saw Jago, so I followed him. Bob's your uncle, as they might say.' Hunter laughed grimly. Ivo heard Jago sigh. He saw Felix clutching Miranda and moved towards them, but they drew back. He hung on his heels, and then dropped back, into the wall, wishing that it could open and dissolve him.

'What about our parents?' said Felix roughly. 'They said they were drugged and bound. We have to find them!'

'They aren't our first priority,' snapped Hunter. 'If we don't deal with Julius now, everything will be lost.'

'Well, I don't care. I'm going to find them.' Felix turned and sprinted off. Miranda made to go after him, but Hunter said quietly, 'You'll die if you go with him. Stay with us.'

Miranda gulped. She was numb. 'OK.' She nodded. 'Just . . . just tell me what to do.'

'Good girl,' said Hunter.

'They're not . . . they're not human, are they?' It was Jago. He put the back of his hand to his forehead and leaned against the wall. His carefully slicked-back hair had fallen forwards. His features had softened. He put a finger to his right temple. Ivo looked behind them. Hunter was keeping guard. 'I've been mad,' Jago said. 'I don't want this. I never wanted to do this.' He righted himself. He looked at Ivo keenly. 'Do you know how to stop them?'

'Yes,' said Ivo, and once more he felt the sharp edge of power inside him.

They ran straight into the gallery where the dining tables had been laid out. It was a cacophony of brayings, commotions, people spilling wine, knocking over glasses with their elbows, rocking back on their chairs, dropping napkins; a dowager with a diamond necklace guffawed, spraying her neighbour with crumbs; an old billionaire who'd pulled himself up by his bootstraps put his arm companionably around the young man sitting next to him, whispering to him the secrets of success; everybody was intent upon their own pleasure, so nobody noticed when the four of them skidded in.

They stood in the wide arch, the red chasm of the gallery yawning in front of them like a mouth, white-jacketed waiters flitting here and there, nymphs shimmying between tables, still part of some performance, still looking as if they had no idea they were in twenty-first-century London.

'Look,' whispered Ivo to Jago, pointing at the walls surreptitiously with his elbow.

There, for all the world like footmen, were more Acolytes, waiting for their moment. Ivo couldn't tell if they were armed or not. He knew now that many of the nymphs and fauns and satyrs amongst the performers were Acolytes too. He wondered if any of the guests were.

'What is he going to do?' whispered Jago.

'He's going to Liberate them all – and us if we stay here . . .' said Hunter.

'And you mean we'll all become like Strawbones?'

Hunter nodded. Ivo empathised with the terrifed look in his uncle's eyes. But not me, he thought, remembering the riots. I will stay sane, and I'll be torn apart if I cannot escape.

'You'd better go back to your seat,' Hunter whispered to Jago. 'Wait there. Defend yourself, defend your loved ones. Don't give in.'

Jago nodded. He turned to Ivo, and put his hand on Ivo's shoulder. His tie had come loose, and the top button of his waistcoat was undone. He was sweating. 'Ivo . . . I . . . I'm sorry.' He bent down and kissed Ivo on the forehead, and then turned swiftly and paced back to his table. Ivo saw him sit down and nod to Lydia, who looked at him enquiringly.

There was a pinging noise, of a spoon being rapped against a glass, and the whole room was suddenly quiet, apart from the odd cough, and one person who continued to tell a joke until he was shushed by the people around him. The noise of the spoon grew in volume until it seemed to fill the whole room, and as it died, Julius stood up slowly, magnificently. Somewhere some clocks started chiming midnight.

All eyes turned towards Julius. Unobtrusively, a few of the Acolytes made their way to the exits, taking up a stand in the middle of the archways. Hunter, Miranda and Ivo slid over to a pillar and ranged themselves around it.

'The Thyrsos,' said Ivo, a sickening feeling in his stomach. Julius was holding it casually in his right hand.

'Your Royal Highnesses,' said Julius, bowing in the direction of the Prince of Wales and his Duchess. 'My lords, ladies and gentlemen. Thank you for coming here for such a worthy cause.' All the tables erupted in applause. Some people cheered, one or two got to their feet and raised their glasses. 'It gives me great pleasure to welcome you all here.' His voice took on an avuncular tone, as if he were a priest giving a Sunday morning sermon. 'I suppose you're all wondering what you are doing here, really, are you not?' He threw the question out, and there was a puzzled silence, broken by Julius laughing.

'It is a question that haunts us all – what is it that brings us to this strange rock of a world, spinning for eternity in blackness?'

There were murmurs in the crowd, neighbours whispering to each other; Ivo heard a man saying, 'What's he on about? Can't we get on to the port?'

'Well, your Royal Highnesses, ladies, gentlemen . . .' he said, a wicked grin on his face. He raised the Thyrsos. 'Tonight I will show you why . . .'

A bloody, enraged figure emerged into the gallery from the side, knocking aside some Acolytes. Strawbones advanced, his mouth dripping with blood, his clothes ripped. He was laughing, a horrible, high cackle. He strode up the centre of the room. Lydia saw him, and put down her glass. Her neighbour bent into her. 'Some kind of performance, eh, Lydia?'

A man, emboldened by wine, stood up as Strawbones walked past. 'Hey,' he said. 'What do you think you're doing?'

Strawbones stopped, and turned very slowly on his heels.

'What?' asked Strawbones.

The man said, louder this time, 'I said, what do you think you're doing?'

Strawbones tossed his head, so that his long hair rustled and shook. He snapped back around, and waved the man away dismissively. The man advanced. Two Acolytes came forwards and grabbed him by the arms.

'Lydia,' said her neighbour, 'going a bit far, isn't it?'

Lydia sat, her eyes reflecting the green lights. Trembling, she knocked over her wine glass and a dark stain spread over her dress.

The Acolytes pushed the man back down into his seat. A roar of sound spilled from the tables. People stood up, knocked over chairs. Through the hubbub, Strawbones marched, tall, terrifying, alien, up the middle aisle, and stood by his brother.

Strawbones, crimson, and Julius, white, stood, each with a hand on the Thyrsos.

'What is going on?' Ivo heard Lydia's voice rise above the rest. 'Julius? What are you doing?'

'Silence!' shouted Julius. The voice was so loud, so full of hellish authority, that, after the last echo had rung out, the room was totally quiet. 'Do not try to leave. The exits are secured. If you do not cooperate, you will die.'

'Who the hell are you?' shouted a dowager. She stood up, sheathed in silk, diamonds crowning her head. Ivo saw that she supported herself on a cane. 'Impudent man!' she cried.

'Yeah!' came some cries of support. 'Is this some kind of a joke?'

In answer, Julius merely inclined his head. A shot rang out, and the dowager crumpled, as if she had been no more than a slender white sapling blown over by a gust of wind. Screams rang out around the room, but everyone was too frightened to go to her aid.

Ivo barely noticed the explosion. He had gone into a sort of trance. His mind was fixated upon the two figures standing tall and strong. This was his destiny, this was his fate; he was reaching out his hand and he was taking it. The rest of the room was a blur around him, as if it was happening in another dimension. He slipped away, glinting silver in the light, like a fish under the surface of a stream.

'Ivo!' whispered Miranda after him, and made to follow, but Hunter held her back. Hunter had seen the look in his eyes, and she thought that she understood. Ivo dropped to the floor.

'None of you can get out,' said Julius, his voice normal now. 'I was telling you why you were here. And you should all listen to me, because tomorrow you will all be thanking me – no, more than that, you will be *adoring* me for what is about to happen.

'How do you all do it?' he continued. 'How do you all fill your lives with the petty things that you do? Trundling, ever and on, to school, to work, being polite, being kind. You know you have to do these things. You know you don't want to. You know that if you really could, you would be freed from all that.

Imagine it!' he said, his tone growing louder. 'A world without restraint . . . a world in which each and every one of you was liberated from that voice in your head which stops you from doing things. Every thought that you ever suppressed, every action that you didn't fulfil, you will now be able to revel in.'

Ivo was crawling along the carpet, under the tables, avoiding people's feet. The Koptor was glowing and burning, tucked into the waistband of his boxers. He was moving swiftly, mechanically, full of an energy that wasn't his. I will give them freedom, he thought. I am the Liberator, I am and I always have been. I hold destruction in my hands.

'So, my friends, ready yourselves,' exclaimed Julius. He began to chant, in a language unknown to Ivo, and Strawbones intoned with him, though he was speaking different words; their voices joined together in harmony. It was like before the riot in Oxford Circus; ivy began to grow out of the cracks of the building. Hysteria was overwhelming the guests; Ivo could feel the rumbling of their laughter as he neared Julius and Strawbones.

He came out from under the table nearest to them. The Thyrsos was glowing, emanating a strange and deviant light that glistened and filled the room, casting everything into a deeper hue, making everything look hyper-real, as if he were hallucinating or dreaming. The carpet beneath his hands felt richer, thicker, the breaths he took sent oxygen through his blood faster. He took out the Koptor and watched as it grew into the thin, blade-like weapon, coruscating in the light, its spark and shine reflecting the thousands of little flames that gleamed in the chandelier above, and showing back to him his own face, distorted, devilish, deathly.

A glass crashed beside his hand. He watched it shatter, spilling wine over the floor. He brought himself up, slowly, to his knees, so that his head was bowed; he looked as if he were about to be knighted. His own mind was immune to the ancient song of the Liberators. He moved as if he were wearing armour, ponderous but lethal.

The two brothers were so intent upon their chanting that they did not notice as Ivo got to his feet, feeling the Koptor in his hands as if he had always been meant to use it, as if he had all his life known that this was what he was meant to do.

He walked up to them, the Koptor gripped tightly, so tightly that he felt blood trickling down his hand; he held it horizontally, feeling it break the air as he moved, feeling it sense its prize near.

The brothers were now so close to him that, if he had wished, he could have sliced their heads off; it was then that Julius saw the glimmer of the Koptor and, faltering, stopped chanting; Strawbones did too, and the light from the Thyrsos dimmed.

'What is this?' screamed Julius. 'What is this? How dare you! Get back!' His hair was lengthening, his eyes becoming green, his civilised mask falling away.

Julius lashed at Ivo with the Thyrsos, but Ivo neatly sidestepped the blow, like a dancer, his body fast and light. It was as if he could anticipate everything that Julius might do, as if he could interpret the future. His mind was singing, as clear as crystal and as cold as ice.

'You have forgotten something,' said Ivo, speaking slowly and formally. 'You who think you are indestructible, you who think you are gods. You have forgotten that you can be destroyed, and by one who is weaker than you. Or maybe you have always known,' said Ivo, as Strawbones lunged at him, teeth bared. Ivo jumped out of the way, the Koptor whistling through the air.

With the Thyrsos dimming, the crowd were coming back to their senses. A commotion broke out. Acolytes pressed in.

'Ivo!' It was Lydia's voice. 'What are you doing?'

'Stay back!' said Jago, grabbing her. 'Leave him.'

'But how are you going to take it from me, Ivo?' sneered Julius. He leaped up on to the table, crushing

284

a plate beneath his feet, and held the Thyrsos above his head. 'There's only one of you, Ivo. And look around – see my Acolytes! See how they will obey my every word . . . there are a hundred of them, Ivo, all around the edges of this room, outside the building, amongst the guests, waiting for me, all ready to do my bidding. How can you stop us?'

Strawbones, like a gazelle, as fluid as water, joined his brother on the table, and grasped the other end of the Thyrsos. Once more it began to crackle and shimmer with light, once more the faces of the people in the room took on a hyper-real sheen. The song of the Liberators filled the room with the heady scents of green forests, wine and feasts.

Ivo's body was hardened, his mind a rock. This is not what is meant to be, he thought. There is a pattern in the world; there is a way into the future. He glanced around him and saw the beginnings of frenzy: he saw a man ripping his jacket apart; he saw a woman screaming; a man jumping up on to a chandelier; faces distorting, sneering, yelling. The man leaped off the chandelier, crashing into a table, sending wine bottles flying.

And he saw, coming towards him, Miranda, Felix, Jago and Lydia, and he saw that they were walking towards him, and his heart began to quail, for there was madness in their eyes; but as they neared, he saw something else in them and in his heart he smiled. Hunter appeared out of nowhere and took out two Acolytes in front of Julius.

Julius looked to his right, and in an instant, Ivo jumped on to the table and advanced towards the shouting pair. Ivo barrelled into Julius, knocking him over and Julius lost his grip on the Thyrsos. Strawbones held it close to himself, clutching it between his hands. He snarled at Ivo. All trace of humanity had left his face.

Miranda arrived at the table, and Ivo saw in her eyes the same madness that was in his own: fury, desperation and determination to survive. She looked at him and a wild exultation passed between them; she leaped up and sat on Julius, and Felix came up behind her and held Julius's arms. More shots rang out.

Ivo moved to where Strawbones had positioned himself, the Thyrsos held out like a weapon.

'Ivo,' said Strawbones, his voice like honey, 'why are you doing this?'

Ivo looked into Strawbones's eyes. The face was returning to its human state, the hair becoming long and blond again, the eyes blue and kind. 'Don't you remember?' continued Strawbones.

'Don't give in to him!' It was Felix. Julius lay limp,

apparently having lost all effort of will. Ivo sensed around him a full-scale battle. He saw, dimly, the Prince of Wales sheltering behind an upturned table, a film star whirling a champagne bottle around her head; he couldn't tell whether the hysteria had gone or not, or who was winning, the Acolytes or the guests.

'Ivo . . .' Strawbones spoke again, weakly this time. Out of his waistcoat pocket appeared the small gleaming head of his garter snake. Strawbones picked it up gently, and held it in the light in front of Ivo. 'Don't you remember?'

Ivo watched the snake slowly sliding in and out of Strawbones's fingers. A champagne glass smashed at his feet but he didn't notice.

'You cannot destroy the Thyrsos,' said Strawbones. Strawbones walked carefully, gently, towards Ivo. 'Come here, my boy. Come here, Ivo.' Strawbones was breathing very slowly. Ivo relaxed his arm a little. The tip of the Koptor wavered. And Strawbones lunged, but Ivo sidestepped him, and Strawbones tripped past Ivo.

Ivo turned swiftly to face him and spoke: 'You're wrong. You have always been wrong. The pattern is finished, the mesh has been made.'

His heart thumping inside his chest, his breath coming in ragged gasps, Ivo edged towards

Strawbones, nervous as a hunter approaching his first kill.

The Koptor was alive, and it was him too, it was a part of him, an extension of his mind, as he took aim at the staff that Strawbones held; the arc of his arms was as taut as a bowstring, his movement as swift as a leopard; he sliced through Strawbones's right wrist.

The hand clutching the Thyrsos fell to the table, and Strawbones fell too, pulling the cloth with him. Lymph and thick purple blood spurted out of the stump of his arm, his mouth open, nothing coming out of it; and Lydia and Jago strode behind him and held him, Lydia heedless of her dress, Jago's white waistcoat spattered with bloodspots.

Ivo knelt, the Thyrsos on the table in front of him, and held the Koptor above it. 'This is for Blackwood,' he shouted. 'This is for all those you maimed, tortured and killed. I am the real Liberator. I am the one who will free you.'

He shifted his weight, and brought the Koptor down upon the Thyrsos with a force that made his arm judder.

It was as if a shock wave emanated from that blow. Ivo was thrown on to his back, as was everyone immediately around him; the room shuddered, paint-ings fell off the walls, a chandelier swung dangerously, little glass droplets falling from the ceiling.

Ivo yelled, a yell that was wild and free, a yell of the mountains, of the woods, of the forests and the hunt. A huge energy was released, as the Thyrsos split in two with a sound that was deep and old.

And then, there was nothing for a moment, except stillness, and silence, silence like an ocean; then, gradually, sound returned to the room.

People got up and dusted themselves off, helped each other up; Lydia, Jago, Felix and Miranda got to their feet.

'Look!' said Miranda. She pointed. Ivo looked.

Julius and Strawbones had raised themselves and were facing each other. The energy from the destroyed Thyrsos was pouring into them. But now they could not control it; now they were turning in on themselves. And they began to scream, to release into the silence the syllables of their power; they encircled each other, overtaken by madness; they went round and round like boxers in a ring. Suddenly Julius leaped and lunged, and Strawbones lunged back; Ivo watched in disgust as Julius tore off Strawbones's arm, showing nerves, bones, blood pouring out in a black, viscous trickle. Strawbones looked down at his arm and picked it up; then he threw it, without seeing where it went – Ivo heard a scream as it landed in someone's lap –

Strawbones prowled forwards, and the two brothers met. Strawbones was biting Julius on the neck, and then Julius was tearing at Strawbones's hair, which came off in clumps. They both shrieked, howling like banshees. And then Strawbones had Julius in a grip with his remaining arm, and he grabbed hold of Julius's leg, and with a strength horrible and supernatural, he tore off Julius's leg at the knee. The sound of the bone breaking made bile rise in Ivo's throat; he put a hand to his face. Julius, as Strawbones roared in triumph, got shakily on to his front, and crawled towards Strawbones; with a burst of energy he landed on him and began gouging at his eyes.

'Stop!' yelled somebody. 'Stop!' It was Perkins, pushing his glasses back, and he advanced upon the two brothers. 'You can't do that! I have devoted my life to you!'

'Then we will take you with us,' snarled Strawbones, and leaping up, he hobbled towards Perkins and grabbed him with his remaining arm and tore into him with his teeth. Perkins tried to escape: Ivo saw the horror in his eyes. But Strawbones had broken his neck with one snap; he tossed him nonchalantly aside as if he were no more than a toy. Ivo looked around again.

The Acolytes had all fallen to their knees; people were streaming out of the gallery; outside, police cars and armed police vans had drawn up and officers in riot gear were storming the building. Through every door they poured, soon the room was swarming with men in battledress, looking like black robots, truncheons and guns bristling all over them. An official shouted through a megaphone; the guests, frightened and shivering in their evening clothes, were corralled out; stretchers were brought in and several people were carried out.

The room was in confusion. Paintings had fallen to the ground; a chandelier had shattered; tables had been overturned. Paramedics were checking through the debris, searching for the injured. Several officers surrounded Julius and Strawbones, pressing in front of Lydia, Jago, Ivo, Miranda, Felix and Hunter. When they tried to move in, Hunter shouted, 'Don't!' and the officers backed away, staring in fascinated, disgusted horror at the savagery in front of them. Perkins' mutilated corpse lay to one side.

Strawbones was the last to die. He was nothing now, a stump of a creature, his head thrown back, his eyes opened wide, green and shining, and they looked at Ivo and they laughed.

Chapter Twenty

Ivo opened his eyes and saw, bending over him, a long tangle of yellow hair. He tensed all over. Strawbones, he thought. He's come back to get me. He's come back to life. He was enveloped by terror, paralysed. Then the head moved and, shaking the hair away, the smiling face of Miranda was revealed. She sat down heavily on his bed, and reached across to him. 'Ivo . . . it's OK, it's finished,' she said, whispering.

'Miranda!' Ivo grabbed hold of her, and she hugged him back tightly.

A chuckle came from the other side of the room and Ivo looked up to see Felix. 'You two getting on all right, then?'

'Shut up, Felix!' said Miranda, but softly.

Ivo realised that he was panting. His throat was dry. He sat up in bed. 'Has it . . . is it really finished?'

Felix leaned back lazily, but Ivo could see deep relief

in his eyes. Miranda and Felix exchanged glances. 'Yes,' answered Felix.

'Your parents . . . are they OK?' asked Ivo. He remembered, suddenly, his own.

Miranda nodded quickly. 'Yes. Felix found them. Ma's got a few cuts and bruises, but otherwise they're fine. Pa's already telling all his friends and making jokes about it. He was on the news this morning.'

'Well, come on then. Let's go! Put on some warm clothes,' Felix said urgently.

Ivo got dressed (having pushed Miranda out of the room) and went downstairs with Felix. At the door to Lydia's studio he paused. 'Wait a minute,' he said to Felix, who tapped his feet impatiently.

Ivo went in. It was empty. The portrait of Strawbones was on the easel, finished. He went up to it, his heart in his mouth. There he was, his long white face, his blue, kind eyes, his red patchwork jacket. The painting didn't move. There was no sign of the figures he'd seen before. It was just a painting. And then, without really thinking, he picked up the portrait and broke it over his knee. It split, with a harsh crunch, and then he threw the two halves, violently, into different corners of the room.

Three minutes later, Ivo was being dragged out of the house by the two siblings. 'What's going on?' he asked.

Outside, the sun had come out. It was three days after the party. Ivo had been in hospital for a couple of days and had been released. He was tired, still so tired. His head was filled with a dull ache, his eyes were drooping. The sky was intense and blue, dotted with white clouds made gold by the light. Ivo looked up and saw a mass of clouds form together, like a bird, wings spread for flight, and then, as quickly as it had appeared, it went.

'Come on! It's nearly one o'clock! We're going to be late!'

'Late for what?' asked Ivo, noticing the black minicab that was waiting for them.

'Not saying,' answered Felix, and then, laughing even more, he pulled Ivo behind him into the car. The streets were now frosted and clear, and Ivo remembered when he had met Felix and Miranda, and how excited he had been. I wanted adventure, he thought ruefully. Now I just want peace. He looked out of the windows and saw the Londoners, milling and swarming as if nothing had ever happened, resilient and strong. The radio was on, and it played Christmas songs, to which Miranda sang along, to the mortification of Felix. Through the streets they drove, until they reached Hyde Park. The car pulled up and the three friends got out. The park was empty, the expanse of grass white with snow in patches.

'What's going on?' Ivo asked. His cheeks were reddened by the cold. His breath blew out like mist. They were nearing the Serpentine lake, and it appeared in front of them, edged with rime and shards of ice. Ivo could see a small group of figures standing at the shore by the boats. As they neared, Ivo saw that two of the people who were standing together were moving towards him, and they were heavily muffled up; his heart beat a little faster. Felix and Miranda slowed down. Ivo realised, with a surge of joy in his heart, who they were, and broke into a jog; soon he was sprinting, and he flung himself at his parents.

He said nothing at first, but held them tightly, enveloped in their arms. His father's stubble was rough on his cheek, and he could smell his mother's favourite scent. 'Mum . . . Dad . . .'

Ivo looked up into his father's usually cheerful face, now grave, and his mother's eyes. 'Jago told us something was going on. We were so worried, Ivo. We're so happy to see you.' They kissed him once more, and he held them, and for a moment only he and his parents existed, and they were safe and they were together and they were alive.

Ivo looked across at the others, and saw Jago, tall in a black overcoat, with no tie on, and Lydia, with a mink fur hat on her head; and Hunter, shuffling from foot to foot in an old brown padded jacket. Ivo let go of his parents and walked over to the other three. Jago bowed a little stiffly, and then hugged him, and Lydia joined in, whilst Hunter stood looking away; then Ivo, remembering her, gave her the biggest hug of all. When he released her, he was surprised to see tears in her eyes.

'Oh, I'm not crying,' she said. 'It's just the cold.' She wiped away a large tear and cleared her throat. 'Now,' she said, 'Jago took you to hospital, after . . . after the end. You were exhausted. But you'll be all right.' Everybody was there now, in a circle, around Ivo. He looked at each one of them in turn.

'What happened? Can they come back?' he asked Hunter. 'Are they dead now?'

Hunter said, clearly and brightly, 'No, that's it. They can never come back. The Thyrsos is destroyed. That power is gone from the world, like so much else.' She said the last with a tinge of sorrow. 'Such a thing will not be seen again.'

'I saw him . . . this morning . . . in my head . . . Strawbones.'

'I know, Ivo. And you will again. They will live on in our minds for ever.'

'And FIN?' He looked up, wondering for a moment

whether he might join, whether he might continue to help Hunter.

Hunter smiled and said quietly, 'Finito.' Ivo could see the sadness in her eyes. It had been her life. 'I've written up what happened. You will be a hero, Ivo, in the secret files of Britain.'

'So what will you do now?' said Ivo, to cover up his embarrassment as Felix poked him in the ribs and Miranda laughed.

'Oh, I don't know. I might retire. Take up knitting. Write a book. Rescue another city from certain danger. Who knows?' she smiled, and patted Ivo, and wiped from her cheek another tear that was not a tear. 'Maybe something else will emerge. There is always something, waiting in the darkness.'

Jago came forward and said, 'I rang your parents when I found you in the Luther-Rosses' . . . in the *Liberators*' flat.'

Ivo was overwhelmed. He could feel pleasure all over him, but it was pure and clean.

'Come on,' said his father, his face twinkling. 'We thought we'd take your mind off things.'

Hunter was already jumping into a boat. 'Who's coming with me?' Miranda leaped in, yelling, and Ivo got in one with Felix, and they pushed off into the lake. The greyish water was dappled and dotted with points of light like guttering candles.

'Hey, Ivo,' said Felix. 'Me and Miranda have got you a present.'

'Really?'

'Well, Miranda did mostly. I wouldn't have thought of it. You'll like it, I think.'

'What is it?'

Felix smiled, and said softly, 'A kitten.' He put down his oar and looked shyly at Ivo, who said nothing, but clasped his forearm.

They rowed across into the centre, and then paused, the four boats in a circle, and Ivo looked at Felix bending over the oars, at Miranda and Hunter splashing, at his parents, at Lydia and Jago, and thought, Now I am free. The lake and the trees and the grass and the sky, my family and my friends, the ripple of water and the rush of the wind, these are the things that matter, and these are the things that will keep us free.

FIN

Acknowledgements

Are due to my editors, Sarah Odedina, Isabel Ford and Talya Baker; my publicists, Ian Lamb and Emma Bradshaw; and all at Bloomsbury, and to my agent, Felicity Rubinstein.

Without these people, *The Liberators* would not be what it is: Anna Arco, Tom Beasley, Olivia Breese, the Chappatte family of Hawkridge Place, Lottie Edge, James Elliot, Julia Finch, Venetia Hargreaves-Allen, Con and Nicky Normanby, and their children Sibylla, John and Tom Phipps, Owen O'Rorke, Lizzie Spratt, Humphrey Thomas, Marie, Richard and Ashley Womack.

And, most importantly of all, to the god Dionysus himself, I pour libations and give humble thanks for his inspiration.

If you enjoyed *The Liberators*,
read Philip Womack's first book

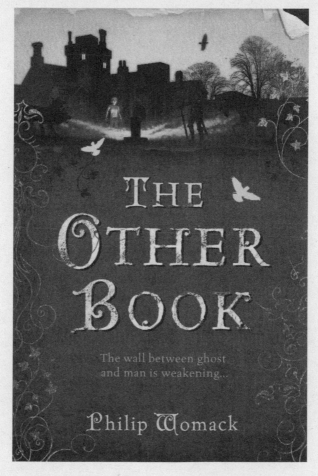

Turn the page to read an extract

Also available from Bloomsbury

ain exploded in the middle of the boy's stomach. It burned briefly, red-hot, and all the breath went out of him. He smashed into a wall and banged his head; eerie shapes danced before his eyes, and then he felt nothing.

When he came to, the boy looked warily around him. What had once been his father was still standing in the middle of Great Hall. Little light could squeeze its way through the grimy glass of the windows. The boy shrank further into the corner where he had been thrown. The Hall was full of smoke that rolled in black billows. The portraits on the walls had long ago been covered in soot. His eyes were stinging unpleasantly. He rubbed them slowly, and blinked three or four times.

He remembered how it had been before *it* had

happened and his young life had been changed beyond all recognition. If he'd been standing in Great Hall in the sunlight, the stained glass of his father's coat of arms would make plays of colour on his hands – startling, blood-coloured reds, deep, sea-green blues, and vivid golds. He'd known the heraldic names for the colours, and had loved their strange syllables – *gules* for red, *sable* for black, *azure* for blue. But now everything was the same dull, dirty shade. His father's glory had been coated over. The heralds had no word for that colour.

He held out his hands in front of him. They were covered in blood.

Huge oak logs crackled and spat in the vast fireplace, which was carved with the coats of arms of his ancestors. His dogs were huddled nearby, yelping and scuffling, their hackles raised, their little fangs bared. Proud Fairfax and sweet Blanche were doing their best to protect him. They crouched at the ready, but there was nothing they could do. What was facing him now was worse than anything they ever met on their rambles in the woods and fields around Oldstone Manor. They were barely older than puppies, had never killed more than a bird.

The boy touched his stomach carefully. It was whole. He had not been wounded. The blood was not his own.

He saw Jemima, his old nurse, standing in the doorway. Her white apron, always the brightest thing in his life, was blackened and torn. She was almost bent double. 'Fly! Fly!' she was shrieking at him in her cracked, quavery voice, but the boy couldn't.

He couldn't dare, because then he would have to run past the thing that had once been his father, which now stood in the centre of Great Hall, so drenched in blood that his clothes stuck to his body, grinning, revealing his decaying teeth, his sword ready for the kill; he couldn't pass the pile of reeking bodies, their organs spilling out on to the floor in a steaming, slimy, gut-turning mess. He retched as he realised that the blood on his hands had come from them.

Those bodies . . . he remembered that only this morning they had been living, moving, smiling beings. They had looked fierce and proud when they had galloped up the drive, the glint of the sun making jewels in the boy's eyes as he watched. Now their faces looked empty, and their fine, embroidered clothes were torn and bloodied; their long, curled hair had fallen dead around their shoulders.

He recalled that he had been sitting in his favourite spot that morning, in the windowsill of the library, looking down into the courtyard below. The five horses of the deputation – all of them grey, except one roan – had trotted into the courtyard, their hooves clattering on the old stone. Sam and Tim, the ragged, stick-thin kitchen boys, had run out to meet them and tether the horses; they gave them water, but they did not bring them food – they had eaten the last of the oats themselves that morning.

Then he had thought he knew why the deputation had come. He had heard gossip in the kitchens, that the King was going to take his father's Manor away. When the ruffians who lurked around Oldstone Manor had heard the news they had all either run off or sunk into drunken stupors. He'd passed one on the stairs, filthy and stinking in his own vomit.

His father had strode into the library, grabbed him and hefted him downstairs to Great Hall. There the men had been waiting, standing in a line, their clothes clean and their faces smiling. They had spoken kind words to him. He hadn't answered, because his father had told him not to speak.

One of them, younger than the rest, with laughing eyes and a blue tunic, and long brown hair, the one who had ridden on the roan, had thrown him an apple; as the young man caught his gaze, his eyes stopped laughing.

The boy gobbled up the apple, peel, pips and all. It was the first thing he had had to eat, apart from crusts, for almost two days. He had enjoyed feeling the sweet acid seep into his stomach.

He had been going hungry since his mother died.

Now, as his father stood, the memory of his mother came to him: the last time he had seen her was when she had been hanged, dressed in the white shift which she wore in bed. They hadn't even allowed her to dress properly.

He remembered how sick he'd felt, and how ashamed, as he had run away into the woods, aiming for one of the watchtowers where he often hid, but his father's men had caught him and brought him to the front of the house. The stink of a blackened hand over his mouth came back to him, and he retched at the thought of it. He tried to think of something else, and came back to his mother . . .

His mother's face, still calm and beautiful, and those hands that he had swung on so many times, the little dip in her nose, the mole above her right cheekbone. But he could not stop himself from reliving the moment when the stool beneath her had been kicked away, and how he had caught the dolour in her eyes.

She had looked right at him, he had seen her lips move, and he had known that she was saying, 'I love you . . .' But sometimes at night he saw her face, pale and anguished, and instead she was saying, 'Save me . . .' He had done nothing to save her.

After that, he remembered, his life had changed. The boy had heard his father being called a wizard, a necromancer. His father was reaching out to others, the boy had discovered; there were rumours of conspiracy, of revolution, of a league of nightmare and shadow. He had been thrown out of his comfortable rooms, and put in a tiny attic bedroom, where his bed was a small pallet of dirty straw, and the cobwebs that garlanded the beams were the only decorations. Where before he had played with pages and squires, he had been left with only his nurse, Jemima.

As he watched her now, shrieking and babbling, he recalled how she would clutch him to her apron, muttering about dark times. Half of the things she said he didn't understand. She wittered about blood lines, and destinies.

The boy had watched his father gamble and drink all day and all night, in the smoke of the Hall, surrounded by cut-throats, thieves, magicians and murderers. Wagons full of bottles came up the drive to the Manor; endless beer barrels came up the river; but the crops failed and the apples rotted. Villainous-looking people came from all around to see the boy's father; he was endlessly closeted with them, his plottings kept so secret that even those who whispered a word were slaughtered.

It was too much for the boy. He had seen his father degenerate from a kind man into a monster. And now his father was a cold-blooded murderer, who had killed the people who had given him an apple. He wasn't going to stand for it. The memory of his mother overflowed inside him. He stopped shaking and, without really knowing why, ran out into the middle of the room.

'Sir . . .'

His father looked at him with hell-fire in his eyes. 'Pray now, what is it, sirrah – thou beetle-headed whelp?' he said, spitting blood. One of his teeth had come loose, and he expelled it with relish.

The boy felt anger and hatred welling up in him. 'You killed my mother. You told them to hang her. She didn't do anything. She was my mother. And now you killed these people. They were kind . . .' The boy ran at his father and beat him with his fists. His father stopped him easily with one arm.

'Oh ho, my little warrior, and what are you going to do about it?' His father raised up his sword and held it against the boy's throat. 'What wilt thou do, thou whelp, thou abortive *hedgepig*?' The boy gulped at the familiar *thou*, feeling the cold, toothy steel against his skin.

'My Lord! Don't touch the boy!' whimpered

Jemima. 'He's only a little one! He's my little one . . .' Her red-rimmed eyes peered out from under her great frilly cap, and they were filled with tears. She rushed at his father, flailing at him with her tiny, bird-like arms.

'God's blood, will you be silent!' shouted his father, and thrust her aside. The boy watched, aghast, as a stream of blackness crackled out of his hand into Jemima, and she screamed and fell dead on to the pile of bodies. He turned to his son, snarling, ''Sdeath! . . . I should get rid of you too, hag-seed, spawn of your filthy, crazy witch-mother that you are. I should send you back into the sweat and brimstone whence you crawled . . .' He raised his sword and aimed at the boy's throat. 'Goodbye, my little one, my sweet gentleman.' The boy tensed, tears dampening his reddened cheeks.

'Father . . .' He felt the swish of the sword as it swung back. Then he heard a creak, and a rush, and a terrible thundering. The huge doors to the Hall banged open.

A strong, foreign voice called out, 'Wentlake de la Zouche, by order of the Blood, put down that sword!'

Wentlake turned round slowly. Two men had entered the room.